THE RISE AND FALL OF THE YELLOW HOUSE

A NOVEL BY
JOHN WHITTIER TREAT

ISBN: 978-0-9965405-7-5

Printed in the United States of America

Cover Design: Minnie Cho, FuseLoft LLC
Back Cover Photo: Steve Shelton Images

Also by John Whittier Treat:

Gurando zero o kaku (Japanese translation of *Writing Ground Zero*)
Great Mirrors Shattered: Homosexuality, Orientalism and Japan
Contemporary Japan and Popular Culture
Writing Ground Zero: Japanese Literature and the Atomic Bomb
Pools of Water, Pillars of Fire: The Literature of Ibuse Masuji

Big Table Publishing Company
Boston, MA
www.bigtablepublishing.com

"Take the needle, arrest these senses,
excise the egg-shaped moon from my field of vision
and silence the bark."
~ Tory Dent, *Black Milk*

"They walked, and some fell by the way."
~ Katherine Routledge, *The Mystery of Easter Island*

CHAPTER ONE

The big cardboard box had begun to wear at its corners long ago. Now the seams were coming apart. Jeff had been using it for storing odds and ends since getting out of college in 1975. A decade of loading it on and off trucks, buses, airplanes, cars, friends' cars and one Red Flyer wagon as he moved from place to place, now New York to Seattle, had taken its toll. As Jeff gingerly slid it off the edge of the topmost shelf of his bedroom closet, he noticed his name written in bold letters with a blue Magic Marker over the logo of a New England egg farm. His handwriting was different then. Big, angular block printing. Not his current tight cursive script.

He reached into the box. A hammer, a spool of wire, two screwdrivers, a wad of sandpaper and a lime-green tennis ball. He reached in farther and withdrew two glass paperweights and a framed picture of himself taken in high school. Two piles of the box's contents sat on the bed now. He continued to take inventory.

When he was halfway through the box, Jeff happened to look out the window that stretched nearly the entire length of the bedroom wall. Though only five in the afternoon it had already been dark for an hour, and the view from his apartment revealed scores of lights dotting the north side of Queen Anne. During daylight Jeff could see the slope was covered with dreary bungalows and badly aging low-rise apartments with epic names like the Iliad and the Ramayana, all thrown up for the Seattle World's Fair decades ago. Now only points of white hovered in blackness. One of the three tall radio towers atop the hill was decorated with colorful holiday lights, a blinking red beacon at its top.

Jeff looked back down at the bed and then peered at the remaining contents of his half-emptied box. There were more bundles of old snapshots. Amid the QSL cards from his amateur radio days, he found a padlock rescued from some past gym, certificates of old school honors, a Cub Scout cap and kerchief, a plastic bong with rolling papers stuffed down its Plexiglas tube, electrical extension cords, a Phi Beta Kappa key. At the bottom of the clutter was what he was looking for. Christmas cards, dozens of them, saved over the years. He got fewer of them nowadays; it was 1983 and people didn't send them as they once had. But he'd saved cards from people he'd gone to high school with; cards from aunts, a brother's wife; cards from old boyfriends and, going way back, even from old girlfriends; cards from his car insurance agent; and cards from people he didn't now remember. Flat, two-dimensional messages from his life before going as far northwest as one could go in the lower forty-eight.

He took the bundles of Christmas cards into the barely furnished living room and laid them out in a rectangular grid on the floor between the television set and the futon sofa. That would be enough for one night. He went back into the bedroom and repacked the box with all the memorabilia arranged in its new logical order governed by utility. To hoist the box back up on the shelf, he stretched on his toes as far as he could.

Jeff returned to the living room and walked a couple of times around the rectangle of cards he'd laid out on the floor. They all looked more or less the same, images of decorated evergreen trees and peppermint canes and snowmen. After a while he lay down on the carpet and formed a right angle with his body bending along the upper-right corner of his Christmas card grid. He reached for a card one arm's length away and twirled it between his fingers while he thought about spending his first holiday alone, without either his family at home or a boyfriend in the house. It felt good but a little ominous, too. He got up off the carpet, pulled a beer out of the refrigerator, and decided to think about other things.

In Seattle the constant rain only comes in the last two months of the year. Until then, Jeff had usually walked or ridden his bike to the University of Washington along the old path that ran by the ship canal. He had a two-year gig as an acting assistant professor of history, teaching what he knew but some things he didn't as well. Jeff had left New York to take this job in Seattle, but he would have left anyway. He had spent his entire life in the northeast, and was eager to be somewhere else. But there was more to it. New York was changing. Not just more expensive, but risky. Friends of friends were getting sick, and it felt like the noose was tightening. Jeff was finishing his dissertation at Yale and needed to jumpstart his career as a historian of the American South. The two-year appointment, they told him at the University, might turn into something more long-term. He was happy to be here, he told his boyfriend Raul over the phone. Or ex-boyfriend. Raul never suggested tagging along with him to the West Coast and Jeff never discussed the matter either. Both knew it was time to move on, though neither man ever said so to each other out loud. Jeff had had a certain problem his whole life: the inability to communicate with the people closest to him. His silence started with a bad stutter as a child, but didn't disappear when he outgrew stammering. He was thoroughly white-bread preppie despite having been raised Catholic, unable to admit anything except for the lies he made up in the confessional for the benefit of a priest to whom he couldn't dare tell the truth. Jeff hadn't stepped into a church since leaving home, but the sight of clergy on the street still set his imagination racing for plausible, false sins to declare. His timidity had crippled his childhood at home with his equally taciturn parents and was now threatening his chances to make friends, much less find a lover. For the past couple of years Jeff had become frightened of what was making people sick in New York, rendering him more introverted still. Recently he had been seized with the desire to flee. But he could not confess that to Raul, who seemed so fearless in the face of all things. Jeff left New York for Seattle relieved and ashamed of himself at the same time.

One night last winter, when he was still living in New York, Jeff's friend Brandon came over from his own apartment across the hall to return some records he had borrowed for a party. He stayed long enough to talk Jeff, who had been cooped up all day, into going out for a beer at the Wildwood. They walked together down to Seventy-fourth Street and Columbus Avenue, and once there soon forgot the time.

"We better head back," Brandon said. "Some of us work, you know."

Brandon threw a handful of unshelled peanuts onto the floor of the bar. By one in the morning there were more brown peanut shells than there was black hardwood. Jeff saw that Brandon looked both impatient and disappointed.

"All right, let's go." Jeff slammed a half-finished beer down onto the bar and followed Brandon out the door.

The temperature seemed to be climbing. All kinds of people were loitering on Columbus as they turned left onto Seventy-sixth, crossed Amsterdam and started up Broadway. Normal people would have grabbed a cab. But Jeff was glad Brandon didn't propose it. He was enjoying the night.

"There wasn't one husband for me in that whole place."

"No," agreed Jeff, distracted by thoughts of his dissertation's Chapter Six. That morning Raul had put a newspaper article on his desk about the resurgence of the Klan in the South, knowing Jeff's thesis topic was about the Carolinas after the Civil War. His mind was toying with the idea he should have called it quits with Chapter Four when he looked ahead and spotted another guy about his and

Brandon's age who looked familiar. He was walking their same direction on Broadway a few feet ahead of them. Jeff tried to catch his eye to see if they knew each other and make some sort of nodding contact if they did. But at the last second, as he pulled alongside him, Jeff changed his mind and picked up his pace of their walk home.

Jeff turned to his left, about to ask Brandon if he knew the guy, when he saw that Brandon had been watching him the whole time. The look on his face told Jeff that Brandon knew him.

"Was that . . . ?" Jeff asked. Now he remembered seeing Brandon with him at the Y once.

"Yeah."

"Why not say something?"

"It was longer ago than you think. I've been through half a dozen boyfriends since then."

The two of them fell silent. Jeff didn't know Brandon all that well despite the fact they had lived across from each other for two years. They neared Ninety-first Street. When they crossed it, Jeff was still puzzled enough to bring the subject up again.

"He looked terrible."

"I hear he's sick. Couldn't have happened to a better fellow."

The neon sign on a restaurant with a shuttered entrance flashed "Comida China" and gave Brandon's face a ghoulish orange tint.

"So what's the story?" Jeff asked.

"Christ, I dunno. Mono, pneumonia, something like that. Maybe hepatitis."

"Oh."

Walking had been a mistake. Jeff was too buzzed and nearly tripped a couple of times. It was well after two when they made it to their building on Riverside Drive. People get mugged at this time of night, Jeff said to himself. Panting from the unusual warmth, he saw Raul in the doorway of their building leaning against the buzzers and smoking a cigarette. He looked like a Latin James Dean the way he was standing, both menacing and vulnerable. Jeff instantly regretted having made him wait.

"Sorry. Went out with Brandon for a beer. Turned into many beers."

Jeff realized he had been late on purpose without even planning to be. Maybe it was his passive-aggressive way of letting Raul know a change was coming. The three of them walked upstairs without exchanging words. Brandon went into his apartment, Jeff and Raul into the one opposite. Now alone with each other, they still didn't talk. Their relationship was winding down, and perhaps there was nothing to say.

Later, just as Jeff was drifting off to sleep with an arm draped over Raul, he heard a drunk down on the sidewalk messing with the first-floor flower boxes, cursing them out. The geraniums died last autumn and the super had never removed the slimy brown scum that remained. He made a mental note to do it himself.

Raul was Jeff's first real boyfriend. Theoretically he had been gay since the sixth grade, but growing up in suburban Connecticut there hadn't been many opportunities to practice. When he was an altar boy no one laid a hand on him. The Little League coach who suddenly vanished from town one day never invited him over to his house like he had the other boys. His first sex with a guy was late in his senior year of high school, when he went to a gay dance at Wesleyan and was picked up within minutes by an effeminate theater major. The college student asked if he could fuck him, and Jeff said yes without understanding what that meant. After then, every encounter with men had been equally brief and mismatched, punctuated with unsatisfactory interludes with a few women he tried hard to date while a college student. He and Raul met at a party in an NYU dorm shortly after Jeff had finished his graduate school classes in New Haven and could live in Manhattan. Raul had grown up in New Jersey but had been in the city for ages. Jeff had been eager to acclimate himself to gay New York, and Raul was the perfect guide. He often wondered what Raul saw in him, though.

He wasn't well off, not particularly handsome, and surprisingly stupid about the simplest things. He often said things that sounded offensive though he didn't mean them to be. But he was very accommodating in bed, where he was an eager learner, and Raul had some unusual tastes. Company joined them at times. Maybe that was why they had never taken their relationship up to any higher level, and why it had deteriorated now to this: from fuck buddies who had really liked each other to veterans in that army of New York gay men who, having done everything imaginable to each other in the sack, now could barely stand each other's company.

The drunk on the sidewalk was making noise again, but Jeff had no further problem joining Raul in sleep.

Nan had time to kill, so she decided to walk up Queen Anne Avenue and stop in at the Thriftway for fresh flowers. Her sister, who had lived in Vancouver for years now, always remarked when she visited how cheap flowers were here. Nan wanted roses. The cleaning women wouldn't be done with the house for another hour or so.

She held the collar of her down parka close to her neck. It felt cold even for December. The weather was wet and raw, and the slick on the concrete sidewalks seemed about to turn to ice. She was wearing her son Mike's coat, which was much too big for her. She didn't know why he hadn't taken it with him when he moved to his own place, or why he hadn't bothered to come back and fetch it once the cold meant he needed it. He only lived across town, down and across the flat of the city and then up another hill on the other side of I-5. Nan made a mental note to ask him about it next time they spoke.

The agency had said it would take its swat team of housecleaners a good five or six hours to make her house sale-ready clean. Nan wasn't domestic herself. She had many talents, or so she thought, but dusting the top of the credenza was not one of them. In two decades she had never done it.

The Thriftway was warm inside. She could smell the bakery department and the faint odor of recently mopped floors. A bouquet of yellow and white roses sold for three ninety-nine. At the checkout the cashier asked, "Do you want a bag?" Nan nodded and watched as the girl, whom she was sure was new, fumbled with two plastic bags, neither of which was big enough to do the job on its own.

The slick sidewalks were now frozen. Nan sped up a bit and enjoyed sliding on the ice using the flowers to balance herself. When she turned the corner a couple of minutes later and saw her house come into view, she noticed her real estate agent's BMW parked in front, too far from the curb.

"Joan."

Joan was outdoors, walking around the neat shrubs to the left of the front door.

"Hi, Nan."

"Cleaners done?"

"Don't know. Just got here."

Nan waved her plastic bags, as if Joan would somehow guess just-purchased flowers were inside them.

They walked into the house together. Nan could hear the high-pitched, metallic whine of a vacuum cleaner upstairs. She went into the kitchen to find something to put the flowers in.

"Any predictions about tomorrow?"

"Multiple offers by next weekend. Trust me. December is always the slowest time of the year, but trust me."

Nan had just divorced her husband. She got the house in the settlement, but she didn't want it anymore. She had plenty of money, thanks to her ex-husband's long and successful run as corporate counsel at Boeing. She was toying with the idea of going to Laguna Beach and renting a cozy bungalow near the ocean after this place closed. Maybe there'd be another man for her.

Joan noticed the flowers when Nan brought the white vase into the dining room.

"Oh, beautiful, Nan. Were you thinking of the dining room table?"

No, Nan had something else on her mind just then, but she wasn't about to tell her real estate agent everything, even if they were good friends.

In the mirror above the dining room hutch, Nan saw her face. Oh, right, this is the part where I'm supposed to think: I really look like my mother now. And how we Swedish blondes don't age well. But as Nan duly noted the lines around her eyes and mouth, she saw only the young woman who moved into this house with a new husband twenty years before, not sure at the time if she loved him enough but ready to love *someone*. She'd be Jackie to his Jack, Liz to his Richard. Nan took the white vase and its flowers and put them on her dining room table, just where the whole world expected her to.

"Joan, I'm driving over to Capitol Hill to run an errand. Lock up when you leave, won't you?"

Nan found a parking spot right in front of Mike's house on Tenth Avenue. The pavement she parked above was dry, meaning that someone had just pulled out. She hoped it wasn't Mike. She hoisted his winter coat under her left arm and got out of the car.

Mike shared the modest house with three other young men, and chances were good that at this hour at least one of them would be home. Their house, too, had a For Sale sign hanging from a post on the lawn, but it had been there for years. Mike once told her it would never sell. The house was the worst looking on the block, painted a sickly pink color and rimmed by anemic shrubs. The rusting hulk of an old Buick lurked in the backyard, its front end visible from the street. Nan turned up the cracked concrete path that led to the front entrance. The door was ajar. Nan didn't need to ring the doorbell or shout to be let in, but she probably should have announced her arrival anyway.

The living room was to the right on the other side of a staircase. It was devoid of people but full of things. As she tried to figure out what she was smelling, she caught sight of a tall red plastic bong standing on an old door with concrete blocks supporting its corners in front of a beat-up plaid sofa. On the other side of the makeshift table was a fireplace with books piled up where logs should be. Men's clothes were crumpled and in several piles on the floor. Was that cat piss she smelled as well? A stack of record albums occupied the seat of an overstuffed chair that looked like it had been dragged in from the street, but she didn't see a stereo. Now the room reeked of wet dog to her, but there was no dog in sight either.

Nan walked back to the dining room, stepping over one of the piles of clothes. She turned left and went through swinging saloon doors into the kitchen. Pots hung from a rack over the counter. Each of the four burners on the stove had something dirty sitting on it. Nan saw no sign of her son or his housemates. She'd met one of them once, and Mike had pointed out another to her on the street when he first moved in.

"Mike? Mike!" Nan considered calling out his old nickname, Richard Junior, but she didn't want to use her ex's name. Mike belonged to her.

Nan debated just leaving the coat somewhere, maybe on one of the kitchen stools. But she had come here really hoping to see Mike, and she had a lot of time on her hands today while Joan prepared the house. She leaned over a greasy frying pan on the stove and felt a slight warmth emanating from it.

A striped cat strolled through the room. It rubbed soundlessly against Nan's corduroy pants leg.

She heard floorboards creak above her head. She quickly went back into the living room and sat down on the sofa, centering herself in front of the door-table with its array of drug paraphernalia. She turned her head as a young man she didn't recognize came noisily down the staircase. He was putting a shirt on over his head and looked for an instant as if he might stumble and fall. Nan used her left foot to stir some old newspapers strewn on the floor, thinking the rustling sound might alert the young man to her presence.

"Hello. I'm Mike's mother."

The man stood at the foot of the stairs and looked distractedly in the direction of Nan's voice. His eyes didn't seem to focus.

"Mike? Oh, Richard Junior."

Nan felt a sharp pain go through her.

"I let myself in. Sorry. The door was open. I just wanted to bring Mike—Richard Junior—his coat." She pointed to it on the sofa. "Is he here?"

The young man covered his mouth as he coughed and seemed stumped by the question.

"Dunno. Might be. I haven't seen him today. Do you wanna go up to his room?"

Nan finally stood up, since it seemed the polite thing to do, but she didn't move any further. The young man had curly hair and large blue eyes, and something about him reminded her of her son's father when he was young. And as she was of Richard, she was somewhat frightened of him. Nearly every man in her life had intimidated her.

"No, thanks. I'll just leave it here for him, if that's all right with you. Will you tell him?"

The young man coughed again. "Tell him what?"

"That I brought his coat." Nan bent over and moved the parka so it draped over the back of the sofa.

The young man cleared his throat and wordlessly shuffled toward the kitchen. Nan took some money out of her shoulder bag and stuffed it into one of her son's coat pockets. She adjusted her scarf around her neck, took one more look around the living room and headed toward the door. It was raining harder than when she

15

had come. The cold winter drizzle had turned into a real shower. Quickening her step, she headed to the Volvo.

As she pulled away from the curb, she saw the door to Mike's house move slightly as someone inside closed it tight.

"Hello?"

"Yeah, hi. Jeff?"

"Yeah, this is Jeff. ...Brandon?"

"Brandon, yeah. It's me. I got your number from Raul."

"It must be late where you are."

"After three. I've been out."

"On a Thursday? Did you get fired?"

"No. But aren't you going to ask me why I'm calling?"

Brandon explained that he had something to send him. "Might be a few days before I can make it to the post office. We haven't talked since you left the city. You haven't called me, I haven't called you."

"Well, I'm still getting settled."

"Yeah, I know. Anyway, I'm not calling because there's much to say."

Jeff didn't know how to take that. "Something wrong, Brandon?"

"Wrong? No, not wrong. Actually, I just found out something tonight I thought I'd tell you about. I heard it at the bar. That guy is dead."

Jeff reached down, peeled off his socks and threw them onto the floor. "What guy?"

"You know, the guy we passed on the street a year ago or so."

How am I supposed to remember that? Jeff wondered.

"Remember him? The guy I used to go out with."

"Dead?"

"Yeah."

"Oh."

"He left me something. He didn't have a will or anything, but they found a letter in a drawer."

Jeff looked down at his feet in the dark room.

"He left me a set of steak knives."

Jeff didn't say anything.

"He knew I was a vegetarian. His little joke, I guess."

"You're not a vegetarian," Jeff said.

"Well, I was when I dated him. You want them?"

They talked longer, but not about anything important. He and Brandon had never exchanged anything important. They weren't that kind of friends. When he thought he detected Brandon yawning at the other end of the line, Jeff found an excuse to end the call. He walked around his apartment in circles with Brandon and his dead quasi-boyfriend on his mind, but without much feeling one way or the other. Jeff thought, *steak* knives? What the hell was he going to do with steak knives? Brandon was a strange guy. Brandon had said he imagined Jeff out here paddling around in a birch bark canoe and living in a tepee on some fir-tree-covered island. Sure, send the steak knives, he told Brandon. I'll make room for your old junk next to my own, he thought, maybe alongside the Christmas cards in my fraying cardboard box.

That night Jeff dreamed about knives flying through the air, darting through clouds, soaring toward the stratosphere, stabbing the bright moon and slicing it into pieces; all of which slowly wafted down onto earth, shiny fragments of white that took their place among the electric lights of Seattle.

Joan called two weeks later to say Nan's house sold on the second offer. The first buyer couldn't qualify for a loan, but the next one, a divorced lawyer—there are a lot of them, Nan observed when Joan told her—was moving to Seattle from California and, flush with equity, was paying the asking price in cash.

He waived the inspection and wanted Nan out in three weeks. Nan really didn't want another house after this one, definitely not this fast. Houses meant husbands and she didn't have one anymore. She was all thumbs, and if she was going to live on her own she wanted to rent where a nice handyman fixed things for her when they broke. Things always break, Nan now knew. She used to think that when you acquired something, like an appliance or a husband, they stayed new forever. Intact. Shiny. But they didn't.

Nan wanted to cocoon herself in a tiny studio, one filled with bright light year-round and not dimmed by clouds. She wanted to live somewhere so tiny she could wear it like favorite clothes, where moving from the bedroom to the kitchen meant stretching one arm this way and the other that way. There would be no guest room.

But first Joan, and then more forcefully Richard's accountant, told her that the profits from the sale of the house meant huge taxes unless she reinvested them back into real estate. Renting a studio apartment in Laguna Beach had to wait. She might as well stay in Seattle for the time being, near both Richard and their son. She had given them so much of her life, a little more wouldn't matter. But she had to admit the truth was the opposite. She needed them more than they needed her. She could not face living alone. She had lived with her strict Lutheran parents and commuted while in college. They would have been happy if she had never left home. But once she rebelled by marrying Richard, a man too handsome and thus untrustworthy according to her parents' Scandinavian prejudices, she found she had simply exchanged one family for another. Until Mike was born Nan found ways to accompany her husband on all his long business trips. Years later she embarrassed Mike by visiting him every weekend at his all-boys summer camp on the Olympic Peninsula.

Nan finally decided she would take everyone's advice and look for a place of her own in Seattle, but one with room for the world to join her if it wanted. She called Joan and told her to start looking for a house to buy anywhere in the city except near the old one. She knew she needed people around her, but they could include more than her ex-husband and son. Nan would stay in the city of her birth after all, but she was determined to discover it on her own. It was the nineteen-eighties, after all, and life was never better.

CHAPTER TWO

The day was breezy and damp downtown. Jeff didn't bring his umbrella since he thought he'd need both hands to haul his new vacuum cleaner back to his car in the parking garage. Two bums parted to let him by on his way in through the Bon Marché department store's double glass doors.

Rows and rows of color televisions faced him when he reached the top of the escalator on the home appliance floor. All of them were displaying the same channel, some report about Reagan and Andropov threatening nuclear war against each other. Jeff hesitated and looked both ways trying to figure out in which direction, left or right, he'd find the vacuum cleaners.

He was looking at a Eureka when a saleswoman came up to him. "Can I help you?" she said. The woman was short and wide. She wore her Bon Marché name tag on a bright yellow sweater.

"I'm looking for a vacuum cleaner."

The saleswoman searched Jeff's face for a moment before she replied. "Come this way." She led him to a corner and pointed wordlessly at a small canister model with a long hose and carpet-cleaning attachment.

"This is what you want. It's the one men buy."

She disappeared for a moment and then reemerged from behind two large swinging doors, carrying a large box.

"Enjoy," she said after he had paid.

Jeff nodded and started for the down escalator.

"Take the elevator," the saleswoman called out to him.

"Okay."

When the elevator doors opened, one person was already in it. Jeff took note. The young man stepped back to the rear of the elevator as Jeff awkwardly maneuvered his large bag into the compartment. As the doors closed, Jeff's elevator-mate moved back toward the front.

"What floor?"

"Huh?"

"What floor?"

"Oh, I can do it. One. The first."

The young man pressed it though it was lit already. "One, okay. Me too."

Jeff liked what he saw, but he didn't want to stare. Jeff guessed the ethnicity was Latino, possibly Italian. Raul was like that too. Jeff knew he definitely had a type. He looked to be in his early twenties, if that. Olive-skinned, with jet-black hair, a trim goatee and large brown eyes, positively bovine. Eyes like that were definitely one of Jeff's weaknesses. But the best thing about him was the smooth olive-green skin stretched tautly over a strong nose and jaw. He was a boy-man—the voice still that of a teenager, but the prominent Adam's apple covered with the faint stubble of an adult's beard.

"You don't have any bags," Jeff said, struggling to overcome his instinctive shyness around strangers.

"What?"

"You haven't bought anything."

Brown Eyes hesitated, probably mulling over whether he really wanted to start a conversation with someone who might be nuts.

"I returned something. A watch. It was a gift I gave someone who doesn't need it anymore. I had to go to customer service."

When the elevator doors slid open on the ground floor, Jeff and Brown Eyes had to push their way through a gaggle of women trying to get on. Standing between the closing doors and the Clinique counter, Brown Eyes hesitated again. One of them had to say something or the opportunity was going to be lost.

"I'm Henry."

"Jeffrey. Jeff."

It was the outside of the house that drew Nan to it that cold January day. It was painted a bright yellow, something out of a Van Gogh painting. That, together with pure white trim, made the Victorian look alive, as if it were vibrating against the neutral gray sky. It was set back from the street and framed by the nearly lime green of the grassy front yard and by the darker greens of the towering spruces and pines on either flank and then, taller still, in the rear. It was a yellow close to cadmium, unearthly in its intensity but like rich gold in its power. The two-story house with the gabled roof and wide front porch sat high on its gentle knoll on the east side of Fifteenth Avenue, not far from Group Health Hospital and quite nearly at the top of the ridge that looked east to the Cascades and west to the Olympics.

Nan stood on the sidewalk in a yellow rain parka and compared her clothing's color with that of the house. She took a step sideways away from Joan and raised her arms as if to greet the edifice.

"I have the key to the lockbox, if you want to go in," Joan said.

"Yes. That's why we're here, isn't it?" Nan giggled.

They walked up the slate path to the front steps. As Joan fumbled with the lock, Nan turned around and looked west over the hill that ran down to I-5 and beyond to the new skyscrapers downtown, and where she could see Elliott Bay had the skies been clearer.

Joan babbled on about the original crown moldings and the old madrona tree in the backyard. Bigger and grander than many of the homes near it on the summit of Capitol Hill, the house had been built in the 1920s. It had all the finishes and amenities of the era.

The many windows, to let in the scant winter light, still had the original leaded glass. The fireplaces worked and the masonry was sound. The woodwork was extensive and stained a deep, rich mahogany that made the house feel warm. The French doors that led from the dining room to another porch and then the backyard had a modern alarm affixed to them, but were otherwise as they always had been. Some of the smaller rooms had their original wallpaper, now a faded tobacco brown; other rooms had been painted electric colors, probably in the 1960s. Where posters had once been tacked, the paint was still vivid, unmolested by long summer light, when Seattle's sun went to work.

Nan sat down on the seat built into the wall below the two narrow, tall windows facing west. She opened her purse and took out a cigarette, lit it, and cupped her free hand to catch the ashes she didn't want to fall onto the floor.

"Who lived here?"

"Say what?" chirped Joan from the far end of the room.

"Who's selling the house?"

"Hmm. A son, I think. His mother lived here until she died three months ago. It's a little mysterious. They found the old lady stone cold in her bed under the covers but fully dressed, as if she were going out."

Nan tapped the cigarette ashes into her hand. "What was her name? Anyone I might know?"

"Don't think so. Why do I want to say they were originally Portland people. Lumber or some such. Maybe it was Aberdeen or Hoquiam. Long ago."

Nan stood up and walked around the perimeter of the living room. Her damp boots left faint marks on the floor. Would Mike come live here with her? Did she even want Mike to live with her? If not, why was she considering buying a house twice as big as the one she just sold?

Nan stopped in front of the fireplace. "What's upstairs?"

"Bedrooms. Oodles of them. Some of the original large rooms were portioned off."

"For one old lady?"

"Maybe she had a lot of family."

"Let's go up," Nan suggested. Following Joan, she was only halfway up the creaky staircase when she knew she'd buy this house.

As instructed, Jeff went back to the gay clinic on Fifteenth Avenue one week later. He had seen its address on the side of a bus Christmas day, and decided to get his move to Seattle off like an Eagle Scout would, with a drop-in visit in January. It had taken courage but somehow Jeff found it. He was usually good at avoiding things he was frightened of. Years could pass between his visits to the dentist. But right now he needed to know that at the very least he didn't have any of the usual gay culprits, the ones treatable with a big shot in the ass, especially since he was finding himself fantasizing about sex with Henry.

"Mother's name?" the receptionist asked.

"Elizabeth."

"Number?"

"Eighteen."

"This way, please. How are you today?"

He was there for the results of his STD tests, but they didn't have a test for what really worried him, which was whatever his friend Sam in New York had. First Sam lost a lot of the baby fat he'd always had, and then the night sweats began. He put off going to the doctor until the headaches were unbearable. How am I, you ask? "Fine," Jeff replied, thinking he should have checked first with his little—*arf*—pet inside—*arf*—the dog that was always whimpering, its *arf* that was shorthand for "Am Really Fucked." That's what Sam was, Really Fucked, and Jeff wondered if his turn was coming.

Jeff sat in a chair in one corner of a small office, the counselor in an identical chair in the opposite corner. There'd be their talk, and the obligatory hug—how many had she given to "clients" that day already?—and Jeff would look down at his feet and the dingy linoleum floor.

The counselor interrupted Jeff's thoughts and said, given his "lifestyle choices," she wanted two other people to see him before he left. Jeff didn't have to move. They'd come in here and have their chat with him. Jesus, what are going to tell me? What do they think I do, for crissake? *Arf, arf,* Jeff thought of saying when they showed up, all I've *got* is my dog, I brought him here with me, don't mind him, we'll go back home soon and have a *real* heart-to-heart. Just the two of us. Yes, yes, less risky behavior, we promise. A condom every time and, sure, drugs and alcohol can cloud our judgment. My dog and I know that. But that's not what Jeff said to them. He wouldn't remember exactly what he said. He had probably responded like any Best Little Boy in the World would have. Despite how terrified Jeff was of getting sick and dying, no matter how smutty his fantasies could still be in spite of that terror, he always came across to others as the golly-gee clean-cut neighbor who shoveled your driveway for you. There should be a merit badge he could earn for all this, in addition to a PhD from Yale.

The counselor left the room to summon her colleagues. Jeff was alone. As he sat there something began to stir within him. It was like a bothered stomach at first. Next it spread like a boozy numbness to his chest and his buttocks. Then it was moving slowly to his limbs, as sharp as shards of glass, and he knew his body was filling with something that could, if it kept growing, fill the room.

Jeff stood up, spread his arms wide, and shifted his feet farther apart to make himself steady. The holes of his swollen body—his ears and nostrils and navel and rectum and the tip of his penis—were all tingling. The energy seemed concentrated in his throat, making plain that what was inside him was going to leave via his mouth and take its place beside him. Jeff's eyeballs bulged, his

25

fingertips became sensitive, and a kind of light-headedness joined the clarity already there in his head. It happened so quickly. There it was, now next to him though opaque and featureless, a dark cloud constantly shifting shape. His body started to deflate and resume its prior contours, and a muddled feeling returned to his brain. He turned and saw a billowy shadow—now man-like but not a man—float through the air toward a wall, the one that had a poster of good sexual health dos and don'ts hung on it. Before Jeff could call out to the thing it passed silently through the wall as if nothing could stop it, and Jeff was alone in the room again until the counselor returned with two other women.

While one counselor talked, Jeff retrieved a vivid memory he had used to masturbate earlier that day. Raul was on the bed in Jeff's New York apartment wearing a Police Athletic League T-shirt and a pair of old gym shorts. He was reading the *Post* and eating an apple noisily in the heat of the late afternoon sun. Jeff was returning from New Haven after a day in the library and a meeting with his adviser. When he saw Raul on the bed, his eyes went right away to the dark place between the bottom edge of the gym shorts and his thigh, where a slice of thick dark cock was curled up like a snake in the nest of a jet-black bush. Jeff got on the bed with his knees just at the edge. He pushed Raul's apple-holding hand out of the way and grabbed the paper with the other. Then he pushed Raul's heavy legs apart and leaned into him. Raul talked with his head on the pillow looking straight up at the ceiling, but Jeff wasn't listening.

Then the memory shifted and something new entered it: another thing, the same shadow he had just seen in the Seattle clinic moments earlier. It moved across the room and stood there quietly at first, watching as Jeff moved his buttocks up and down to seduce his boyfriend. Raul placed his hands with long, delicate fingers on Jeff's hips and kept talking, not to Jeff in particular, or even to himself, but to everyone there. It was just then that the stranger moved in closer. It joined them on the bed on the sheets made hot by the sunlight pouring in through the window. Still, Jeff and Raul did not pay any attention to this half-alive, half-dead presence. Jeff used his hands to gather what was fleshy on Raul's pectorals under his shirt and mold them into pyramids. Raul kept murmuring things, and the third entity among them soon was talking, too, but neither man noticed. Raul and the shadow mumbled their words in Jeff's apartment, the sunlight illuminating the sexual congress while their voices ricocheted like bullets, or like the start of a romance in some foreign language. They were words that somehow made the room smaller, so small they oozed out the open window and dribbled down to the street below, where they made black, oily stains on the sidewalk.

The counselors finished their counseling and Jeff went home. When he woke the following morning, piles of unspoken words were scattered about on the carpet of his Seattle apartment, things that had leaked out of his memories and now waited to be sucked up and tossed away the first time he used his new vacuum cleaner.

When Nan closed on their old house in late January, she called her ex-husband to tell him what she had done. "Richard, the house is not ours anymore. I've said goodbye to it." He seemed somewhat surprised, though she had kept him up-to-date on the sale all along.

"Richard, you know I'm staying in Seattle, right? That idea about Laguna Beach was just an idea. My bid on a new place on Capitol Hill has been accepted."

"Capitol Hill?" he said with a mixture of surprise and skepticism. "The north part?" he asked, referring to the fancy half of the neighborhood.

"No, right in the middle. Near Group Health." Nan guessed that he thought that was a place for kids in their twenties, and not a middle-aged woman. She enjoyed correcting his assumptions about her.

"Not much of a move," he added.

"Enough of a move," she countered, meaning she would be free of the house she'd shared twenty-plus years with him.

"Do you need any help?"

"No. I've hired movers already, thanks."

"Well, good luck. What are you going to do with a whole house? There all by yourself?"

"Fill it with people," she announced firmly, though she had no idea where those four words had come from. Fill it with people? What people? She was sure Richard was thinking the same thing.

Later Nan figured out that she had meant to hurt him with that answer, make him think her life now was overflowing with all kinds of new friends. But she also knew that Richard's life was already busy with a new woman who had so effortlessly replaced the old. The break-up had come so suddenly, had been so unexpected. Nan guessed she was naive. Friends who had gone through their own divorces, like Joan, were fond of giving her those insufferable looks of sympathy mixed with knowing, invincible superiority. *Men*. In hindsight the trouble between her and Richard accelerated once Mike left home. *Now you know, too.* Why hadn't she seen it? *I could have told you so.* When they agreed that their son could postpone college for a few years, Nan should have realized that Richard took this as an opportunity for him to defect from life's standard trajectory as well.

Nan, on the other hand, never deviated from anything. She played it by the book her whole life. Good daughter, good wife, good mother. Not even a flirtation with a deliveryman or a secret cocktail at noon. Seattle had always been the 1950s even when it became the 1960s and the 1970s. Mayberry by the Bay, where the men went to work with lunch pails and the women wore handmade aprons. But now in the 1980s, things were changing in Seattle. The world was moving here now, just as Richard was moving out.

Jeff had written Henry's phone number on the back of a grocery store receipt. It was ten on a Sunday morning and too early to call anyone. He sat down on his sofa and let his eyes roam the far wall until they focused on a patch of wallpaper less faded by the sun, where a picture frame might have once hung. Who used to live here, Jeff wondered, and where are they now? He fell asleep until his own phone rang.

Jeff bolted from his supine position on the couch and went to answer it. "Jeff? Henry. From last weekend."

"Henry! You found my number."

"You gave it to me, remember?"

"I did?" Jeff was groggy from his nap.

Jeff sat on the carpet with the phone between his legs. He let Henry do the talking.

"I worked at Starbucks last night until closing. Actually, past closing."

Jeff knew Starbucks was some kind of store that sold coffee beans.

"They use me to clean the place up sometimes."

Bean salesman *and* janitor? Jeff said to himself.

Henry continued. "You know, I was going to North Seattle Community College, but I'm taking a break now. Thought of enlisting." Jeff was listening to someone less than two-thirds his age. But he felt ready to move past Raul. "Anyway, it's cool just to hang out until something better happens." Jeff was definitely attracted to this young man. Henry was more than the opportunity for sex with a hot younger man, but a chance for Jeff to audition for his new role as Svengali.

"Let's go to Numbers later. The Twenty Twenty-four," Henry said.

"Hmm."

"You ever been?

"No. Not yet." Jeff knew instantly to lie. He'd been there several times already. But why sound like a bar rat?

"Okay, you know where it is?"

"I think so. A club, right? I've been by it. I'm not that new here."

"Great. Later."

Jeff drove to Broadway to run errands after hanging up the phone. It started to rain, and Jeff hadn't brought an umbrella. He didn't bother anymore. Carrying an umbrella was usually the sign of someone from out of town, or recently arrived. The natives never minded getting wet.

Still, Jeff nipped into a place called A Different Drummer bookstore to wait out the worst of the rain. He was overpowered by the strong musty scent of used books and by the darkness unrelieved by anything more than a couple of uncovered lightbulbs in the ceiling. The clerk at the front was a slightly older guy, mostly bald but sporting a neat walrus mustache. He greeted Jeff as if they knew each other. It was still early in the day, and only two other customers were in the store, both of them in front of the magazine rack leafing through some gay skin mags.

Jeff unzipped his jacket and pulled down the hood on the sweatshirt he was wearing underneath. He picked up a magazine called *RFD* and skimmed an article entitled "I Came Out in a Restaurant in Coos Bay." As he went over to the shelf marked New Arrivals, he felt a rush of hot dry air emanating from the electric heater that Walrus must keep under the counter. Jeff moved a bit down the narrow aisle to avoid the heat. Not much piqued his interest, and he didn't want to buy anything that would just get soaked when he resumed walking in the January rain.

He retraced his steps down Broadway. There weren't a lot of people on the sidewalk at this time of day and traffic was light. Seattle generally struck him as an empty city. Jeff knew in theory humans lived here, even if this was the last part of the continental U.S. to get many of the white ones. He wasn't ready to say he was having regrets over moving here, but for the first time it occurred to him he might.

He stood at the corner of Broadway and Republican and waited for the light to change so he could cross. There was no reason to wait, but he wasn't in a hurry. The Number 7 bus lumbered up Broadway toward him on the other side of the street.

It glistened with rain, and he could see through its big windshield wipers an overweight black woman driving. It came to a halt in front of Fred Meyer. The intersection was quiet once the wheels of the bus stopped making the slurping sound of tires on wet pavement. Jeff put his hands in the pockets of his coat and continued to wait for the light to change.

A couple of people appeared on the sidewalk in front of the bus, people who must have just gotten off. Before the bus closed its doors with a whoosh and revved up to go the scant twenty feet to the stop light, Jeff saw a woman alone, wearing a woolen cap and a faded green army surplus jacket with a hippie bag slung across her shoulder.

The light changed. Jeff was about to step off the curb when he heard the woman shout, "Ryan! Ryan!"

Jeff looked across the street and saw that the woman had stopped and was looking straight at him with a big smile.

"Ryan!" she repeated. She meant him. He kept walking. He heard her call out "Ryan!" once more, but he kept ignoring her. He must look like Ryan. Or maybe the woman was just a street person and called everyone Ryan. The rain was falling more heavily again, and Jeff picked up his pace.

On the spur of the moment he decided to stop at the Elite for an early drink, pre-Henry. He found a spot along the wall of the gay pub to stand and nurse his beer. He didn't feel like meeting anyone, though if someone walked in who looked like him and was named Ryan, he might make an exception.

He drove home to his apartment in Fremont, despite the one beer that had turned into three. He was walking up the stairs to his place when he passed one of his neighbors. Jeff didn't know his name, but knew he lived on a floor somewhere above him.

"Hi."

"Hi."

The neighbor continued down but then stopped. "Oh, I've got a package for you. It came yesterday—the mailman gave it to me when I was coming in the building. I'll go upstairs and get it." Very kind, Jeff thought. He knew exactly what the package was, even if he pretended otherwise. He wasn't expecting anything else.

"Here it is."

Once in his own apartment Jeff went into the kitchen for a knife to cut the twine wrapped around the package. He sat down on the sofa in the living room to open it. He tore the brown paper off and tossed it onto the floor. The box Brandon had used was an old candle box, making Jeff think for a moment there'd be candles inside. He lifted the cover off and removed the newsprint Brandon had used to pack the box. Steak knives. A lot of them, with fake black onyx handles and serrated edges. Jeff picked all of them up with one hand and saw a note underneath, written on a torn piece of the same brown paper Brandon had used to wrap the box.

Jeff—

These belonged to the old boyfriend I told you about when we went out to the Wildwood that night. The one who died. He never used them. Someone who was sick gave them to him. It seemed like a joke at the time. Maybe you can use them. Better you than me! Later, buddy. Sam says hi. You should call him.

Brandon

Too creepy, Jeff thought. He walked into the kitchen and put the knives in the sink to wash later. He was tempted to give Brandon a call and thank him for sending the package. But it was already eleven p.m. in New York, and maybe Brandon was out or asleep. Jeff went back into the kitchen and took the knives out of the sink after rinsing them off. He lined them up on the counter in a straight row from the edge back to the wall, sharp edges pointed away from him. Then he went to meet Henry.

They sat down on one of the pool tables as soon as the bartenders put the large plywood sheets down to protect the felt.

They barely made it in time as other men rushed to do the same thing. Henry talked about himself. Jeff learned that he was half-Chilean but had lived all his life in Seattle, punctuated only by brief visits to his father and other relatives in Santiago. His mother, a local Norwegian, had been a teacher's aide in the elementary school he'd attended, which had been embarrassing for him. For the past year he'd been living in an apartment near Northgate with an ex-boyfriend. Jeff made a note of that, but didn't ask any follow-up questions since he knew the definition of "ex" was open to interpretation.

"I live by myself."

"Fremont, right?"

"Yeah, Fremont. It's near work. The University of Washington. I've got a two-year contract."

"Wow, the UW. I've got friends going to school there. What do you do?"

"Teach. History." Jeff knew that answer had just put distance between him and Henry. He let his eyes leave his date and scan the entire bar, a rude habit he had acquired early in gay life. Henry nursed his beer and fell silent. Jeff felt sorry for him, a dangerous thing because it was already an emotion that risked complicating things.

"So what's your old boyfriend's name?"

"It really doesn't matter, does it?"

"Just curious," said Jeff, not too happy at being blown off. Henry yawned, making Jeff worry this was the end of the conversation. At just that moment, Henry put a hand on Jeff's thigh. Jeff moved his hand with the beer, to make more room for this gesture. He gave Henry his most seductive look and saw he was wearing a thin gold chain with a crucifix dangling from it. A fellow Catholic for sure, Jeff thought. Raul's parents had become evangelicals when he was a child, and so he hated anything religious. Jeff was indifferent.

"Jeff. His name is Jeff."

"Oh. Guess there are a lot of us."

The music in the bar was suddenly louder, making conversation harder.

"Was Jeff."

"Huh?"

"He died. Half a year ago." Henry played with his beer bottle in his lap. "I'm gonna move out soon." He was nearly shouting into Jeff's ear. Jeff took another sip of his own beer rather than ask any of the obvious follow-up questions. A little dog was barking inside him.

"Can't afford the rent on my own. Anyway, he wasn't a good influence on me."

"Oh yeah?"

"That's what they tell me in group."

"What group?" Jeff asked, though that was not the question he really had in mind.

"I'm in recovery. On and off, anyway. Jeff—the other Jeff—he was a dealer."

Jeff pondered whether this was a good time to cut his losses, say his farewells and go home. He watched Henry take another swallow of his beer.

"You're drinking."

"What?"

"Recovery. You said you were in recovery."

"Oh, not for beer. Not for that."

Jeff eased himself off the pool table and then leaned against it. He instantly worried Henry thought he might be restless, or even about to say goodbye. The thought had occurred to him for a split second. He put his beer down on the plywood where he'd just been sitting, close to Henry, so that he'd understand he had decided not to leave.

"Well, it's beer that I should probably give up." Jeff patted his belly. His attempt at a joke didn't work. "Let's talk about something else!" Henry shouted above the din.

34

"Okay, sure. Just how old are you, anyway?" Somet told Jeff to check.

"Twenty. Almost twenty-one."

Jeff looked at Henry carefully for the first time. He had that look of a boy on the cusp of manhood that Jeff could fall for. There was also something disquieting about him. But right now the way he cocked his head, hunched his shoulders together and compressed his posture said he was a very adorable young man. Jeff scanned Henry's face for signs of imminent trouble and was relieved not to find any, or maybe he just willed himself not to. As he picked up his beer, he decided to put the brakes on his hall monitor impulse for the time being. Henry was just too cute.

"What else do you want to talk about? Do you want to know how old I am?"

Henry shrugged. Jeff turned the beer bottle around in his hand and clinked it against Henry's.

"Let's go then," Jeff said in a tone that half suggested, half commanded. He surprised himself talking to Henry the way Raul used to talk to him. Henry hopped off the pool table and they left for Fremont. Two other guys rushed to take their places on the plywood.

CHAPTER THREE

By the beginning of February, Nan was in the new house. Richard was right; it was too big for one person. She spent the first week sleeping each night in a different room, dragging a sleeping bag purchased from REI long ago when her family briefly took a fancy to camping. Any of the rooms she tried out could become her bedroom, except for the ones on the second floor that faced Fifteenth Avenue and had traffic noise all hours.

She didn't leave the house much that first week, except to walk to the QFC for groceries and down to the post office on Broadway to fill out more change-of-address cards. Once the phone was installed, she immediately thought of calling Mike to invite him to come over. He was so near her. But she knew that he knew where she lived now, and if he wanted to visit he didn't need to be prompted.

She settled on the large room in the basement. It was a little cold, she was sure it was damp, and she had to walk up two flights to reach a full bathroom. But it was the largest room, had the washer and dryer nearby, and by sleeping there, she left all of the other more cheerful rooms with windows for guests.

Most of the furniture she'd brought from Queen Anne was arranged without much thought. She reassembled the brass bed piece by piece in the basement, and talked the electrician into helping her drag the mattress and box spring down the narrow stairs that led off the kitchen.

A lot of her time was spent wandering around the rest of the empty house. Some things she had to have done—new paint, wallpaper, light fixtures—but she decided to leave everything the way it was for now.

One night she sat in her ex-husband's old recliner, which she had always hated, and moved an old floor lamp over to it to give her light to read by. She was going to read the copy of the *Seattle Times* but instead she fished around in one of her movers' boxes to find her old notebook. She saw it underneath the hand pistol Richard had given her years ago for protection when he was away. Nan reminded herself she needed to find a safe place to hide it in the new house, but she pushed it aside for the moment, surprised how heavy and cold to the touch it was. She extracted the notebook. At the Queen Anne house she'd used it to keep track of things she wanted the cleaning lady to do. But tonight, on a fresh page, she started a different kind of list.

She had already mentioned to Mike and Richard that she was going to use the house as a place for community groups to meet. Neither of them had registered any interest in hearing more, but she was serious. She'd read in a neighborhood weekly that the gay AA group was looking for a new place to meet because the church at Sixteenth and John had asked them to vacate. The first item she wrote down on her list: Find out whom to talk to about gay AA. As she thought about Number Two, she idly ran her hand lightly along the inside of her left thigh, letting it slow down in places that had not had human attention in a long time.

Like other women of her generation, she had imagined she was strong, a feminist even, but in fact she hadn't really ever needed to be. There had been men in her life to whom she deferred from the start: a father whom she always obeyed; a husband whose control of her she mistook for love; and then a son whose willfulness reminded her of both his father and grandfather. There were always those men. But now one was long dead and the other two were leading lives in which she played no indispensible part. Her hand left one breast and found the other. She'd be busy, she promised herself that. She was in her new house now, and had a project in mind. But nights would be like this, even if days were filled with the people she'd boasted to Richard she knew—summoned from where, she had no idea. Her hand felt cold on her skin and she let it slide away. She had to learn to divide what was once three people into one woman, and let it be her world.

Raul eventually wrote. The first thing Jeff pulled out of the envelope was a Polaroid of Raul and Sam sitting on Sam's couch and holding up sheets of white paper with four words written on them with a black Magic Marker: NEW YORK MISSES YOU. The letter accompanying the Polaroid was full of news, mostly of Sam, with whom Raul was now living on a need-be basis. Sam was a beefy strawberry-blonde Irish guy who shared Jeff's ironic take on life, but with more of a sense of humor about it all. They'd been introduced at the same party he'd met Raul, and while Raul became a lover, Sam was someone Jeff saw around and spent a weekend together once in a house in the Grove with six other guys. The last time Jeff had seen him was at Julius's on West Tenth, just before he moved to Seattle.

Jeff learned from Raul's letter what experimental therapies Sam was on, about his new interest in Zoroastrianism, and how his sister-in-law in Buffalo had put him in touch with someone who had cured himself by eating swamp grass. Then the letter moved on to news of other people. Some names Jeff recalled, and a few he could associate faces with. But none were his friends.

Sam couldn't work anymore at Bonwit Teller and Raul's own money was running low. That boss from hell at Condé Nast had finally let him go. In a couple of months Sam could qualify for disability. Could Jeff help out until then?

Jeff walked to one of the windows of his apartment and looked out at the ship canal. The drawbridge was up and a barge slowly cruised past it. Jeff left the letter on the windowsill and went into the kitchen, where he used the Snoopy magnet to put the snapshot on the refrigerator. Too thick for the magnet, it fell to the floor after a few seconds. Jeff picked it up and left it on the table, where a week or so later it would be buried under newer mail. It wasn't that he was offended to be asked for money. It was simply that news from New York caused him to think about the city all over again. Fantasizing about Henry, whom he hardly knew, became his preferred way of thinking about Seattle rather than New York.

Another letter arrived ten days later. It was from Sam, but not really Sam. Sam didn't have the energy to write, so friends now added handling correspondence to the chores they did for him. The letter was long and chatty, and parts of it were funny like Sam was always funny, but most of it was gossip about friends and acquaintances filling pages to their edges, forsaking margins, as if now the news of those people scrawled in a messy hand made them present to someone absent. It was a letter that, as Jeff turned its pages over to see both sides, showed how life in New York was so full of dread over how life might stall and then end that it stops being dread and becomes Muzak. Jeff worked hard to convince himself he was safer in Seattle. No *arf* here, not really, not yet. I'm really alone here, Jeff told himself with too much self-pity, not even a disease to keep me company. Sam had Raul there on his couch, ready to do things when asked, but Jeff had no one. But he knew he would not change places with Sam for anything, and it was that selfish preoccupation with himself, on top of fear, that had driven him to the Pacific Northwest.

The letter ended with a thanks for the check. Jeff surmised it was someone else who signed the letter, maybe guiding Sam's unsteady right hand with his own to scribble a SAM with space left below for the "New York Misses You" added in Raul's unmistakable hand. The same hand had added a little drawing beside this girly farewell message: a caricature of Jeff, an equally unmistakable skinny face, long nose and receding chin, an unruly cowlick, plus that more-than-slightly-supercilious look. Raul, Jeff chuckled, had really nailed him. Alongside the drawing were block letters added in another color: "RAUL MISSES U 2." Jeff chuckled again because this was so unlike Raul. Could it really be true? Well, Jeff thought, we'll just believe what he says for a while, until Sam is dead and Raul doesn't need to write any longer.

Note to self: write Sam I'm thinking of him. Jeff wanted to say things in addition to the usual, clichéd get-well-soon stuff. *Why you and not me?* But he knew he wouldn't. He probably wouldn't even write him at all. Jeff was very practiced at wishing all problems to go away.

He sat down on the sofa and reached to pick up a large padded mailer that had been on the floor for two months. His mother had sent him his Christmas present, a V-neck sweater, in it. Now it was going to be a time capsule. He stuffed it with the Polaroid of Raul and Sam, his old New York address book, a book of matches from Uncle Charlie's still on the coffee table from the last time he had smoked a joint and, casting about for something iconic of 1984, last week's *TV Guide* with Joan Collins on the cover. He tried to reseal the envelope by licking it with his spit. Jeff amused himself to think he was donating his DNA to posterity. Scientists could regenerate the tribe with it in the future. As usual, Jeff liked to think the survival of the world depended upon him.

He put on his new sweater, a windbreaker, heavy socks and some rubber boots. He fished for the biggest tool he could find in his kitchen drawer. He had to settle for the metal spatula. He picked up the mailer and went outside.

It was late afternoon and already dark. The damp air smelled like spring to Jeff, as it did almost every day. He walked up Fremont Avenue, past the Buckaroo tavern and Marketime Foods. He crossed Forty-sixth Street and went as far as he could until he was at the entrance to Woodland Park. The gate to the zoo inside the park was closed. In the immense conifers next to it, where Jeff judged the most secluded spot in a grove of spruce, he knelt down and used the spatula to scoop up chunks of weeds and dirt.

With great effort he dug a shallow hole just big enough for the mailer. He slipped it into a plastic grocery bag he'd stuffed in his pocket before leaving the house. He stretched the plastic bag so that the top side was smooth of wrinkles. From another pocket he extracted a crushed red ribbon bow he'd also brought with him. He peeled the backing off its white adhesive square. This was supposed to be for Raul's Christmas present, but he never bought one. He pressed it onto the smooth side of the plastic bag and placed it in the hole. He hoped that no one's dog would dig it up. It was his gift to future historians, and he didn't mean the future to be next week. But he didn't have the patience to dig a deeper hole.

Jeff went home after walking in a circle in the park, passing a small stand of young pine that looked like it had just been planted. He stood in front of the most symmetrical of the pines, which put him between the stand and the lights of the apartment building across the street on the western edge of the park. In the clamminess of the late afternoon, drops of water had condensed on the pine needles of this young tree, posed ready to fall. Jeff leaned forward and his nose almost touched them. The light coming from the windows was refracted in the drops, like dark prisms.

When Jeff got home, he scribbled another note to himself to go buy a new electric blanket for Raul as a belated Christmas present, even if he didn't have the bow anymore. He also made a note, this one mental, to send him a letter with his own news. Maybe he'd say something about Henry. He jotted one last note (*Tell* someone *where you buried your past*) and slid both under Snoopy and his earlier reminder to write Sam. He really needed to invest in more magnets, he decided. He also thought: I am never going back to New York.

He hadn't heard from Henry since their night together but couldn't muster the courage to be the first to reach out. Every new man Jeff passed on the street or saw on a billboard looked good to him. The night before he had gotten on the lines and cajoled some guy into a phone fuck, but it was perfunctory and not what Jeff had been eager for. Around three a.m. he went to the living room to watch some TV with the volume turned low. He didn't want to disturb his neighbors. Jeff kept getting off the sofa to change the channels, not content with the old movie on one channel or the repeat of the eleven o'clock news on the others.

The next day he slept well past noon, and by evening had bad cabin fever on top of his horniness. He watched TV for a few hours, ate dinner out of a can, and watched a couple more hours of TV. When he guessed it was late enough, he drove down First Avenue South past the Kingdome and parked in front of a warehouse. He had a complimentary pass to a new club someone had handed him in a bar. Jeff was intent on finding trouble the worst way. He needed to feel the strong, rough hands of a stranger on him. In New York sex was always just around the corner, but in Seattle you had to go ferret it out. The white card clutched in his hand, he stood outside the black door of the black building and tried several times, over the din of truck traffic on the Alaskan Way Viaduct, to hear if anyone on the other side was acknowledging his knocks. It was well after midnight, there had to be people in there. Two strong cups of coffee before he left the apartment had revived him, but now he felt a wave of exhaustion roll over him. Late nights were harder now that he was thirty.

Two other men showed up, ignored him and rang a doorbell that Jeff hadn't seen since it was painted black too. The door immediately opened and Jeff followed them in. For some reason Jeff had assumed the warehouse space would be pitch-dark inside, but it wasn't. Bright ceiling fixtures illuminated a long room with a bar that ran its entire length, looking like it was made of clear glass. The walls and floor were painted the same black as the door, and the crowd of men who packed the room was mostly shirtless but all wearing black denim or leather. One guy was in a black jockstrap and heavy work boots but nothing else. Cigarette and dope smoke filled the air and made it hard for Jeff to see what was going on at the far end of the bar. The low bass sounds that he'd heard waiting outside for the door to open were deafening inside, and Jeff could see a glass filled with a clear liquid at his end of the bar vibrating with the sound.

He bought a beer for five dollars and maneuvered his way to the wall opposite the bar through a small group of men. He saw the two men he'd followed inside talking to two other guys who looked much like them. No one seemed to notice Jeff. He wasn't particularly handsome: just the hot looks of the boy next door, but he wasn't a boy anymore. What he had going for him was his six-foot height, a full head of hair and piercing blue eyes. Most of the men in the club looked more professionally gay: facial hair, piercings, leather. For Jeff in his mood tonight, that was fine. The men had an edge about them, something that only long experience with managing desire could produce. Jeff didn't particularly want to think he was one of them, but tonight he found it tempting to be in their company. He wanted to get picked up in the worst way, and he'd stay here until he was. Maybe his vanilla looks would be the shit that drew the flies.

Everyone seemed to know everybody else. Jeff was nervous and drank his beer too fast. He wished he'd taken a little speed before leaving the apartment. He leaned against a wall with a large doorway in it. It led to darkness. Jeff put his mostly drunk beer bottle down and went through the opening to explore.

The music was muted in the back room. At first all that Jeff could see was the tiny orange glow of the cigarettes and joints, a dozen points of dim light, some not moving in the blackness but others flitting about like fireflies. As his pupils enlarged, he noticed smaller glints of light reflecting off the metal buckles, studs and snaps on the leather that some of the men wore.

Jeff slowly inched his way to an empty space along the far wall. He leaned back with his hands in his pockets and one leg bent at the knee, foot on the wall. His heart pumped faster. He looked around to see if anyone he was attracted to was alone. No man-boys like Henry here tonight, but that's not what he was looking for. He needed someone to take charge. Three guys to his left were huddled together like rugby players, sharing a deep whiff of the poppers Jeff could smell. Standing up straight, two of them let loose low-pitched giggles; the third teetered back on his heels and looked for a moment as if he might fall. Jeff thought he could smell other chemicals, too, but he couldn't identify them.

Jeff was about to go back into the front room to buy another beer and check out new arrivals, when someone spoke into his right ear in a voice so out of nowhere he jumped a little.

Jeff didn't catch what was being said, or asked. He turned toward the sound. The owner of the voice was shorter than Jeff. He was broadly built, with black hair in a crew cut and prominent eyebrows. In the dark, Jeff guessed the man was about ten years older than he was. He wore a body shirt and black jeans, with no belt and the top button of the fly undone. He had big arms and thick wrists, both of them with studded leather bands on them.

"Excuse me?" Jeff shouted over the music. He nodded his head to acknowledge the man's presence.

"Bill. The name's Bill."

"I'm Jeff."

Bill grabbed Jeff by the arm and dragged him to another corner of the dark room, where it was easier to talk.

"Better."

"Yeah."

They chatted about the new club, quickly agreeing Seattle needed something like it, as if Jeff had any idea what Seattle needed. Other men walked by them, but Jeff noted that Bill's stare never left him. He felt a gnawing hunger in the pit of his stomach as he realized that Bill was not only what he was hunting for, but within the realm of possibility.

Bill gestured to Jeff that he needed to go to the men's room. Jeff stood alone, not moving, worried that Bill wouldn't find him when he came back. He could see Bill stop by the bar on his way to the toilet to talk to another guy, someone his own height and with an equally muscular build. Shit, Jeff swore, I've lost him. Jeff looked around the dark room to see if there was anyone else he might attract. It was too dark to tell. Suddenly Bill was back by Jeff's side. He had two more beers in his hand. That's as good as a wedding ring, Jeff thought to himself with a smile. Less than a few sips into his second beer, Bill was leaning into Jeff, pushing him back against the wall with the certain weight of his body. He slowly ground his crotch into Jeff's left hip and whispered what he proposed the two of them do with the rest of the night. The loud music made it hard for Jeff to catch everything he said, but he grasped the idea. Bill moved one of his legs in between Jeff's own and rubbed his thigh against Jeff's. His cock stiffened. Jeff reached down with his left hand and groped Bill's own equipment. Bill's prick felt perfect.

"Fuck me with that." Jeff grew hotter at the sound of his own words.

Bill extracted himself from Jeff and, without a word, left the room. Damn, how many times can I blow it? I'm too fucking horny and I've scared him off. On the verge of being depressed as well as angry at himself, Jeff looked around the dark room a third time, scouting for other possibilities, but his disappointment over Bill had now put a damper on things, including his erection.

Bill returned as quickly as he had just left. He strode toward Jeff laughing, with two shot glasses in one hand and a bottle in the other. Jeff broke out in a grin too.

"What's that?"

"Vodka!"

"A whole fuckin' bottle?" asked Jeff as Bill sidled up to him.

"One of the bartenders is a friend."

"I guess so. Still, isn't this against the law or something? Taking a whole bottle from the bar?"

"Against the law? So are we, baby. Now drink up."

Bill did two shots in quick succession. Jeff did three, as a hungry sensation in his gut grew stronger. He put the glass down on a ledge and placed his hands on either side of Bill's hips.

"I have a boyfriend," he blurted out, confusing his fantasy with reality.

"Sure you do. What's his name?"

"Well, not really a boyfriend. Someone I just met. Henry."

"I had a Henry once. Tall. Black."

"That's not him." Jeff watched Bill pour another shot for himself and one for him.

"Then what are we talkin' about? Here's to Henry!" Bill raised his glass and signaled Jeff to do the same. They clinked them together and downed the vodka.

An hour later they were in Bill's house in West Seattle. Bill said it would be a bit of a drive, and it was. The yard had a big German Shepherd behind a chain link fence, but Bill quieted its bark down quickly. The front door seemed to have a million locks to it. Once in, Jeff sat down on a long leather sofa while Bill went to the freezer in his refrigerator and extracted another bottle of vodka.

"I've had enough."

"Okay."

The room, Jeff noted, had narrow windows running along the top of two of its walls. At this hour, the only light came from tiny recessed bulbs in the ceiling, which was painted black like the club they had just left. They were sitting in a large room, with a couple of doors leading to what must be the other rooms in the house, but Jeff would never see them. Part of the big room they were in was furbished in expensive modern furniture. Bill had good homo taste.

Bill sat down next to Jeff on the sofa and pulled a small onyx box on the glass coffee table closer to him. He opened it up and took out a ball of aluminum foil. Once he'd diced it and made six perfect lines on the table, he leaned forward with the canonical rolled-up dollar bill and snorted. Then he offered it to Jeff, who snorted a line as well.

"I guess I'll have a shot of the vodka after all."

Bill smiled and returned to the refrigerator. Jeff put his right hand down on where Bill had been sitting. It was warm with his body heat. The coke had Jeff's heart beating fast. Bill came back with a tumbler filled with the clear liquid.

"Here. And take these with it."

Bill put two pills in Jeff's hand. He didn't say what they were, and he had none for himself. Jeff threw them back in his throat and let the vodka wash them down.

Bill led Jeff back to the playroom. Two folding massage tables stood in the rear and two leather slings hung from the ceiling facing each other. Everything was flat black or shiny chrome, except for the pink latex dildos and butt plugs lined up in rows by sizes from small to large. The playroom was clean, like a surgery theater— reassuring and unnerving at the same time. Jeff leaned back into the wall as he imagined the pills, whatever they were, taking effect. Bill kneeled down on the floor between his legs, extracted Jeff's dick from his fly, and slowly sucked him. Jeff turned his head back toward the tables and thought he could see a pair of boxing gloves lying on the floor.

"You been in Seattle long?" Jeff asked dreamily, as if to himself rather than to Bill.

Bill kept working on Jeff's prick, then came up for air and said, "All my life."

Jeff was about to ask another question, but Bill raised one of his hands to Jeff's lips and put his index finger on them, signaling silence was best. Jeff focused his stoned gaze on Bill's thick wrist and, inspired, shifted his hips to bring his groin closer to Bill's face. Then he closed his eyes and let old pictures from his mind project against the back of his eyelids.

Eventually Jeff took off all his clothes without any of Bill's help. Bill stood in the middle of the room and watched Jeff as everything came off. He turned around and showed Bill his ass, and Bill moaned approvingly.

"Another drink?"

"God no."

"Whatever God says."

Jeff walked over to the play area. He ran his hand over some of the dildos and looked up at Bill. Their eyes met and both broke out in big, boyish grins.

Jeff climbed into one of the slings. Bill came over and helped him work both of his feet into the stirrups. Jeff's cock was so hard it felt it was bursting. What the fuck were those pills? He ran his hands up and down his smooth chest and stomach and tugged on his balls. Bill was out of view, but Jeff could hear the refrigerator door open and close. He started to pinch his nipples hard.

Bill appeared between Jeff's outstretched legs. Jeff felt his body relax into the curve of the sling, and he looked up at the black ceiling as his heartbeat raced and his ass felt open to everything.

"I've got something else, too." Bill had an amulet in his right hand that he broke into two halves and, this time taking the first hit himself, shoved the other under Jeff's nose.

"Hey baby, let me do that for you," Bill said. "Oh baby, yeah." He used his other hand to rub the inside of one of Jeff's thighs. "I wanna fuck you first."

"Are you gonna fuck me now?" Jeff implored, already knowing the answer. "Are you gonna fuck me good?"

"Yeah, me and my friend are."

Jeff had trouble focusing. One of the doors at the other end of the big room opened and a man with a black hood on his head walked over to the sling without making a sound. Bill stepped aside and let him take his place between Jeff's legs. "You're gonna go somewhere now, yeah," Bill said. Jeff wanted to protest and at the same time did not. It was hard to tell where the hood stopped and the man in it began. The lights in the ceiling were dim and the man's skin was nearly the same color as the hood, either naturally or because of the shadows. Jeff felt something warm, part liquid and part solid, pour and push inside him. "You're gonna get it now, yeah," said one of the two men. A hand put a damp cloth under Jeff's nose.

Jeff lost all control. His body felt like a thick liquid oozing out of the sling onto the floor and slowly rolling in puddles toward the walls. Stiff things and not-stiff things inside him spread and probed his interior. Something broke through and flowed into his veins and traveled to his heart, his mind, the back of his eyeballs. The man in the black hood was as much a part of him now as his own arms and legs. It might have been a minute, it might have been an hour, but eventually the man in the hood moved away and disappeared through the door he had come in. Had he really been here? Something incarnate, something not. Both solid and vaporous. Something that had come and gone. Jeff was satisfied now. He felt as if his insides had been cleaned and purified. Sometime later he tried sneaking quietly out of Bill's house, but the German Shepherd started barking in the yard. Jeff, very groggy, struggled to find his bearings once outside on the street. It was only dawn, on a Sunday, and Jeff had to wait a long time for the city busses to take him back to where he had left his car. But it had been, he would tell himself after getting home, worth everything.

Late Sunday afternoon Jeff walked up Fremont Avenue to the Marketime. He needed four of the five ingredients asked for in the recipe he cut out of the local newspaper that morning. Once in the store, he found three of them and decided that was enough. He was feeding only himself, unless he decided to invite Henry over. One night of sex usually demanded another immediately, Jeff had learned. Whether he felt guilty about the previous night would depend on how Henry struck him the second he walked through the door.

He stood in line behind a street person waiting to buy a bottle of Listerine—the vintage of choice, Jeff had noted, for Seattle bums. He looked at the tabloids for sale and almost picked one up because in the upper-right corner there was a small photo of John Travolta with his shirt off, and it reminded him slightly of Bill. Jeff's cock stirred. But then the homeless guy in front of him, mumbling something, left the line and wandered off, making Jeff the next customer to be waited on.

The checkout girl was very blonde, with curls dangling from either side of her head. She had lots of makeup on, with red lips. She was chatting to the clerk in the line next to her without actually looking at her. When her eyes met Jeff's, she suddenly stopped.

"Oh my *gawd.*"

"What?" said Jeff, surprised.

"Sorry." The girl giggled. "I wasn't expecting you."

Why would she, Jeff wondered. Then again, he was a customer and she was an employee.

"Oh, gee, you're not you," she went on. "I mean, him. Do you know there's someone who looks just like you?"

Jeff debated ignoring her question. He smiled at her and said, "Lots of people look like me. Someone once said I look like Barry Manilow."

The girl laughed and rang Jeff up. As she reached for a jar of sun-dried tomatoes on the conveyor belt, she said, "Barry Manilow? Gee, I dunno. But you sure look like this guy who used to come here all the time. Roger. No, not Roger. I think his name is Ryan. You guys should meet, it's amazing." She put Jeff's things into a paper bag.

"Thanks," Jeff said, as he grabbed the bag and headed for the automatic doors leading to the street.

That night Jeff did call Henry and told him to come over. Henry had to take two buses, but Jeff insisted he do it. "It's Sunday and they don't run very often," Henry apologized when he showed up. "How have you been?" Jeff asked as he lit a joint.

Later, after nothing more than a mutual jerk-off, Henry fell asleep but Jeff did not. He ran his fingers lightly up and down Henry's torso as he nuzzled his sticky groin and belly against the twenty-year-old's smooth, firm buttocks. He pushed the blankets away from their upper bodies to have easier access to shoulders, biceps, the nape of a neck and two perfect, young-man pectorals. It was cold in the bedroom, but Jeff made sure his new friend stayed warm. His hands roamed everywhere, careful not to wake him. Jeff couldn't help compare Henry with Raul. Henry was smaller, younger, less muscular. His breathing was shallower, barely audible. The back of Henry's head was thick with shiny black hair that picked up light even in the dark. Jeff already saw Henry knew much less about the world than Raul did, and so logically it was Jeff's turn to be the teacher if this went on. Raul had shown Jeff New York. What was Jeff going to show Henry?

Jeff's finger resumed its lazy circles. Tonight was only his second time with this guy, and it was too early to draw up an errand list. Terminally cute, though. Jeff separated from Henry and turned over on his side. He drew the covers back up and concentrated on the cotton trade in the postbellum South in order to induce sleep, but fresh images of a West Seattle basement ruled his mind instead and his cock began to rise. He turned away on his side and forced himself to sleep, but when he woke in the morning, his body was pressed seamlessly against Henry's.

CHAPTER FOUR

Later in February, Henry called to tell Jeff he was moving. He'd found a place on Capitol Hill that needed a new housemate. Jeff mused: Well, that's why I haven't heard from him. Get a grip. A week or so is nothing to a twenty-year-old.

"One is a Nazi vegetarian, doesn't want *any* meat in the house."

Jeff briefly considered offering to help Henry move, but he didn't relish the idea of seeing where Henry had lived with the first Jeff. He hadn't asked any questions about his death. He guessed the answers involved drugs.

"So, where on Capitol Hill?"

"Tenth Avenue. It's a big two-story house."

"How many other people?"

"In the house? Me. Someone called Clark who works in a bookstore on Broadway. Tim—don't know anything about him, except that he's the vegetarian. And Mike. It's Mike who ran the ad in the *SGN*. But he's straight."

"The others?"

"Both gay."

"Well, good, I hope it works out."

"Yeah, me too. Let me give you my new number."

Jeff wrote it down on a paper bag that was on his kitchen counter. Later he transferred it to his little black book, but it took a while because he wasn't sure he had Henry's last name right. Sosa? Flipping through the pages he was struck by all the tricks he had forgotten. A New Haven townie pretending to be an Italian Jew called "Dale Finzi-Contini"; and a real Jewish undergrad from Poughkeepsie with the gay-bar alias "Elihu Dixwell." Jeff put the new number in the *H* section, writing "Henry" in capital letters.

Jeff visited Henry a couple of days after he moved into the Tenth Avenue house. It wasn't a particularly attractive house, and it definitely needed some paint. He knocked on the door but someone other than Henry answered.

"Uh, I'm Jeff. Is Henry home?"

The tall, husky young guy with morning hair told him to come on in. Jeff stood in the entryway and looked into the living room to his right. He could smell dope and something slightly acidic, like burnt rubber.

"Henry's upstairs in his room. Go on up. Second door on the left. I'm Mike, by the way." They shook hands. Jeff stole a good look at Henry's housemate. He had a wide, open face. His hair was nearly blonde and his complexion pale, but with close to purple lips. It took an instant for Jeff to notice the eyes: large, pale blue, attentive. Henry had said Mike was straight, and he was right. The housemate loomed like a linebacker in front of Jeff until moving aside to let him pass.

Jeff found Henry spread out on a futon on the floor, shirtless, reading a magazine and smoking a cigarette. Two cardboard boxes stood at the foot of the futon and clothes were piled at the other end.

"Nice place."

Henry chuckled and put the cigarette in an empty cup that was between the futon and the bright blue wall.

"Yeah? You think so? I was afraid you'd think it was a dump. That dresser's not mine. It came with the place."

Jeff sat down on the edge of the futon and crossed his arms atop his bent knees. Henry stretched his own arms and grasped his hands behind his head, exposing his dark armpits. Jeff wondered if this was an invitation for sex. He began to close the door to the bedroom, but Henry told him wait, he had to go to the bathroom.

Jeff looked around while Henry was gone. The room definitely belonged to a young guy. Nothing hung on the walls yet, a lot of stuff was in piles here and there, including a baseball mitt, a shoebox without a lid full of cassette tapes, and a jockstrap that for some reason was tied into a knot.

"I met someone downstairs," Jeff said as Henry came back into the room.

"Must have been Mike. What did you think? He's straight."

"Yeah, you told me. Seemed okay."

"Tim is the queerest guy here. He gives Tupperware parties."

"He looks familiar."

"Who? Tim?"

"No. Mike."

"Well, he's a type," Henry said dismissively as he resumed his supine position on the futon, letting the back of his thigh rest against Jeff's hip this time. "Your high school jock heartthrob. He wants to grow up to be a rocker. His mother just bought a big house up on Fifteenth. Mike says she's thinking of turning it into some kind of community center. For gay guys."

"That's kinda weird. Her son is a breeder. I assume his mother is too."

"Yeah, I guess." Henry twisted his upper body to look for his pack of cigarettes. "Mike has a girlfriend. Some chick older than him. I think her name's Steph or something. She sings in his band."

Jeff wondered if Henry was thinking about the difference in their ages. He was looking at Jeff in a friendly but otherwise unreadable way.

"What kind of 'community center'? Is she a nun or something? Social worker?"

"Don't ask me," Henry, replied, still fishing for a cigarette. "Fuck if I know. Twelve-step shit, probably."

Jeff interpreted that as an opener.

"So are you in the program?"

"'In the program'? Sounds like you've been there yourself."

Jeff looked up at the ceiling. "I've had my issues. Who doesn't? Still do. I've done some reading." He debated whether to go on. "Look, I've had a problem with drinking. Runs in the family I guess. Then living in New York didn't help much."

Henry looked at Jeff quizzically. "How big a problem? Like, pass-out-in-the-street big?"

"It's happened," Jeff said exhaling audibly. "I'm doing better since moving out here. No drugs, though. Well almost no drugs. You know, weed. Speed on the weekends back in the old days."

This was enough information, Jeff, decided, for one day. He lay down on the futon alongside Henry, who had given up looking for a cigarette. He watched Henry's shirtless chest rise and fall with his slow breathing. His nipples were small and chocolate brown, unlike his own. Raul had had hard muscles, but Henry was an ectomorph.

Jeff raised his arm and then lowered his hand onto Henry's smooth chest, settling in the shallow valley between his pectorals. He let it lie there lightly and didn't move it at all. After a few moments, Henry raised his arm, too, and placed his own hand on top of Jeff's, making sure each of his fingers covered each of Jeff's. They stayed that way for a long time, until Henry went to fetch some lotion from the top dresser drawer.

The bulb in the floor lamp flickered. Nan turned it off and went through the French doors to the backyard to smoke a cigarette. There was a slight breeze. She was looking at the tall pine trees that lined the far end of the yard when she thought she could see something moving on the ground. It was a small animal racing in a straight line along the back fence. At first she thought with a start it might be a huge rat, but then she realized with relief that it was a raccoon. It was just about to squeeze under the fence where the ground was slightly depressed and continue onto her neighbor's property when it stopped and turned in Nan's direction. It looked like it was staring at her. Nan froze just like the raccoon. She didn't move her lighted cigarette, the one thing that might have attracted the animal's attention. Nan did not want to break the truce that existed between her and the animal.

The animal was the first to make a move. It ever so slowly turned toward the fence and its tight exit. It shook its hindquarters back and forth in a kind of farewell to Nan as it slithered through. Nan wondered if it might return to her yard, but it did not. She took a long, final drag on her cigarette and turned her own back to go into the house. She closed the French doors, made sure they were locked, and looked one last time through them at the back fence. Nan was not sure whether to feel more or less lonely now that her raccoon was gone. Probably rabid, it occurred to her. If it came back with bigger friends, she was prepared. She had that pistol in the house. Richard had taught her how to use it. Did raccoons attack? She didn't know, but in a showdown between her and anything foaming at the mouth, she'd be the winner. She made a mental note to make sure the gun she had hidden under clothes in the top drawer of her bedroom dresser was loaded and ready. Then she laughed at herself for being so silly.

That evening Jeff and Henry went to Daddy's Tavern on Stewart Street for a drink. The bar was nearly empty, probably because it was so early. Porn was showing on a TV suspended in one corner and old Village People disco music was coming over the big speakers. Jeff was paying for two beers when he heard Henry, standing behind him, shout hello to someone. When he turned around, he saw two guys near the black leather curtain at the entrance to the bar.

"Tim, Clark, meet Jeff."

These were Henry's two other housemates. The four of them stood in a circle in the middle of the nearly deserted bar after everyone had a beer in hand. Jeff remembered Clark and his mustache as the Walrus from that bookstore on Broadway he had gone into that rainy Sunday, the day of his first date with Henry. Tim, who was much younger, was going to school. No one mentioned Tupperware.

"So you've been in Seattle how long?" Clark asked.

"I moved here last summer. I got a job at the UW."

"Cool. I'm a grad."

Clark continued, "English major. Creative writing. After getting out I moved to Boston, thought of going for an MFA. Didn't like it much, though."

"The MFA program?"

"No, Boston. Too cold."

Tim raised a closed fist to cover his mouth as he coughed. He looked bored and did not do much to hide it. Eventually he wandered off over to the bar to talk to a new bartender, who must have just shown up for his shift.

"What are you going to do with the rest of evening?" Clark asked after a lull in the conversation about Boston.

"Dunno," Henry replied. "Maybe get something to eat. Maybe another bar. Tugs or the Park Bench, I guess. You?"

"Back to the house, I guess."

Jeff and Henry debated checking out the Axel Rock, but Henry said he was hungry. They headed to the Dog House on Seventh Avenue.

The diner, unlike the bar, was packed. They sat at the counter between two bikers. Jeff told the older Asian waitress he wanted pancakes; Henry, two burgers.

"Well, they seemed like okay guys."

"Clark's all right. What you see is what you get. Tim, I can't figure out. Maybe a little strange."

"He's the vegetarian." Jeff remembered the strong smell of dope that had hit him when he first entered the house that afternoon. "Who's the stoner?"

Henry took a big bite of his first hamburger, head bent low. "All of us, I guess." He didn't take his eyes off his food.

Jeff was curious about Henry's "recovery," but didn't want to appear judgmental. Besides, Henry might have some questions for Jeff.

They were done eating quickly. The waitress refilled their water glasses and slammed the check down on the counter without asking whether they wanted anything else. Jeff paid.

He drove Henry home. They didn't talk in the car, and when he pulled up in front of the house he just gave Henry a wave goodbye. He watched Henry walk up the concrete path to the front door and go in. He wished Henry had invited him in. He wanted more than an occasional roll with him. He wanted it every day. Maybe Henry was too shy in front of his new housemates to have an older guy stay over. Just as likely, Henry just wasn't as much into Jeff as Jeff was into him. Jeff didn't like to think about the age difference between them, but he knew it mattered.

He resolved to go straight home. But the car suddenly had a will of its own. Somehow the two of them ended up in front of Daddy's, where a parking space opened up just as miraculously. Jeff went in the door and was the last to leave at two-thirty in the morning. Getting into his car, Jeff wondered if it was morning madness at Arnold's yet. It was only the fact he had classes to teach on Monday that prevented him from finding out.

Nan went to the basement of the church at Sixteenth and John to meet Vincent. Only one person was there when she arrived, a good-looking man with sharp features, probably in his late thirties. He was sitting on a folding metal chair among many other empty ones.

"Vincent? It's Nan. Hi."

"Vinnie, please. I'd offer you some coffee but the kitchen seems to be out of it. AA meetings consume a lot of coffee, you know."

No, Nan didn't know that. Lesson number one, she told herself.

"So, Vinnie, you must be wondering why I called you." Nan was surprised she was so nervous. Her voice nearly cracked.

"I get calls all the time from people I don't know. That's cool. Looking for information about a meeting. My number's in the gay paper every week. I don't usually hear from women, though. They have their own groups." Nan realized that Vinnie thought she was a fellow alcoholic looking for help.

"Vinnie, like I said on the phone, I read about you in the *SGN*." Nan wondered if Vinnie could tell she was straight. "I was reading that the church isn't going to let your gay men's AA group meet here anymore."

Vinnie let out a sigh. "Oh sure, they'd let us meet. But they want to charge us more money."

"Anyway, so you're looking for a new meeting hall. On the Hill. Cheap."

Vinnie nodded. "That's right. Is that why you're here?"

"I've got a place. For free."

"You *got* it for free?"

"No, I'll *give* it to you free. Lend, I mean. Share, actually. I have a big house on Fifteenth near here, south of Group Health. It's yellow. Maybe you know it."

"I think I might know it, sure."

"I live there alone. Just moved in. I don't work, my ex-husband supports me." Nan worried she was telling Vinnie more than he needed to know, but she kept going. "I'm thinking I'd let neighborhood groups use it for meetings."

Vinnie's expression didn't change. "Out of the goodness of your heart?"

Nan didn't say anything, because whatever she said might come out wrong.

"What's the catch?"

"No catch. It's yours to use. Oh, sometimes my son might be around. He won't be in the way."

Vinnie shifted his weight on the folding chair. "You're a real do-gooder. Rare."

"I'm not sure how to take that, Vinnie. Are we getting off on the wrong foot? Is there something wrong with do-gooders?"

"Sorry, Nan, that didn't come out right. Just trying to figure out what's in it for you. Some people get off on other people's troubles."

Nan thought for a second about what Vinnie had just said. Why *did* this one cause appeal to her? Because homosexuals and drunks were everything her father and ex-husband were not. Meaning, men who might accept her help. Nan didn't "get off" on anyone else's problems, but she did have time and space, so why not?

Surer of herself now, she went on the offensive with Vinnie. "You're not from here, are you?"

"Here?"

"Seattle, I mean. We're not that suspicious of everyone."

Vinnie let out a laugh. "You got me, Nan. Philadelphia. Okay, let's start over."

Nan sat down on the chair next to Vinnie.

"Look, Vincent—Vinnie...I'm in my forties. Divorced. Relatively comfortable. My son is grown. For the most part, that is. I want to help and I have this big house I'm not using and willing to share."

"With homosexual drunks? Just exactly why?"

"Well, you need a meeting place, don't you?"

Vinnie poked one of his cheeks with his tongue. Nan let herself observe that he was rather handsome, despite the long, faint scar that ran diagonally across his forehead.

"We meet three times a week. Monday and Thursday at eight, then Saturdays at eleven. P.M."

"That late?" Nan asked with a bit of dread in her voice.

"The temptation hour. Actually, there are many temptation hours—that's just the one that my particular group covers."

"Well, sure, I don't see why not. I might be asleep by the time you're done. I guess I can trust you with my house, can't I?" Nan decided to like Vinnie. Something in her told her she could trust him and it was time she started listening to herself. She was *not* going to be frightened of him or of his groups. This *was* a good idea.

Vinnie was quiet for a moment. "Yes, you'll have to trust me," he finally answered.

Now it was Nan's turn to be quiet.

Vinnie said he would speak with the other members of the group to see what they thought. But he added he was grateful for the offer.

"By the way, any users in your family?"

"Pardon?"

"Drinkers. Addicts. Anyone in the program? Or need to be?"

"The program?"

"In a twelve-step group."

"Ah, no, not that I know of." Nan reviewed her family tree for a moment; then she did the same for Richard's, though her knowledge there was sketchier. "Why?"

Vinnie gave Nan a look that, coming from anyone else, she might have thought flirtatious. "Just asking," he said.

"Now can I ask you a question, Vinnie?"

"Shoot."

"How did you become…an alcoholic? Was your father one?"

"Addict, Nan. I'm a recovering addict."

"Addict, then."

Vinnie had told his story a hundred times in group. He decided to give Nan the short version. "I was in Vietnam."

"Is that where you got that scar on your forehead, too?"

"No," Vinnie replied, as his thoughts went back to his earlier life with Ryan.

Nan went home to meet Mike at her house. She left the front door ajar for him since she would be in the kitchen trying to clean the oven, and it was hard to hear the doorbell with your head in a metal box.

"Hi, Mom."

Nan stood up with a little difficulty, and took two steps forward to give her only son a hug. She saw so little of him, and she wanted tonight to go well.

"It's big. Bigger than our old house," he observed.

"Let's sit down. Have you had dinner yet?"

Mike nodded and sat on one of the two bar stools on the far side of the kitchen counter. He put his knapsack down on the floor. Nan took the other stool and leaned forward to cradle her head in her hands.

"I haven't seen you in a while."

"I know. I've been busy, you've been busy. Thanks for bringing the coat over. And the money, too."

"That was ages ago." Nan looked at Mike for a moment and decided he looked okay. "Tell me something new."

"I'm in a band."

"A band? Wonderful! What kind of band?"

"Hard to explain. Grunge. Sort of."

Hard to explain to your mother, that is. Her first boyfriend had been in a band. "You're the drums, I assume."

"Yeah. It's only been a few weeks, but me and the bass player, plus the girl who sings, we've written two songs."

"Have you performed anywhere? Can I come see you?"

"Aw, Mom, I said it's only been a few weeks. It's hard to find time to practice. We've all got jobs. We were gonna get together tonight, but you made me come over. It's even harder to find a place to practice."

Nan thought for a moment. "How about the garage at your place, behind the house?"

"We don't have a garage. That belongs to the neighbor."

"You can practice here. I don't mind. And there's plenty of room, as you've pointed out."

"I don't think you'd like what we play," Mike said, rubbing one of his index fingers under his nose.

"Well, I'm assuming it will be very loud and the lyrics very offensive, but I probably wouldn't understand them anyway." Nan lowered her hands to the counter and folded them. "So practice here. In the basement." Nan was thinking she could easily sleep upstairs if she had to.

"Well, let me talk to the other guys."

"Fine," Nan said. "But I can't imagine anyone objecting. I *want* young people in this house. Plus, I guess I'd see more of you if you practiced here." Nan wondered if she was being too obvious in her attempt to recapture her son into her orbit. Richard was never going to come back, but Mike might.

She took her son on a brief tour of the upstairs and the basement. "It almost looks haunted," he said at one point. "That's because it's so empty," she replied. "That will change."

"Okay, I'll see what the other guys say. You know, it could be a lot. Like four or five times a week."

"I'll let you know if I see too much of you," she teased.

Nan gave her son a kiss and watched him go. She stood on the front porch and waved, but he didn't see her do it. She turned around, went back into the house, and decided the oven was clean enough for one evening.

One day a note was left in Jeff's office mailbox by one of the department secretaries. It said to call Henry.

Funny, Jeff thought. Henry never called him at work. He didn't even know Henry had the number.

Tim, the housemate, answered the phone. Henry was out, he said.

After work Jeff went by the Starbucks in Pike Place Market where Henry worked. No customers were in line and Henry was behind the counter. Jeff smiled at the sight of him.

"Oh, sorry about that. Didn't mean to bother you at work. I just had an idea all of a sudden, so I called you where I thought you'd be."

"You thought right. But I was in the library when you called."

"Well, wanna go to a party?"

"What party?" Jeff countered, though he'd already decided the answer was yes.

"The White Party. Third annual. It's gonna be at the Monastery. Think about it fast, because tickets are cheaper if we buy them now."

Jeff knew where the Monastery was. It was a former church on Boren Avenue that he passed on his way from Fremont to Capitol Hill. But he'd never been inside. Someone at the Park Bench had told him it was a dance bar, popular with underage kids. Jeff wondered how they got away with it.

"When is it?"

"Week after next. C'mon, let's go."

"A white party. That means we have to wear white?"

"I'm glad a PhD can figure that out," Henry laughed, wiping his hands against the front of his Starbucks apron. "It will be fun."

"Sure." Jeff leaned over the counter and whispered into Henry's ear, making him laugh some more. He killed time outside the Starbucks until Henry got off his shift.

On the night of the party, Jeff and Henry wore white T-shirts and white running shoes. Neither of them had white pants, but Henry assured Jeff they were cute enough to get in without any trouble.

"I'm gonna take my shirt off anyway when we're in."

That's an option for you, Jeff thought, but not for me. His stomach was bigger than it had ever been, and he'd never had the definition that Henry did. How had he wound up with such a hot little number?

They had some trouble finding a parking space, but once they did and got to the steps leading up into the club, the big biker doorman let them in right away. Jeff was reaching into the back pocket of his jeans for the two tickets, but no one asked to see them.

The inside of the former church was huge. All the pews had been moved to the perimeter of the room to make space for the dance floor. Hanging from the high ceiling were all kinds of flashing, whirling lights. The music was deafening. Jeff wasn't sure how long he'd be able to take this. The place was packed with a lot of teenagers. Really young, Jeff thought.

It dawned on Jeff that Henry probably had a lot of friends here. After all, he wasn't any older than these club kids. Jeff would see Henry in his element. He knew Henry was attracted to older guys—that's how he'd snared him. Now he might find out Henry was attracted to his own age too. Usually it's one or the other, but not always. As Jeff made room for two Goths with lots of eye makeup to squeeze by him, he realized how little he knew about Henry.

Henry was standing close to Jeff and pressing hard against him. He noticed that Henry was scanning the entire room with his eyes. Maybe he *didn't* know anyone here.

"We can show our tickets and get two free drinks. Each."

"Okay," Jeff said. "Bring me a beer."

Henry came back with two Budweisers. As Jeff gulped half of his down, he looked around and saw the place was more crowded. Two teenage girls nearly knocked the beer out of his hand as they bulldozed between him and Henry.

Henry said something to him.

"Speak louder, I can't hear you!"

"I said, do you wanna dance?!"

They put their beers—Jeff's empty, Henry's half full—on a pew and went out into the middle of the dance floor. They found some room for themselves. They moved awkwardly to some disco music—neither of them had any natural rhythm. They smiled. Jeff looked at Henry and wordlessly mouthed the question, "Having fun?" Henry nodded.

After the song ended, something Jeff didn't recognize came on over the immense speakers, which were where the altar must have been. Jeff cocked his head to signal Henry he wanted off the dance floor. They found room to sit on the pew where they had checked their beers. It was underneath a huge stained glass window. Christ, carrying a crucifix up a hill, was fallen on the ground.

"What kind of church was this?" Jeff said into Henry's ear.

"Still is a church, in a way. George, the guy who owns it, is a Universal Life minister or some shit."

"Well, it doesn't *look* like a church." Jeff needed to shout. "Except for all these stained glass windows."

"Let's go upstairs, George might be there."

Jeff now knew Henry had been to the Monastery before. Maybe many times.

A narrow staircase led to a loft overlooking the dance floor, probably where the choir used to sing. At the top another biker dude was keeping guard. Oh, Jeff guessed, this is the VIP room.

It was darker in the loft but the music was just as loud. A number of couches were strewn about a large area, though Jeff couldn't make out how many people were sitting on them. But apparently they themselves could be seen.

"Henry! Over here!"

A black man in an overstuffed chair made a limp wave of his hand to summon Henry. He was probably in his fifties, though it was hard to tell with no light; and he wore aviator sunglasses, which made telling his age harder still.

They both walked over.

"Henry, it's been a while," the black man said once they were in conversing range. "A long while. I'd heard you'd gone straight. Who's your friend? Sorry about Jeff, by the way."

"That's okay," Henry said with a gulp. "George, this is my new friend Jeff. Yeah, I know, another Jeff. Jeff, meet George. He's the guy I was telling you about."

There was no room to sit on the couch next to George's chair, and George made no effort to rouse the four punks who seemed to be passed out on it to make room for them. Jeff stayed slightly behind Henry, who stood directly in front of George.

"Straight, sure! Still a drunk though." Henry raised his Budweiser in a mock toast to George.

George pulled a long drag on his cigarette. "We miss you at services. Your friends have been asking about you."

"I got work, just moved, shit like that."

George studied Jeff for a moment. "And so you've met a new Jeff, you say?" Jeff believed George was smiling at him.

"Listen, boys, I have business with the DJ. Go sit somewhere in the back, I think there's room there. I'll have someone take care of you. Wait for me." George rose with some effort, as if he had arthritis or was high. Henry grabbed his arm when it looked like he might fall back into his chair.

"I'll be back," he said, shuffling off unsteadily.

Jeff and Henry were sitting on a dark-red sofa all to themselves when a blonde twinkie in a tight black T-shirt came over with two tall plastic cups on a wooden tray.

"Compliments of the house. Courtesy George." The young man swiveled on his heels and hurried away.

"Well, cheers," Henry said, beer bottle in one hand and full plastic cup in the other.

Jeff sniffed it. It was unadulterated vodka, he noted, and suddenly he saw the basement of a West Seattle house in his mind. After a couple of sips, it tasted smooth. Jeff knew he was going to want at least another, whether it was complimentary or not.

Jeff could see George moving around the DJ's booth at the front of the loft overlooking the dance floor. Was George talking to the jockey and pointing in his and Henry's direction? Jeff turned to Henry and saw he was oblivious to it all.

"I gotta go," said Henry, noticing Jeff looking at him.

"Where?"

"Take a whiz. I'll be back."

Henry was gone a long time. His vodka drained, Jeff stood up not sure whether to go in search of another drink, which he really wanted, or in search of his boyfriend, whom he was a bit worried about now. He opted for both.

After a long wait at the bar downstairs, he had his vodka refilled and hunted for the men's room. He found it in the far back corner, marked neither male nor female. Jeff turned the unlocked doorknob.

He walked in and saw Henry sitting on the toilet but with his pants up. Another young man stood close by his side. A single pale, bare lightbulb bathed the small space in an unpleasant yellow light. The room smelt like stale beer and piss. The unknown guy was almost an albino, with a red plaid bandanna tied around a head too big for his boy's body. He wore a tight off-white T-shirt. He was thin, nearly birdlike and leaning slightly forward toward Henry. Henry's right elbow rested on his hips, forearm extended straight out, turned upward. The albino had a hypodermic needle in his left hand. From the way Henry's left hand was gripping his right bicep tightly, it was clear to Jeff that the needle had recently been in Henry's arm, or was just about to be.

Henry had turned his head and let his eyes settle on Jeff with a look on his face Jeff had never seen before. It was a mixture of surprise, fear, annoyance and something Jeff could not fathom at once.

"Jeff, just a little partying."

Jeff thought himself a quick study but the tableau before him took time to comprehend. He stayed speechless as Henry turned his gaze back to his forearm, letting out a snicker at the same time. The albino stood up straight and looked at Jeff warily.

"Looks like a cop. You a cop?"

Henry turned his head toward the albino. Henry intervened quickly. "Nah, that's Jeff. I know him."

Just then Jeff was aware of another presence in the crowded bathroom. Jeff swerved around, half-expecting George and worrying about the confrontation that might ensue. Who'd be thrown out, Henry or Jeff? But the fourth person was not George. It was Clark with a teenager, no more than sixteen, under his arm. Clark smiled at what he saw and, saying nothing, turned to leave with his young prey in tow.

Jeff led Henry back to the car and took him home. He was pliant enough that it was easy to put him to bed and leave him alone in the house. As Jeff drove home, he wondered what they would say when they saw each other next. Jeff would wait for the right time to talk about this, and maybe about a couple of other things too. He wasn't going to lose Henry over a relapse, not when his own lousy sobriety was shot to hell every weekend. But at the same, he worried he was back to making excuses for not confronting the truth about either Henry or himself. His cowardice weighed on him like a stone, but a stone he had succeeded in bearing with little awkwardness his whole life. Back home and unable to sleep, he threw himself onto the sofa and began to read a history of white migration to the Pacific Northwest, Clarence Bagley's *In the Beginning: Early Days on the Puget Sound*. He had brought it home from the library on a whim, but now he couldn't put it down. He poured himself some Wild Turkey from the bottle he kept out of sight under the sink amid the cleaning supplies, and learned how in the 1860s, as armies slaughtered each other in the East, other Americans were making this far corner of the continent their new home.

Jeff went into the kitchen to refill his glass. There were ants swarming all over his counters where he hadn't cleaned very well. A previous tenant had left a box of sticky ant traps under the sink among the cleaning supplies and next to his bottle. Jeff strategically placed them along the backsplash. He hung around to see what would happen. The ants were red and tiny. Jeff observed a few of the insects approach the cardboard trap closest to the sink and seem to debate whether to go in or not. Two of the ants did. Jeff felt pity. They wouldn't be coming out again, if the lethal goo did its job. But one did come out. Good for you, Jeff thought. But then the ant did a 180-degree turn and went back in the trap. Maybe the other ant was his friend, and he didn't want to abandon him. Jeff grabbed a damp sponge and wiped the counter where, just moments ago, ants were wondering what to do. As he put the sponge in the sink, he saw one red ant in a corner that had escaped both the traps and his housework. He picked it up and, all pity gone, crushed it between his fingers. If anyone had seen him do this, Jeff observed, they would understand a great deal about him.

CHAPTER FIVE

Vinnie reached Nan. "I've talked to some of the others," he said over the phone. Nan could hardly hear him. The music in the background on his end of the line was loud. "We appreciate your offer, and we'd like to take you up on it."

They met the next day at the DeLuxe on Roy and Broadway to discuss the details. Vinnie filled Nan in with more information: sometimes drug counselors from the hospitals would show up to observe, and many of the guys had to have slips signed because they were attending on court orders. Vinnie had the right to send people home he thought had shown up high, or buzzed, and he often did. He was curious about Nan's homeowner's insurance. She promised she'd look into her liability coverage.

"Can we use your coffeemaker? We drink a lot of coffee." The waiter put Vinnie's cheeseburger down in front of him. "We ask everyone to contribute a dollar at each meeting, if they can. Some give more. That should pay for the coffee." He explained that either he or someone else would clean up afterward.

"Actually, you don't have *two* coffeemakers, do you?" Vinnie added.

"Two? Who has two? No, sorry. I only have one. It's one of those Mickey Mantle things."

"You mean Joe DiMaggio. You have a Mr. Coffee."

"Yes," Nan said. "That's it. Mr. Coffee." The waiter delivered her omelet. "I'll buy you a big coffee urn. Two, Vinnie." Nan felt she could contribute that much to the cause, in addition to her living room.

"Don't sweat it."

Next, Vinnie said he'd try to scrounge up some folding chairs. Some of the group could sit on the floor.

"So, Mondays, Thursdays, Saturdays, right?"

"Right. They're all yours."

Vinnie studied Nan's face for a moment. "You're awfully kind."

Nan didn't respond. She knew Vinnie was still searching for a motive.

He picked up the check and walked with her up the hill to the Yellow House.

"I've walked by here a million times. Never been in."

"Why would you? Did you know the previous owner?"

Vinnie chuckled. Nan didn't know that he'd tricked all over Capitol Hill.

"Want a look? You should see it before your group meets here, don't you think?"

Nan unlocked the front door and led Vinnie to the living room. Nan was glad she'd picked up before leaving the house.

"The kitchen's back there. I suppose I should lay in a supply of Styrofoam cups or something."

"I'll bring those, Nan. And the big cans of Folgers too."

They sat on the sofa in front of the fireplace. Nan felt comfortable enough with Vinnie to ask him some personal questions, such as how long he had been in AA. "Eight years. Nine in NA." What line of work was he in? "I work for the city. Urban planning."

"Are you in a relationship?"

"No, not for a while now."

Nan was increasingly timid in asking these questions, worried she might be breaking some rule about confidentiality she didn't know about.

"Just so there's no misunderstanding later, you know that this is a men's only group, right?"

"Oh yes!" Nan answered brightly, though she knew she was being warned off.

"So, it's your house and all...."

"Oh, don't worry, Vinnie. I'll make myself scarce."

"Three nights a week? Month after month? Are you really sure, Nan?"

"It's a big house. You won't even know I'm here."

Vinnie gave Nan a man's hug and said he had to go. "I'll call again before the meetings start," he said, halfway out the door.

Okay, Nan thought as she dropped into Richard's recliner, the one she had commandeered out of spite. I can cross Number One off my to-do list. She made a mental note to let Mike know when the group was going to meet, so he could arrange for his band to practice in the basement at other times.

Suddenly she heard someone at the door, turning the doorknob. It's still unlocked, Nan realized.

It was Vinnie. "Sorry. I tried the doorbell. It doesn't work, I guess."

"Oh, Vinnie, you gave me a start. Did you forget something?"

"No. I just wanted to say something to you."

Nan felt a knot tightening in her stomach, as if something she didn't want to hear was about to be said.

"You...asked if I was with anyone. And I said I used to be. His name was Ryan."

"Do you still see him??"

"He's around." Vinnie stood in the doorway, letting the raw cold into the house. "That was a long time ago. Or so it seems."

Nan stood up by the recliner. Vinnie swiveled and went out the door. Ryan. Nan turned the name over in her mind. Some part of her wished it had been a woman in Vinnie's past. She found him attractive and had to stop herself from fantasizing. She walked over to the door and turned the bolt to lock it. She had the funny feeling she had just been warned. Nan turned off the lights on the first floor and went down to her cell-like bedroom in the basement. As she lay atop the bedspread, she decided the next day she would move her bed and her clothes to a room on the second floor, where it would be warmer, drier and closer to the stars.

Henry pouted a bit on the phone when Jeff said he should take the bus to his place and then he'd drive them both to the party.

"That's two buses."

"Two—count 'em, two," Jeff teased. "Come over early when you get off work, if you want."

"I don't want us to be the first people at the party. Not cool."

Jeff let a moment pass before responding. "No, we won't go until you want to. They're your friends, right? We'll do something else between work and the party."

Henry hesitated. "Okay."

Henry showed up long after Jeff knew he'd finished work at the Starbucks. He was obviously crocked.

"You're high."

Henry pushed past Jeff and went to the sofa and sat down. "Only a little sloshed," he said, turning his head to Jeff, still standing by the door. "I stopped at Sonya's on the way."

"Sonya's —is that a person, or a place?"

"Both, I guess."

They walked out to his building's parking lot and got in Jeff's car. He pulled out into the street and headed in the direction he was almost sure Magnolia was.

"Henry, I'll need directions. This is a new neighborhood for me. Henry! Are you conscious enough to give directions?"

Henry concentrated hard, the way stoned people do. There had been more than drinks at Sonya's, that much was clear. He had Jeff cross the Fremont bridge, skirt the north side of Queen Anne hill, then coast down to Fourteenth Avenue until they reached Garfield Street. Then they headed west and eventually made it to Magnolia. Off the arterial Jeff had to make a number of turns on narrow residential streets. Henry told Jeff to start looking for a parking space, and he found one near an intersection. He was relieved they had gotten there safely.

"Ready?" Jeff reached into the backseat to grab the bottle of tequila he'd left there earlier in the day, preparing for the party.

"Will I like this party?" Jeff asked.

"Don't be a snob."

"I'm not a snob. I'm just shy."

"People will think you're a snob."

Henry led Jeff across the street and halfway down the block until they reached a concrete staircase. When they reached the top of the steps and the large deck attached to the brown-shingled house, Jeff could hear a lot of people both indoors and on the unseen far side of the building. The deck wrapped around three sides of the house. Henry tugged at Jeff's sleeve and took him around to the back through the drizzle, rather than go through the interior.

About fifteen people stood on this side of the wide cedar platform, all men save one woman, talking and drinking in several small groups. No one but Jeff was looking out over the view of Elliott Bay, its dark water and the intervening hills pockmarked with car headlights, lit houses and rings of the pearl-like streetlights floating on invisible poles. White pinpoints moved on the water, probably a ferry headed to an island in the Sound.

Henry took the bottle of tequila out of Jeff's hands. Saying he'd go find John and Nick, the hosts of the party, he went through the half-open Dutch door that led from the back deck into the kitchen. Looking through the window on the right of the door, Jeff saw Henry put the bottle down on a small table covered with other bottles and plastic cups of various sizes and colors.

Jeff walked around the deck, squeezing awkwardly past two other guests to find a damp wooden railing that looked out at the Sound. In a city of fabulous water views, Jeff had somehow rented the only place without one.

Two guys, one white and one black standing farther down the railing, nodded their heads in unison as if to say hello to Jeff. They walked over and introduced themselves to Jeff as Jack and Stevie.

"Haven't seen you around before," Stevie said. "But man, you sure look like someone I used to know."

"I moved here last year."

"We're not natives either," chimed in Jack. "We've been in Tacoma together for three years now."

"Tacoma? Haven't made it down there yet." He didn't add that he'd been told it smelled.

Jeff was about to ask whom they knew at the party when he heard Henry's voice behind him.

"Say, Jeff, this is Nick."

Jeff spun around and nearly knocked Henry's plastic cup, filled with something brown, out of his hand. Henry had his arm around the shoulder of a thin man not much more than five feet tall. A gust of wind could blow him off the deck.

"Hello, Nick." Jeff extended his hand. "Thanks for letting me tag along with Henry."

Nick gave Henry a quick look.

"Actually, he didn't tell me he'd have a date." Nick winked at Jeff, and Jeff took an immediate dislike to him.

"You have a nice house. Great view."

"When the weather's good, for sure. We've been here a long time." The three of them stood silently.

"Why don't I get you a drink?" Henry offered.

"Ah, thanks," Jeff said, glad someone spoke. "How about some of that tequila we brought?"

As Henry disappeared for a second time, Jeff and Nick studied each other.

"I'm glad you're seeing Henry," Nick said, as if confiding. "He's had it rough. Not everyone likes him, but you probably know that already."

"No, I don't know that," Jeff said stiffly, annoyed by his host even more.

"Well, like I said, rough. But you'll change that. We were all worried for a while. The first Jeff and all that. Even before then. He has a history of being…available, and then suddenly not. Certain promises not kept. Made some folks angry. Plus too many tempting pills in the medicine cabinet for his own good. Sure, we're all a *little* self-destructive, but that child was making an art of it. I mean, guns in the house? Like I say, you'll be good for him." Nick challenged Jeff to say something by arching his eyebrows.

Henry reappeared as quickly as he had departed and put an end to the conversation. He handed Jeff a plastic tumbler half full with the tequila. "No limes. Sorry."

"No problem," Jeff said, raising the tumbler. "Cheers." Henry and Nick raised theirs in kind.

"You from Seattle?" Jeff quizzed Nick. He was confounded by what he had heard, and needed time to recover.

"Close enough," he frowned. "Enumclaw."

Henry chortled, knowing that Jeff didn't have a clue where that was.

"I'm really enjoying Seattle," Jeff said halfheartedly but in the spirit. "No winter." Weather suddenly seemed the safest subject.

"No *winter?*" Nick said, his eyes wide with incredulity.

Henry, making no secret of his boredom, drained whatever the brown liquid had been in his glass. "Jeff's from New England," he intervened.

"Never been there," Nick tossed off indifferently.

Jeff had to be careful, but Nick's little solicitous scene had unnerved him. This was not going well so far, and he didn't want to ruin it for Henry. Or for himself. He was reminded he had to make friends, and all friends come with baggage when they are gay men his and Nick's age.

"He was surprised we have television," Henry threw in. "Right, Jeff? And electricity. Indoor plumbing was a huge relief."

"Wanna go inside, everyone?" Nick asked. "It feels like this pissing is going to turn into real rain."

The three of them walked like ducks in a row through the crowd in the kitchen toward the living room. Someone waylaid little Nick and Jeff found himself alone with Henry.

"That Nick was talking about you."

"I see some guys over there I know. I'll be back," Henry said abruptly.

Another conversation started but not finished. The room vibrated with overlapping choruses of low male voices. Jeff used a finger to stir the remaining fraction of an ice cube in his glass of tequila. He drained the rest of it to help put aside what had just happened. Reverting to type, he saw several people in the room he could be vaguely attracted to, but since he'd tagged along as Henry's quasi-boyfriend, he decided that flirting would be bad form. He made his way over to the large stone fireplace and pretended to study the terra cotta Mexican figurine on the mantel. Then he turned around to lean back against it and face the room.

The sofa was loaded with five guys passing a joint among them. Beyond them was a circle of people who looked like they were at the receiving end of an interminable sermon from an older man in a tailored suit. Unseasonably tan and too carefully groomed, he delivered his remarks emphatically, gesturing with his hands.

Suddenly the older man's bright blue eyes met Jeff's own from across the room. After a split second of mutual recognition, the older man smiled as he stopped whatever he was saying midsentence, theatrically freezing his mouth wide open.

He bowed his head slightly, as he made what Jeff guessed were apologies to his doubtlessly relieved audience. He made his way around the sofa to where Jeff was motionless against the mantel. As he broke into a grin, Jeff remembered his name. He stood erect and extended his hand to Charles.

"Jeffrey! What are you doing here!"

"Charles. I could ask you the same. I live here now."

"*Here?* In Seattle?"

"Yes. I have a job here. Since last year. I've graduated from Yale. Well, will soon. New York was just getting to be too much." Jeff didn't feel like being any more specific.

Charles gave him a look that suggested some sort of scored triumph.

"You don't have to apologize. You have your reasons, I'm sure."

Jeff barely knew this person. He was a musician or something, maybe a cellist or a second-string conductor, with the New York Philharmonic. They had been at a few parties together and not anything more. Charles made a pass at him once, but after Jeff reacted coolly he didn't try a second time.

"What brings *you* here, Charles?"

"This party, you mean? That delightful fellow I was just talking with"—Charles motioned with his wine glass back to the small crowd he had abandoned—"is with the front office of the Seattle Symphony, and I suppose his job is to make sure that I'm taken care of. While I'm here in the wilds of the Pacific Northwest. My own private Sacagawea.

"I'm here for a week. Performing with them next weekend. It's all rehearsals right now. They're putting me up in a very nice boutique hotel somewhere downtown, but darling, it's all deserted at night. Everyone here goes to bed early. Carl—that's his name, I'm almost sure of it—said he'd been invited to this faygeleh party tonight, so I said let's go, and here I am!"

Jeff wished he had some tequila left in his cup.

"Do you like it here?" Charles asked with a curled upper lip. "Or did you move here because of Raul?"

Jeff let out a forced laugh, hoping that might deflect Charles's question, which really wasn't a question anyway.

"Have you seen Raul? Heard from him?" Jeff asked. The living room was growing fuller with guests, and Charles moved closer to Jeff.

"I think he's living with someone new. In the Village. Well, not new, really. Used is more like it."

"Charles, I'm sure little in New York escapes your notice, but Raul's rooming arrangements might just be that 'little'."

Now it was Charles's turn to emit a forced titter.

"No, there you're wrong, Jeffrey-boy. I know Brandon, and he keeps me informed by carrier pigeon." Charles looked around the room. "Even here, in the untamed backwoods of our Manifest Destiny."

Jeff felt weak in the knees. "You mean Brandon up by Columbia?" Jeff wondered if Charles somehow knew he and Brandon had been neighbors in the same building. "How do you know Brandon?"

"Now there's a long story," Charles said exhaling, surely just to sound mysterious. "One summer at the Pines. Before you were born."

"Okay, I won't ask any questions. Except one, I guess. How is Brandon?" Jeff lifted his empty cup off the mantel, only to put it down again and thrust his hands into his pockets, preparing for bad news.

"If you're so out of touch with Raul, then I'm not surprised you don't know what's up with Miss Brandon. Or down." Charles was not smiling, and he stared at Jeff. "Sam takes up all her time these days, I hear."

"Well, I did hear Sam went into the hospital." Jeff was not going to pretend he didn't know whom Charles was talking about. He looked around them, searching for something that might distract him from this conversation. He saw Henry strut across the room to the opposite corner, where he tousled the hair of someone he presumably knew well enough to touch. Jeff returned his eyes to Charles, who was still staring hard at him.

"What do you mean by 'down', Charles?" Jeff asked.

"As in not well, Jeffrey, as if any of us women are. But Sam's the one *really* not well. As in dying. Soon."

Jeff nervously reached for his drink on the mantel, and reflexively raised it to his lips though he knew it was empty. He awkwardly played with it in his hand.

"You hear that about a lot of people. It's often not true. Everyone is *La Bohème's* Mimi in her garret." Jeff noted to himself that the news was in fact usually correct, more or less, but that he just didn't want to believe it. Believing it meant he might have to do something, if he was a real human being. Just how different was he from Charles? Jeff wondered. The reality was that Charles was probably the better friend to everyone.

"You want another drink?" Charles offered helpfully, not missing a beat. His face relaxed and even looked kind for a moment.

Jeff cleared his throat. "Yes. I do. But first I want more details about Sam," he pressed. Jeff noted to himself that suddenly he was taking interest in a friend whom, like others in New York, he'd been trying his best to ignore. He really needed to open his mail.

"Okay, you asked for it," Charles began, clearly relishing his role as the bearer of bad news. "Blind, incontinent, emaciated, drools *all* the time. Mid-stage dementia—he thinks he sees things moving on the wall, though he can't see anything at all. There's a bunch of Concord grapes growing out of his side. Got the picture, boobalah?"

Oh, just the usual, Jeff concluded, getting depressed and wanting more liquor. "Have you been to see him?" he asked, trying to sound blasé as he digested the details.

"In the hospital, yes, once. His caregiver, some nice black lesbian, called me out of the blue one day and said I'd better come quick. Jeff, you know very well I do nothing quickly, but this time I did. Left rehearsal and *flew* to St. Vincent's. Well, it was a false alarm. But," Charles continued, moving his head in a vague circle, "soon I gather it won't be."

Jeff had not known Charles did nothing quickly. He really did not know who this man truly was. He wished it were Charles dying and not Sam.

"Is he in St. Vincent's again? Somewhere else?"

Charles bore in closer. "The latter. Mommie Dearest's moved into his apartment. She's changing his diapers now. *Doña* Raul and the Lady Brandon say he wants to die at home." Everyone says they want to die at home, Jeff said to himself, but almost no one does. The moment comes when breathing is hard, and you panic. You're not really sure this is quite your moment to die yet. Instead you beg your lover, or your parents, or some stranger sent by an agency, to call the ambulance. And you go to the hospital and die there a little while later, with a fat hard plastic tube down your throat alone at three in the morning. Jeff didn't want to think about it, so he went back to wondering how this person Charles, whose name he couldn't remember two minutes ago, was in touch with so many people from his former New York life.

"All right, I'll call tomorrow."

"Do if you wish, but I doubt he'll know who you are."

"That's not the point."

It seemed to Jeff that it took Charles a moment to grasp what he meant. In Jeff's world, even empty gestures meant something. He'd never be the New Yorker Charles was.

Charles recovered quickly. "Spoken like the true narcissist you—I mean *we*—are." Charles squealed a queer cackle. Is that what I sound like? Jeff asked himself.

Jeff saw Henry walk across the room again, in the opposite direction. He was glad Henry was staying away; he didn't want him to hear any of this fag banter. Just then Nick came by with another short man in tow, wearing almost the identical clothes. Gay twins, Jeff thought.

"Jeff, I see you've met Charles. This is John, my lover. Your other host."

Charles shot Jeff one of his oh-gawd looks, but he did not respond to it.

"Hello, John," Jeff said extending his hand. "Thanks for having me. Us. *Actually*," Jeff emphasized. "Charles and I already know each other from New York. Small world and all that."

"Well, great! Let me freshen your drinks. Jeff...tequila, right?"

Nick and John, joined at the hip, took their glasses and disappeared into the kitchen doing a little skip. Not just gay twins, Jeff observed, but gay munchkin twins.

"So, Charles, thanks for all the wonderful news. The hits just keep coming, don't they? Always great to hear from the old crowd." Jeff wished he still had that cup in his hand, even if it were empty.

Charles turned serious, and it aged him ten years. "Look, Jeff, I bet you think you are a million miles away now. No Big Gay Apple, no worries. Well," Charles said, warming to his theme, "you're not, Blanche, you're not." He laughed his nellie laugh again. "Let Mother lay it out for you. You brought all your fitful nightmares with you. Right here. Into the goddamn Great Pacific Northworst. Got it, Mary?" Charles raised his right hand, extended his long feminine index finger and lightly touched the tip of Jeff's nose. Charles was drunk.

"They'll find you wherever you are. Even here, in this godforsaken excuse for real estate. Not even a decent hotel," Charles slurred. "Or party," he snorted.

Jeff debated defending Seattle, and though he didn't, he realized that he now thought of this city as his home. He could defend himself, but Charles had a point. Seattle was a big town on the cusp of being a small city, but it wasn't quite there yet. Everybody seemed to know everyone else. Until anonymity descended, tarpaulin-like, over its seven hills it would still be a place where gay people gathered at their own risk, if only because a city made up entirely of friends and acquaintances was a city without queer adventure.

He saw Nick and John, or was it John and Nick, returning with two drinks. It was time for an exit before things got messier.

"Nick, John, give mine to Charles." Jeff stepped away from the mantel. "He's always been a two-fisted drinker. Emphasis on fisted." Jeff was inventing this about Charles, but he was sure it was true.

"Bye, Chuck."

"Bitch!" This time Charles let out a great, rich laugh, which made the guests nearby turn their heads. Jeff nodded goodbye to his hosts and bolted past Charles, who was now holding one drink in each hand. He walked by Jack and Stevie on his way out and nodded a goodbye to them. Jack looked so wan and sallow next to his younger black boyfriend; is that how Jeff looked next to Henry? He found Henry out on the rear deck, talking to the woman they'd seen when they first arrived. Jeff interrupted them.

"I'm sorry, but I've got to tear Henry away from you. It's a school night and he has homework to do."

Henry predictably frowned, but the woman seemed to enjoy the joke.

"Henry, let's go," Jeff growled over the din of the music that poured out of the house onto the deck. Jeff half-expected resistance, so he was surprised when Henry sheepishly said fine.

Jeff, feeling the buzz of the tequila, took his time walking down the steep, dark steps from the house to the sidewalk. Henry must have had at least as much to drink as he had, plus whatever "Sonya" had given him earlier, but he bounded down the same steps like a gazelle.

"Henry, you drive." Jeff could have, but he didn't feel like asking constantly for reverse directions. They were quiet in the car until Henry, staring straight ahead as he drove, spoke sharply. "What was that all about?"

"What? Leaving the party?" Jeff noted that Henry went through a stop sign.

"Aw, I'd had enough."

"Yeah, it was enough."

"Who was that old guy cornering you?"

Jeff bristled at the reference to age, since Charles really was not much older than he was, maybe forty to his thirty. He let what Henry said go.

"His name is Charles. Charles Something-or-other. He's a conductor, I think."

"Like on a train?" Jeff almost didn't catch Henry was joking.

"No, of an orchestra. Apparently we knew each other in New York." Jeff immediately regretted putting his relationship with Charles that way. Whenever the words "New York" came out of his mouth, he thought he sounded pretentious. He knew that Henry was sensitive to not knowing much about the world outside Seattle. But "back East" sounded worse. "A real camp. Way beyond his expiration date."

"A real what?"

"Forget it."

"I bet you know a lot of people from New York," Henry said. Jeff thought about how small Henry's world was this far in his still-teenage life, and that Jeff's few years in New York, with fewer real friends, must seem so vast to him. Jeff felt a bit ashamed of himself, letting Henry believe he was so worldly when he was anything but. When was he going to start being honest with Henry?

It was after one in the morning, and they encountered little traffic on the road as they made their way back to Fremont. Jeff was soothed by the slow rhythm of the squeaky windshield wipers, which Henry really hadn't needed to turn on. Henry had his large hands on the steering wheel in the ten and two o'clock positions, just like they teach you in high school driver's ed. His hands, like the rest of his skin, had a slightly greenish hue to them that Jeff attributed to the Chilean father and the bit of Inca blood in him.

They were beautiful. The cuffs of his long-sleeved shirt, sticking out from his jacket, crept far up over his wrists, making him look like a boy: the shirt was too big for him. Jeff put his left hand on Henry's right knee. Jeff was pleased that Henry didn't growl or snarl at him, given how rude he had been at the party.

Henry was more than a physical attraction now. He was more than a rebound from Raul, his *other* Hispanic lover. He was someone Jeff was now caring about, someone with the uncanny wizardry to draw him out of his shell and start being candid not only with the people around him but with himself. It was going to be time soon to start telling this precious young man what he really felt, and what he feared, and that would be when Jeff would hear it out loud for the first time himself.

The hand stayed on the knee until Henry had to shift gears.

"Are you going to stay over, or do you want to drive all the way back to your place? I'm fine driving the car back to my apartment," Jeff offered.

Henry kept staring straight ahead but responded immediately.

"If it's okay, I'll like to stay at your place tonight. I think Mike may be jamming with his band back at our house."

Doubtful, Jeff thought, at this hour. The neighbors would be complaining to the cops. He knew Henry had said that because he wanted to be with Jeff, and because he could tell Jeff wanted to be with him. Back in the apartment, Henry produced a joint from somewhere and they smoked it on the sofa. Both of them were wired and not ready for bed. Some time ago Henry had extracted a promise from Jeff to teach Henry gin rummy, and he made Jeff do it now. They moved to the kitchen table after Jeff found his cards in the back of the drawer where he kept his knives. He watched Henry shuffle them. He stared at the young man's hands again as they moved quickly over the cards. Jeff's own were smaller, paler and not sexy at all. He slid them under the table until Henry told Jeff he had to cut the deck. Henry drew the lower card.

"Deal ten. Then turn the first card up in the rest of the pile," Jeff instructed.

Jeff explained the rules and won the first round, Henry the next two. When Henry knocked on the table, he did it loudly and with a big grin. Jeff was relieved Henry didn't seem pissed off about their evening.

They smoked part of another joint and went to bed. Henry made Jeff do the ice cube trick under the covers, which meant running to the refrigerator. Once all was done Henry fell promptly asleep. His arms secure around Henry, Jeff had a dream. It was another party. He was in a room and noticed a phone on the wall, and though people were crowded all around him he impetuously picked it up to call Sam. But he couldn't remember all of his number. That's where the dream ended. When Jeff woke up briefly in the early morning, he studied Henry's naked body next to him and compared it with what he imagined Sam looked like now. Henry's flesh was smooth and warm, and no grapes grew out of his side.

Jeff, perhaps on account of the liquor and the dope, slept late. He found Henry stretched out on the sofa when he got out of the shower. He was looking through the pages of Jeff's dissertation, which Jeff had left on one of the cushions meaning to work on revising it this weekend.

"It's long," Henry commented as he dropped it back on the sofa with a bounce. Jeff walked around the room in a towel around his waist, flossing his teeth.

"Longest thing I've ever written. Longest thing I'll ever write."

"What grade did they give you on it?"

"They don't give dissertations grades. They either pass you or they don't."

When Jeff stepped out of the shower later, Henry was tapping his foot restlessly on the floor. He was sitting up straight now but otherwise hadn't moved from his place on the sofa.

"Let's go for a drive. I want to get out of the house. I want to get out of the city."

"Just us?"

"Hmm. Wanna ask someone to go with us? What about that New York friend of yours, the conductor. Choo-choo."

"*No.* You're just saying that to get a rise out of me." Jeff wasn't happy to be reminded of the party.

Henry chuckled. "If I wanted to get a rise out of you, I'd suck your cock."

"It is your turn, I believe," Jeff shot back with a smile, and he toyed with taking Henry up on his offer. But he wanted to escape the house, too. He could see through the blinds that the sun was high.

"All right, Jeff, let's see if Clark wants to go someplace."

Jeff didn't say anything, but he thought back to the night at the Monastery. He hadn't seen Clark since then, nor had he talked to Henry about what happened that night.

An hour later, Jeff pulled the car up in front of the Tenth Avenue house. Henry was about to go fetch Clark when Clark came bounding out the front door.

"Okay, boys, where to?" Clark asked brightly, easing into the backseat.

"Henry says we should go to Deception Pass. That's fine with me, if you guys know the way."

On the fifteen-minute ferry ride to Whidbey Island from Mukilteo they stayed in the car at first. Jeff took the joint Clark lit for the three of them. A few minutes later Jeff walked to the bow of the car deck to look at the gray, choppy water. It really smelled like the ocean today. He saw another Washington State ferry, the mirror image of their own, passing on the starboard side.

Suddenly Henry appeared next to him, his hands in his pockets and shoulders scrunched up.

"It's freezing."

"It usually is on a boat. You should have brought a heavier coat." Jeff cursed himself for treating Henry like a child.

At Clinton they drove off the ferry in line and followed most of the other traffic up the spine of Whidbey Island.

"You been here before?" Clark asked.

"No, I haven't," Jeff replied. "Haven't taken many trips out of town yet."

Jeff stopped at the first opportunity for gas. It didn't feel like an island. Fire Island was an island. Nantucket was an island. But Whidbey seemed like everywhere else in Seattle.

Henry came out of the gas station with a bag of barbecue potato chips, which he ripped open and passed around once they were back in the car and on their way.

"The trees seem taller here than in Seattle."

"Maybe. Probably."

Another car drove in front of them. Henry said he thought he knew the guys in it. "Hard to tell from the back, though."

"Gay?" Jeff asked.

"Über-gay," said Clark, chiming in. "They grow orchids."

They arrived at Deception Pass. The car in front of them kept going over the bridge. Jeff slowed down and parked on the shoulder of the road.

"Wish we had another joint," Henry said wistfully.

Clark pulled one out of his shirt pocket and they smoked it before walking toward the bridge.

"Nice dope," Jeff said to no one in particular.

"Someone at the store brought it back from B.C. last weekend," Clark explained.

They were the only people on the bridge. It was late in the day. And it *was* cold, Jeff decided. The three of them stood halfway down the long bridge's length, leaned on the rail and stared down into the deep ravine and the churning water. A few tourist boats played with the several eddies. Jeff reflected on how different things looked here compared to New England. The Northwest was all mist, heron feathers, tree bark. The Salmon River near his Connecticut home had an old covered bridge over a bed of rocks and pebbles, hardly a trickle of water compared with anything here. Jeff never actually saw a salmon in it. But here, between Whidbey and Fidalgo Islands, it was a real ocean that roared, all these miles inland from the Pacific. Jeff listened to the roar of the water amplified by the walls of the ravine. This was the kind of place people might come to commit suicide, Jeff thought. Like the Golden Gate Bridge or the Empire State Building, just not famous.

It began to drizzle. Henry put his baseball cap on. They didn't move right away. For Jeff, it was in part the marijuana, in part inertia, in part a desire just to let things go on for a while longer. There was no traffic. Henry broke the spell when he motioned to head back to the car.

Jeff had Henry drive them home. He slouched in the backseat, having told Clark to take the front passenger side. He dozed off, waking only when the car slowed down to pull into line at the Clinton ferry dock.

"Well, that was a nice drive," Clark said, as if to himself.

"Wish we had another joint," Henry moaned, his head resting on the steering wheel as they waited to load. Jeff was glad they didn't; it was a long drive back home.

Jeff saw an old newspaper on the floor of the back seat of his car. He lazily reached down to retrieve it out of boredom. Dirty shoe prints covered it, but it was still easy to read. A *Seattle Post-Intelligencer* from 1983. He absentmindedly scanned the front-page headlines. Articles reported on local politicians, and one was about something called WHOOPS. A weather forecast in the upper-right corner: rain. Mariners' score: another loss. A lottery number. Then Jeff spotted an article under the fold. There'd been an attempted robbery at a bank in somewhere called Spanaway. The police apprehended the two suspects after a car chase. Jeff's heart skipped a beat when he read that, according to the police report, the two would-be robbers had the first names Henry and Jeff. Jeff ran his eyes quickly down the rest of the article for more information. It seemed that they were both men in their twenties. Jeff was going to say something to Henry, but he stopped himself. He threw the paper back onto the car's floor. Not every coincidence had to be commented upon. Why would he want Henry to know they had failed doppelgängers in crime?

Henry turned the ignition off when he saw they couldn't drive onto the ferry anytime soon. After pulling on the emergency brake sharply with his right hand, he threw his head back and sighed. Jeff, Henry and Clark sat quietly in the motionless car, each thinking his own thoughts. Clark's were the simplest: he worried. He was worried about the bookstore, he was worried that he had already run through his pricey dope, he was worried that his love for boys was going to get him in trouble sooner rather than later. There was no joy for him in his thoughts. Jeff thought about Henry. He thought about Henry's fat and beautiful cock nestled in a thick bush of dark hair; he thought about the curve of his perfect half-moon ass; he thought about the excitement he felt every time Henry was in the mood to penetrate him with his erection. He thought about Henry's lips and the long eyelashes, the deep man-boy voice and the way he nestled like a girl in his arms when they went to sleep. There was a lot of joy in his thoughts, and just a little apprehension that such things don't last. Henry's thoughts lay elsewhere. They drifted back to the first Jeff. Today and other days he had trouble remembering that this Jeff was not that one. The first had done him so much right and wrong, raised him in lieu of a family but at the same time made him a junkie; the second was someone he admired even in his remote arrogance and was now beginning to love. His joy and sadness that one Jeff was dead and the other alive made him feel both guilty and grateful. He couldn't figure out if this was the way he was supposed to feel. All tallied, the sum of these three people's thoughts balanced the scales of how gay men in America lived their lives nowadays, on a long narrow bridge above an ocean in turmoil.

CHAPTER SIX

Jeff used the index fingers of both hands to probe under his jaw. Something definitely felt swollen, and he deployed his fingers to define the lump, so smooth and round and potentially prophetic. The bathroom mirror was spotted here and there with specks of blue-green toothpaste. He tried to decide if it was only his lymph nodes that were bigger, or his entire neck. It could be a million things, he told himself, or just one. Is this what Sam went through once? How all his friends would open their third act?

Definitely his glands, he concluded, and not his whole head. Well, he'd wait to see if things got better on their own. They had before. Things usually did cure themselves, he knew that, and he laughed a little unhappily at himself. Before leaving New York, he had had these moments. His tongue would be white, or his cold would linger. Once he had walking pneumonia, or so they told him in the infirmary. He was a hypochondriac for sure, like most of his circle. Came with the territory, Doctor Freud would say. Still, none of these "little problems" completely disappeared after coming to Seattle. What had he brought with him? What had he carried into Henry's life? The thought was unthinkable and he stopped himself.

He was splashing his face with some lukewarm water in the sink when he heard Henry call his name.

"In here. The bathroom."

When Jeff went into his living room, Henry was sprawled out on the sofa, one leg up over the top of it. Jeff considered for a moment whether he should tell Henry about his swollen glands. Maybe later, he decided, and so once more put off a conversation. Jeff was such a weakling. He hated himself for it, but there seemed so little he could do. How could he ask the young man in front of him to be the brave one? When he had told him so little of his life before this? When he knew *nothing*? But of course, Henry knew a lot already: all that Jeffery Number One had taught him, and before that a man named Ryan. All gay men in the world seemed convicted, of whatever crime they were charged. It was just that often the knowledge of their crimes was discreet, and secret from each other.

"Hey. What's going on? You okay?" Henry asked.

"Yeah, I'm okay. No need to be my fuckin' mother."

"Whoa. Now I know things aren't okay."

"Just hold me, okay?"

"Sure, baby." Henry grinned and made room on the sofa. "Come here and let daddy love you."

The next day Henry told Jeff he was going away for a few days.

"A few?"

"Two or three."

"Where?"

Henry kept looking in Jeff's kitchen drawers for something, making an awful racket as he did.

"Can I help you?" Jeff asked, moving to Henry's side. He knew this was an important moment somehow, but he was hesitant to make it so.

"No. I have to go by myself."

"I meant with whatever you're looking for."

Henry stood up straight and took a deep breath before he slammed the top drawer shut. "I thought it might be in there."

"*What*, for crissake?"

93

"A book of matches. I used them to light a burner on your stove to boil water and I think I put it in the drawer."

"Well, is it there?"

"I dunno. I don't see it."

"What's so damned important about matches?"

"I need that book of matches. I wrote a phone number on the inside cover."

Jeff took a step back. "The number of some prospective trick you met? In a bar?"

"No, you asshole," Henry shot back, now even more annoyed. "My fuckin' brother's phone number."

That's news, Jeff thought. Henry has a brother.

"I ran into him downtown last week on my way to work. I…haven't seen him in a long time. We couldn't talk much, he was in rush and so was I."

"So he wrote his number in a matchbook," Jeff interrupted, "which he gave you, and which you've now lost."

Henry's face scrunched up in frustration and for a second Jeff was frightened his boyfriend might hit him. He extended an arm and put it on Henry's shoulder, knowing he was taking a risk.

"Okay, look, I'm sorry. Let's start over. You're going away for a few days and you need to call your brother. Right. I can put two and two together. You're going to go visit your brother. He doesn't live here in Seattle?"

"No, I *need* to go visit my brother. And no, he doesn't live in Seattle."

"What's up? What's going on?"

Henry twisted his body this way and then that, all the while keeping his two feet firmly planted on the kitchen floor. It was something a child on the verge of a tantrum might do.

"C'mon, let's go sit down."

Once they were on the sofa, Henry explained. His brother's name was Greg, only he wasn't really Henry's brother. Greg lived with him and his mother when they were both young, and Henry *thought* the older boy was his brother. Later, when Greg ran away from home, his mother explained to him that Greg was in fact her sister's son but by his own dad, and therefore Henry's half-brother. She just pretended Greg was her own.

"Where'd Greg go?"

"I guess he has a girlfriend in Eastern Washington. Crystal. When I saw him last week, he told me he was still living there with her. On and off."

"There means where?" Jeff asked, thinking east of the Cascades, but not much farther than Seattle.

"Spokane."

"Why go now? Something wrong?"

Henry shifted his weight on the sofa, a sure sign he was having problems deciding how to answer.

"It's his birthday."

"His *birthday?* So send a card."

"You don't understand. Your fucking family probably gave you presents and a big white cake with fancy white candles on it and red balloons that floated up to the ceiling. Hey, maybe your goddamn parents rented Bozo and a donkey for you and all your nice friends to ride on. Well, Greg and me didn't do things like that. Our excuse of a mother, or whatever she was, didn't even remember exactly when we were born. So I'm gonna ride that fuckin' bus for seven hours to see my brother on his birthday and do shit with him and you know what? You're not invited."

Jeff put his hand on Henry's knee and looked at him.

"Do you need money?"

"I got some," Henry said softly.

Jeff let time pass before he spoke again.

"What time is the bus? I'll drive you there."

"Thanks. I need those matches. I gotta let Greg know I'm coming."

Henry eventually found what he was looking for wedged inside a box of Saran Wrap. He hurriedly stuffed some of the clothes he kept in Jeff's bedroom closet into a plastic bag he found underneath the kitchen sink.

During the drive Jeff thought about how, of course, Henry had to have a family even if he knew nothing about it. Henry didn't know much about Jeff's family either. How could he, since Jeff never talked about it? He moved to put some distance between him and his family. Living at the edge of a tectonic plate was about having no family at all, especially if you were Jeff. He supposed a lot of gay guys know their boyfriend's family, go there for Thanksgiving and chat pointlessly with grandmothers or aunts. That had never been Jeff's style, but he supposed he could inquire a little.

"What's your brother do in Spokane?"

"Greg deals. Big time. Not the small crap, like what Jeff did."

"Dead Jeff," Jeff said. And then wondered why he was being so cruel.

Jeff turned into the nearly empty Greyhound parking lot. "Call me when you head back. I'll pick you up if I can. We haven't talked about what happened at that party. At the church…"

Why had Jeff brought this up now, when he knew there was no chance of a real conversation? Henry picked the plastic bag off the floor of the passenger seat and hopped out. He gave Jeff a quick wave with his free hand and skipped through the double glass doors of the bus station. Jeff sat there looking at two empty buses parked alongside the building. He decided to sit there for a few minutes in case Henry came back out, either because he'd missed the bus to Spokane or because he'd changed his mind. But after a while Jeff put the car in gear, turned around by making a big circle in the parking lot, and pulled out onto Stewart Street to head back to Fremont, where he found that Henry had left his precious book of matches on the kitchen counter.

Lots of strangers were coming and going in her house now. Nan passed people in her kitchen, the hallway, the dining room, whom she neither knew nor felt she should say hello to. A simple nod sufficed, and sometimes not even that.

She trusted Vinnie to take good care of the house the three nights of the week he used it. She trusted him, but didn't know exactly why. Still, Vinnie had friends and those friends had friends, and now they were coming to her asking to borrow the house for their own meetings. Can we use your living room for an NA get-together on Monday afternoons? Is late Sunday afternoon available for a Big Book meeting? We could really use your space.

Nan said yes to all of them. Why shouldn't she? The house didn't really feel like it was hers anyway. She had the uncanny feeling she was just passing through, as if this were some kind of hotel she'd checked into and would soon be leaving. Why had she even bothered to unpack her boxes? Or change the address for her magazine subscriptions? Nan concluded these strangers had as much a right to the Yellow House, which is what Vinnie told her everyone was calling it, as she did.

One of the groups that wanted to use her living room was for the "worried well." These men weren't all addicts, Nan was told. They were gay guys who were frightened about their health. "Not like the twelve-step group that Vinnie runs at your home already, but just a chance for the guys to share their stories, talk things out," said the man on the phone, interrupting Nan's vacuuming one day. "Some of them have ARC. AIDS Related Complex."

ARC, Nan thought. That meant they were going to die. Not recover, like the alcoholics and addicts would.

"Worried-well. Guys who are healthy but are thinking they might not stay that way."

"I thought your group was for people who are already sick?" So maybe they won't die after all, Nan said to herself. "Fine, it's all yours. Saturdays at noon."

Nan went back to the hallway and turned her vacuum cleaner back on. She moved the old machine, which predated her marriage, back and forth over the worn carpet runner she inherited from the

Yellow House's previous owner. She bore down hard on it with all her might. Then she stopped and let the machine bear her entire weight. So these men, she thought, will be my new family. These homosexuals will come and go, but how is that different from the other men in my life, my husband and my son? One has already left me and the other is working on it. But some of these men will die. Turning the vacuum cleaner off with her foot, she lifted it off the ground, pulled the plug out of the wall and carried it down the stairs. She put it away in the closet in the entryway, beneath the two coats that strangers had forgotten when they hung them there a day or two ago. She went over to the large window that faced onto Fifteenth Avenue and watched the traffic pass by in the gray, late-morning drizzle of a late March morning that was halfway between winter and spring.

While Henry was in Spokane with his brother, Jeff decided to throw himself into work at the university. He had lunch two days in a row with other faculty and pretended to be interested in the problems they had raising their teen-aged children, or their innuendo about who was cheating with whose wife in what department. It was all very heterosexual and Jeff played along like one of the boys. But mostly he kept to himself and reminded himself he had a career to tend to. He tinkered with his lecture notes, met with students, and wrote his advisor back at Yale about what he was up to. Late afternoons he started hanging out at the Allegro café in the alley between University Avenue and Fifteenth, where he was inspired enough to outline a new article he might write. Evenings he stayed in the U-District to eat dinner or, back home, dedicated himself to getting his dissertation in shape to show to a university press or two. The rise of the Klan in the Lowcountry during Reconstruction had been a topic he and his Yale teachers were sure scholars wanted to know more about, but it was hard for Jeff to stay interested in it now that he was living in Seattle, a place whose history was only beginning when the Confederacy's was ending. In his most enthusiastic, caffeine-fueled moments at the Allegro, or when mellowed out with wine alone in his Fremont apartment and feeling omnipotent, he even toyed with the self-flattering idea that he should be the Young Turk of an historian to write Seattle's history just where the South's left off, unaware that others had done so before him.

In addition to teaching and writing, he spent a lot of time dwelling on his health. That was the downside of his days, and it was usually in the early morning when he stood naked before the mirror. It was time to find a real doctor in Seattle. And he needed to have a talk with Henry when he was back on this side of the Cascades. Everything they'd done so far was safe—if anyone knew what safe was—but when they were drunk or high, they'd come close to skipping precautions. Try as hard as he might, Jeff just could not make a condom sexy. It was sheer force of will on his part, so far, that had kept them from "forgetting." If he and Henry both had AIDS, what Jeff called *arf*, or both didn't, they could throw the Trojans away. But they had no way to know.

He didn't want Henry to have *arf*, though he was pretty sure that, after New York, he had to have it himself. Henry was younger and vulnerable in ways Jeff had worked hard in his twenties to outgrow, but which he now found attractive in Henry. Experience isn't all it was cracked up to be. Was he falling in love with Henry? Jeff wasn't sure. It still seemed like a really bad crush, but one he hadn't confessed to Henry. Jeff thought: For someone who never shuts up, you sure don't say anything important, do you, especially to your boyfriends. He needs me. He sells coffee for a living. I'm his real older brother, not any Greg. I am ten years older than Henry. I've been around. I went to college. Henry comes from a fucked-up family. I went to *graduate* school. I want to take care of Henry. Who the hell is Greg, anyway? Greg is the asshole who got Henry strung out, I bet. I don't even know the guy and I hate him. Henry is with him right now, instead of me. I want Henry to love me if I'm going to love him. That's the deal I never had with Raul. I grew up on the East Coast, where people talk faster than they do here and say smarter things. I know better now. Henry has the beautiful eyes of a child. That first Jeff, the dead boyfriend, never fucked Henry. The new Jeff always used condoms; he was so good about it despite the desire to be more intimate. Henry is pure and is going to stay that way. Henry can't have AIDS, unless it was a needle that nailed him.

But then it occurred to Jeff: Is all this because I want someone to take care of *me*? Because I worry I may need taking care of? Maybe I should have found a boyfriend in Seattle older rather than younger. Hey, remember why you left Manhattan. *Arf, arf.* Jeff was comfortable as the boss in the relationship just now, but he knew he had another side to him that would surface sooner or later. He wondered which parts of Henry he didn't know about yet. The guy definitely had a bit of the macho Latino in him, but he was so passive sometimes. He was different from Raul, who had been in control all the time. Jeff knew he was never meant to love Raul, really, but he wanted to be capable of loving Henry and the little boy inside him. The question was what to do with his own little boy.

Three days after he'd taken Henry to the bus station, the phone rang. He knew it would be Henry on the other end. Jeff could tell immediately that Henry was wasted, and drunk to boot. He had predicted Greg was not going to be a good influence on Henry, though Jeff had to admit he wasn't a particularly good one either.

"Jeff."

"Yeah, Henry, hi. What's up? Where are you?"

"Ah, not sure. About where I am. Outside of Spokane. Some place where my brother's girlfriend lives. He's balling her right now in the bedroom."

"Okay, just don't you be next in line," he finally said, thinking it might sound like a joke, but it did not.

"I miss you," Henry said in a low voice, slurring his words into a telephone receiver he was holding too close to his mouth.

"I miss you, too," Jeff replied, wondering if they were saying this only because Henry was fucked up. "When are you coming back to Seattle?"

"Greg might marry this chick. He's talking about it."

"So when are you coming back?" Jeff asked again but no more insistently. Still, something in the tone of his voice seemed to make Henry pay attention.

"Ah, tomorrow. Or the day after. I need to check on a few things."

"Got money?"

"Money? Sure, I got money." There was more tittering, and it came from the people around Henry. Was a whole room listening to them?

"Well, call when you do. I'll try to meet you at the bus."

"Don't need the bus this time," Henry said, slurring his words. "Greg will drive us. In his car. He's going to hang in Seattle for a while."

"With the girl?" Jeff asked, thinking of the sex going on.

"What girl?" Henry said, oblivious to what he had just said.

"Look, you take care." Jeff felt his brain was working overtime with the idea that Henry's brother was now going to be in the neighborhood. "With the girl?" he asked again.

"I dunno. Some girl. Her name is Crystal."

"Call, okay?"

"Yeah, I'll call."

After Jeff hung up the phone he went back to bed but couldn't sleep. He jerked off to make himself drowsy, but that didn't work. He walked around the apartment, finally sitting down on the sofa to watch late-night television. Someone was talking about Reagan's "Star Wars" and how it was going to end civilization as we know it. He changed channels. Half an hour into *South Pacific*, stretched out on the sofa and just on the verge of sleep, he saw himself with Henry, legs intertwined and lying in each other's arms on a hammock on some warm beach with coconut palms. They swayed slowly in the breeze and had the whole world to themselves.

That evening Nan had decided to sit in on a meeting, though women weren't supposed to. She found a place on the sofa early. In addition to being the only woman, she'd also be the oldest person and was entitled to a comfortable seat. Stevie and Jack from Tacoma were the next two to arrive. They sat down on either side of her, and Nan said hello as a signal that they had permission to chat with her.

"I'm Stevie," the black man said. "This is Jack." Unprompted, Stevie began to explain his and Jack's issues with alcohol and drugs. Nan nodded occasionally. Others who seemed to know Stevie and Jack well joined them around the coffee table.

"Two years for me," Stevie said, "and a year and a half for Jack. You?"

"Oh," Nan said with some embarrassment. "I'm new here. I'm not actually an alcoholic." One of the new arrivals chortled.

"I know how that sounds. Sorry," Nan apologized. "It came out wrong." These men think I'm in denial, she realized.

Stevie resumed his chattering. "Jack thinks he may be sick," he said almost brightly, "but I'm okay so far." They lived in Tacoma, Stevie added, but they came to Seattle several times a week to attend this group and a couple of others. "Tacoma, City of Destiny," Jack snorted.

"Oh, you've been here before?" Nan wasn't sure if she remembered them or not.

"Oh yes," Stevie said. "We've come from the start. Back when we were meeting in the church basement. I've seen you here before—you were over there." He pointed toward the dining room. "But we haven't talked before."

"Yes," he added. "You haven't talked in this group yet. New people don't talk much."

"This is my house," Nan explained. "I'm just a visitor to the group."

"We're all visitors," Jack said. "Just passing through!"

Stevie appeared to be digesting the news that the Yellow House was Nan's. "Lived here long?" he asked.

"No, just a couple of months." Nan played with the charm bracelet on her right wrist. "I moved here from Queen Anne. After my divorce."

Jack and Stevie nodded. They asked questions about how big the house was, and whether she lived alone now. Jack was interested in what was the upstairs, but Nan said that was off-limits to the groups. "When the weather's nice you can meet outdoors in the back, though."

"We're in an apartment. Jack has never lived in a house. Not a real one." Jack shot Stevie a dirty look, but he continued. "I bet he'd like a tour. He loves to explore other people's places. Don't you, honey? Spent time with the county once when he did it uninvited! Actually, that's where we met."

"In someone's house?"

"No!" Stevie roared. "Jail!"

"I've got a new lesion," Jack announced suddenly, startling Nan but apparently no one else in the room.

"On his back," Stevie explained to her. "Between his shoulder blades, smack-dab in the middle. He hasn't seen it, but I have."

"Do you have a good doctor?" Nan asked, not knowing what else to say.

Jack laughed. "Well, I have a doctor."

"Do they hurt?" Nan asked, now that laughter had lessened the tension. "Do lesions hurt?"

"Oh no, no pain. Just ugly as all hell." Jack grinned as he spoke.

"Well, I think it's cute!" Stevie leaned across Nan's lap and gave his boyfriend a kiss on the cheek. "I'm going to give it a name." Just then Vinnie appeared and started the meeting by reading the preamble.

After a polite few minutes more, Nan left the room. She would have stayed the whole hour, had she not embarrassed herself at the start. She went to her new second-floor bedroom but didn't pick up the book she had begun the week before. She had never met a person with AIDS, at least to her knowledge. Jack didn't look sick. When do they start to show it? she wondered. Was Vinnie okay? Was there a way to tell without asking? Nan lay on the bed and thought about Richard and Mike. She was so glad they were healthy and safe. When she woke the next morning, fully clothed and atop the bedspread, that was the first thought that crossed her mind again.

Henry woke up to find himself atop a sleeping bag on the floor. He was in Crystal's house. Someone must have put him there to crash after the party ended. He stretched his limbs and yawned. The living room here was as much of a mess as the one in the Tenth Avenue house in Seattle. Must have been quite an evening, Henry thought, trying to remember the details. He knew he'd called Jeff but had no idea what he had said to him. He turned his head to the left and saw a big dog asleep near him. The only sound in the house was the old animal softly snoring. Greg must be with Crystal in the bedroom.

Henry had no idea what time it was, but the faint daylight meant it couldn't be that early or that late. He lay on the sleeping bag and started to daydream before drifting back to sleep. He'd come all the way out here to celebrate his brother's birthday, but maybe the real reason had been to get away from Jeff and truly get fucked up like this. He knew his brother dealt and that there'd be all kinds of junk at the party. He'd done stuff not knowing what it was. Why was he hell-bent on screwing up over and over again? Was he trying to kill himself? You know, it doesn't take that much to overdose, especially when you don't know what the shit is or where it came from. This girl he'd gone to high school with was found dead in some guy's bathtub their senior year. Was it an accident, or had she just given up caring? Maybe the guy had offed her. No one ever knew. If Henry was ever to buy the big one he'd find a more dramatic way to do it. The world would know why he didn't give a flying fuck anymore. There were faster ways to do it than by poisoning yourself gradually with bigger and bigger doses of good times.

The first Jeff had threatened him with a gun once. They were high and had been arguing. Henry thought the worst was over, but when he turned back to face his boyfriend he saw Jeff holding a pistol pointed at him. It hadn't seemed real at first, but then Henry remembered Jeff kept a small arsenal in their apartment. You never knew in his line of work. Now, Henry and Jeff stared across the room at each other. It was like the gunfight at the O.K. Corral, except no one was shooting yet. Jeff lowered the weapon and put it down on an end table. Even Ryan at his craziest had never pulled a trick like that on him, and Ryan was the one Henry thought might actually kill someone someday. Henry had never owned anything more lethal than a slingshot he made for himself as a kid to use on birds. Never hit one once.

Henry wondered later if he deserved this. He had done bad things to lots of people. Sometimes the only way he could express human emotion was by lashing out, by stealing and cheating and generally acting out, all for the attention it got him. When he was sixteen he'd spent a night in the King County jail for kicking an old bum senseless under the Viaduct downtown. His mother came to bail him out and asked him why he did it. Henry had no answer for her. Once the first Jeff had woken up in their bed and found Henry with a kitchen knife about to carve something into Jeff's chest. And Henry would have, if only he'd known what he wanted to inscribe. In the back of his mind was just the weird thought that drawing blood, no matter what initials he wrote or picture he drew, would guarantee his boyfriend had to love him forever. Maybe Jeff had meant to do the same thing by pointing that gun at him. How close, Henry wondered in his daydream but not for the first time, was he to pulling the trigger? After Jeff died in the hospital, Henry took all of his guns in the apartment so Jeff's family wouldn't find them. He fenced the lot, except for the one Jeff had aimed at him that day. He thought of it as some kind of perverse souvenir of his deceased lover. Sometimes he got it out and fondled it. When he put the end of the barrel to his lips or teased his ass crack with it, the danger of living with men who dealt came back both to frighten and thrill him.

Now Henry was with a new Jeff. He was trying hard to be good this time around. When they were together he was really cutting down on the junk. Jeff drank and smoked a little weed but there was nothing else at his apartment to tempt him. He knew he pleased Jeff in the sack. The job was going well and he hadn't missed a day of work. No hand in the till like before; with fewer drugs there was less need for cash, and Jeff was generous with him anyway. Henry was serious about getting back into school one day. Henry wanted Jeff to be proud of him, and that was a goal he thought he could really achieve. He had disappointed a lot of adults when he was a kid and he didn't want that to happen now. Then he and Jeff could take it from there. He admired Jeff. He'd gone to an Ivy League college. He was a *professor* and Henry had barely made it out of high school. He'd wasted the past several years and didn't want to waste anymore. Maybe this Jeff would love him forever, and not go die on him like the previous one had. He couldn't take that again. Everything depended on Jeff sticking around. Henry would rather die first himself. Let someone else do the cleaning up this time.

The dog in Crystal's living room started snoring more loudly. Henry rolled off one of his socks and threw it at him. The dog stirred slightly, harrumphed, and then stopped making any sound at all. Must be years since that old mutt of Crystal's has barked at anything, Henry thought. He turned on his side to face away from the animal. Concentrating hard on the endless blank landscape of Eastern Washington to avoid any more memories of men gone from his life, Henry fell back asleep.

CHAPTER SEVEN

After Henry had been back for a couple of days, Jeff dropped in on him at Starbucks and suggested they take their own overnight trip.

"What? I just got back from Spokane. Where to?"

"Index."

"Index! It's not even summer."

Jeff leaned his own head playfully in the same direction as Henry's. "I'll pay," Jeff said in an attempt to cinch it.

Henry looked at Jeff carefully for a moment.

"That's nice of you," he drawled. "Make it Palm Springs."

They laughed. Jeff put his elbows on the table and cupped his head in his hands.

"Index. There's a hotel there I read about in *Seattle Best Places*. With fireplaces." Jeff tied his empty straw wrapper into a knot.

"I should talk to Greg," Henry said, as if thinking aloud. The mention of the brother irritated Jeff. It's one damn night. But he took the path of least resistance and said, "Sure, talk to Greg. Then let's pack and go."

Whatever Henry had to talk to Greg about, it didn't interfere with Jeff's plans. Henry showed up, short of breath, at Jeff's apartment around three that Saturday.

"You're here early. Well, great," Jeff said. "We'll beat some of the traffic if we leave now."

Around Monroe they made a pit stop. Henry was in the gas station restroom for a long time. When he came back to car he had two candy bars, one of which he offered Jeff. They fastened their seat belts and got back on Route 2. Henry, his mouth half full of a Mars bar, started humming some melody.

"What's that?"

"What's what?" Henry mumbled.

"That song."

"Oh. You wouldn't know it. Chilean."

Jeff was reminded once again how little he knew about Henry. "Sing the words."

"I don't think there are any."

"There are always words. You just don't know them."

"Well, if you're so smart, make some up."

The road wound this way and that through the damp green landscape, and in the dim gray light Jeff made sure to keep his eyes on the road. Henry dozed off briefly next to him. The Mount Index Café came up quickly on the left side of the road. Jeff made a sharp turn on the road leading into Index proper, waking Henry up. Jeff eased the car into the space closest to the entrance of the old railroad hotel. He opened the trunk and took out their backpacks. Mount Index loomed over the tiny town.

"Hotel Trout Fishing in America."

"Huh?"

"Nothing," Jeff said under his breath.

At the check-in desk inside, Henry hit the bell. A pimply girl came out of a side door behind the counter, greeted them and asked Jeff to fill out a registration card. Henry amused himself by reading newspaper reviews that had been embossed and hung on the wall.

"Two beds or one?" she asked.

"One," Jeff said.

"Room 208."

Henry grabbed the key out of Jeff's hand and bounded upstairs with their two backpacks. Once in their second-floor room, Jeff thought of taking a shower, but Henry beat him to it. Jeff put his hand down the front of his pants to move his thickening cock into a more comfortable position. While listening to the water run and to that melody Henry was humming again, Jeff opened one of the two bottles of red wine they had brought along, using the corkscrew in his Swiss army knife. He poured generous portions into the two water glasses on paper doilies that he found atop the dresser. He placed them on the nightstand by the big bed. Going into his toilet kit, Jeff extracted a tube of KY and two condoms and put them on the nightstand as well. Jeff carried one of the two glasses over to the big overstuffed chair by the window to wait for Henry to come out of the bathroom. He moved his hand over his crotch again.

A few minutes later Henry emerged with only a thin hotel towel wrapped around his hips despite the chill in the room. He ran his hands through his long, wet black hair and instantly took note of Jeff's preparations on the nightstand. He went over to it, picked up the other water glass and emptied it in two long gulps.

"Aren't you going to take your clothes off?" he asked Jeff, grinning.

Jeff quickly slid out of his jeans, sweatshirt, socks and underwear and made a pile of them on the floor. He stroked his dick hard as he looked at his naked boyfriend lying on his stomach atop the bed. Henry rested his head on his folded arms and rotated his smooth ass in small circles, inviting Jeff to join him.

Jeff put all his weight on top of Henry. He grabbed Henry's arms with his own and planted wet kisses in Henry's upturned right ear. He moved his own hips, letting his hard penis grind into Henry's ass. Henry turned his head more and they deep-kissed.

They were both aroused and ready. Jeff got up on his haunches and, using his left hand, took hold of his cock and let it bump against Henry's hole, which his boyfriend was making available by raising his hips off the bedspread. Jeff teased Henry some more with the head of his prick and then one of his fingers. Henry was soon up on all fours, ready to receive him. Jeff looked down at his beautiful back, not a single freckle or blemish to mar it. He wanted to give Henry pleasure. He stroked his dick some more, and beads of pre-cum gathered at its tip. He smeared some onto his finger, reached around and let Henry taste it on his lips.

Jeff reached for the lube and one of the condoms. He sat back on his heels behind Henry's ass and ripped the condom packet open with his teeth.

"No. No condom."

"What?"

"No condom. Just give to it me. Fuck me."

"What are you talking about?" Jeff asked incredulously, but he knew exactly what Henry was talking about. Jeff looked at the glistening hole he was being asked to enter.

Henry turned over onto his back and grabbed his ankles. "I want you inside me. Now. Fuck me! Do it."

Jeff left the bed and stood up. His cock started to droop even as he was excited by the way Henry was talking to him.

"Jesus fucking Christ."

"Yeah, fuck me. I want your cum," Henry growled.

"Henry, stop. We've never done that. We can't." But Jeff was thinking: Yes, we could.

"I don't care what we said. I need to get fucked."

"And I wanna fuck you. With a condom. Like always."

Henry let out a loud, bothered sigh and rolled over onto his side. After a moment he sat up on the edge of the bed. He put his elbows on his knees and then his head in his hands. There was another sigh and he got up without a word, went back into the bathroom and slammed the door behind him.

Jeff picked his underwear up off the floor and put them back on. He sat in the overstuffed chair and stared into the empty room. He was depressed by the sound of Henry jerking off in the bathroom. It was a good bet, Jeff supposed, that it wasn't him in his boyfriend's fantasies just now. Standing up and feeling like something worse was going to happen, Jeff put on the hotel's thin terrycloth bathrobe. He went back to the armchair and plopped down. He reached for the television remote but it didn't work. He went over to the set, turned it on, and was trying to be interested in a documentary on birds when Henry reemerged from the bathroom. It was clear from the way they looked at each other that both were angry. Jeff went to lower the sound on the television.

"You don't have AIDS, or *arf*, or whatever it is you fuckin' like to call it," Henry nearly shouted.

Jeff shifted his weight in the chair and played with the frayed hem of his bathrobe. Nothing he might say would sound right, but he had to say something. "God, I hope you're right. But we don't know that. I told you I had something gross in my mouth last year." Jeff shot a glance back at the bird documentary. Henry sat back down on the edge of the bed, the damp towel opening to reveal his inner thighs. Jeff thought he could see his boyfriend's spent penis resting between them.

"Yeah, you told me. You talk a lot, you know that, don't you? Short on action though."

They stared at each other for a moment. Suddenly Jeff felt much older than Henry.

"Look, I know how you feel. Sometimes I want to feel all of you in me, too." Jeff didn't take his eyes off the dark patch between Henry's legs.

"Then let's just do it. I don't care about the future. It's a long ways off."

That's what you think now, Jeff wanted to say, but now was not the time to lecture Henry. He thought of Sam back in New York. When was the last time he made love to anyone, he wondered.

"If I've got one anyway."

That's where this was headed, Jeff realized. Henry didn't want so much to fuck without a rubber as he wanted his older boyfriend to take away what hope he had to live for and tell him that, too, was okay.

"Henry," he said, "we're here and I want things to go right. Let's mess around. With condoms. Please."

Henry closed his legs, taking Jeff's view away.

"Too little, too late, Jeff."

Jeff wanted to tell Henry how many incompatible thoughts were in his head at the same time. He was thinking about dying, and he was also thinking about how close he was to giving in to Henry's demands. He was thinking about life and its intimacies versus death and its finality. He picked up the remote, which now worked, to turn off the television completely.

"Any more wine?" Henry asked.

"The bottle's on the dresser."

After Henry refilled his glass, he went back to the bed and stretched out along its length.

"You know, we're all gonna get it anyway."

"That's not true. Nobody gets everything. That's not how history works."

"The professor speaks. What planet do you live on?"

It now occurred to Jeff, with the force of the simplest lesson, that if Henry didn't find what he wanted with Jeff, he'd find it elsewhere. If he wasn't already. But just as quickly it dawned on Jeff that right now Henry was asking for him.

"Look, let's talk. You know we need to be careful."

"White boy from Connecticut wants to be careful. That's because by your rules, you always win. Well, in my family everybody loses."

Henry left the bed and went to his backpack on the floor by the dresser. He pulled out a baggie half full of dope, went back to the bed and rolled a joint. "You know, it's not that I need it raw. Or that I even need to get fucked. It's just a test for you. It's that I need us to trust each other."

"I do trust you," Jeff blurted out, knowing it was the automatic and not entirely truthful response. "I do trust you. And I need you to trust me to do the right thing."

Henry returned to his backpack and scrounged for a book of matches. Standing in the middle of the room, he lit the joint. Jeff stared at Henry's lean smooth torso above the towel and at the muscular legs below, and felt a stirring in his groin again. Henry let out a long slow stream of smoke into the room.

"You need help," Henry said, looming over Jeff in the chair.

You're just saying that to hurt me, Jeff wanted to reply.

"You need help to deal with your hang-ups."

"Safe sex equals hang-up?"

"To start with. That's not all I'm talking about. You have a lot of stuff inside you that you never let out. You're like my fuckin' mother. You don't talk to me. You don't talk to anyone. And you're no great listener either, by the way. That's one reason I'm glad Greg is back again."

The brother, Jeff silently cursed. He knew the name would come up. He was being compared with a loser of a drug dealer and he wasn't winning the contest.

"And sometimes I miss Jeff. Jeff Number One."

That "number one" hurt. "Okay, Henry, you have a point. Yes, I don't talk, not about the important things. I don't open up. But please don't make this all about me. You have issues too."

Henry did not offer Jeff any of the dope but instead took a second long drag for himself. In the low light of their room, the orange glow at the tip was bright.

"Me?" he said after making a show of exhaling again. "Just because I asked for it up the ass?"

"No. That's not what I mean. Everyone gets drilled, be my guest. Though some of us don't want to commit suicide at the same time." Jeff thought maybe some of us do, but let that drop. He went on. "I mean something else."

The silence between them lingered for what seemed too long.

"You take too many drugs," Jeff said finally. He wondered why he said this just now. Part of it, he realized of course, was to hurt Henry in recompense for Henry hurting him.

Henry gave Jeff an icy stare as he took another long drag on the joint.

"We never talked about that night at the Monastery. I know you use. You know that I know you use. There was a fuckin' needle in your arm. Recovery my ass."

"We coulda' been humping right now and not talking this shit."

"Don't change the topic."

"Don't change the topic? Well, how about this? You're a fucking drunk! You're always drunk."

Then Henry stuck the knife in deeper: "You'd be a better fuck, by the way, if you weren't plastered all the time."

Jeff let out a sigh rather than counter with an observation about how the drugs kept Henry soft.

"Yeah, I know I drink. A lot. And I should stop. I've been thinking about it. But so should you."

"Stop what? A couple beers? While you're pouring vodka down your throat?"

"Stop *all* the shit you do. Just what *don't* you do? You're always out of it. Speed? *Smack*?"

Henry made a show of laughing, no doubt because he wanted to make clear his contempt for Jeff and his out-of-date vocabulary.

"Sure I get high. Who doesn't? My mommy got high, my daddy got high, the first Jeff *really* got high, and now my goddamn brother makes a good living getting everyone high. So what do you want?"

"I want you to stop."

"I will when I'm ready."

"Now."

"What the fuck are we really talking about? All this started because you wouldn't fuck my ass."

"I *was* fucking your ass. I was suiting up."

"That's not fucking. That's a medical procedure." Henry rose angrily and walked in a small circle in the middle of their room. Jeff looked at Henry's sturdy legs below the edge of the bath towel. His thin treasure trail was dark against his olive skin. Jeff really did want to fuck him. But he was not going to, certainly not now.

"We can't go on like this. Either we have a real relationship, or we're done."

"And a real relationship means coming inside each other?"

"No, that's not all of it. But it's some."

Jeff wished he had a drink. He glanced up at the wine bottle on the dresser. It was empty. But there was another bottle.

"Listen, I know I gotta stop. I know what using did to my mother, and I heard from her what it did to my father. You can't be my enemy about this, though."

"I'm not the enemy," Jeff protested, though he didn't understand what Henry meant.

"Well, you sound like it. You sound like every damn adult I've ever had in my life."

"Okay, I'll shut up. You do the talking." Jeff gripped his fists tight and waited for what was coming.

Henry scurried over to his backpack on the floor and pulled out some clothes. He threw the towel onto the bedspread and was completely naked for a moment. He quickly put on the clean underwear and socks, and then the shirt and pants he'd been wearing all day.

"It's time to get help." Henry slowly buttoned the front of his shirt. It was one Jeff had given him as a present.

"What kind of help?"

This time it was Henry who sighed. "Mike, my housemate. He says his mother lets these gay groups meet at her house up at the top of the hill. AA, NA, you name it. AIDS groups too."

"First you want me to fuck you without a condom, and now you're telling me to go to an AIDS club?"

"You're the one who's worried, not me."

"Well, why the fuck aren't you worried?"

"I'm talking about drugs."

"And booze."

"Yes, and booze."

Jeff went to the bathroom and filled his empty glass with water from the tap. He put the glass down on the floor next to the chair. He saw a way to bring all this to a conclusion. "So you think we should go to these groups?"

"I dunno. Maybe. It's an idea. I used to think it was bullshit. Higher power, that kind of hocus-pocus."

He must have been thinking about this for a while, maybe even gone to a meeting. Jeff knew that Henry needed help, that he needed help himself, but he hadn't expected Henry to be the one to propose it.

"Let's lie down on the bed together," Henry suggested. Jeff understood that Henry was signaling time out.

For a long time they lay side by side on the bedspread. Henry in his clothes, Jeff in the hotel bathrobe. They didn't touch. Both of them stared at the ceiling above them. In time, Jeff took Henry's hand in his own and squeezed it gently, then harder.

Henry was the first to say something. His voice emerged from his throat in a deep register.

"I want to stop using. It's gonna to be hard to give up all my sweet stuff."

"Move in with me," Jeff offered without thinking.

Henry reluctantly took his hand out of Jeff's and turned onto his side to face him.

"You're an addict too, or haven't you heard? The booze to start, but I think other things, too, baby. It's like you're completely shut down. How much time do you spend thinking about anything but your basic needs? If I go for help they're sure to tell me I can't be around you. Maybe at all. That's what they said about the first Jeff. And I didn't take their advice."

You're getting ahead of yourself, Henry. Jeff panicked at the thought of losing Henry for good. One crisis at a time, please. But everything Henry said about him was right. "Each day as it comes, right? Each day. Isn't that what they say?"

"Read that in a book, did you?" Henry rolled onto his back and stared at the ceiling again. After more silence he spoke again.

"You're freaked out by AIDS. Too freaked out. Okay, I understand that, I guess. You're from New York. Sort of. But this is Seattle. It's not New York. Get over it. You need help yourself. You know what? Either you're fine, or you need to get ready for the day you won't be."

Henry's candor dumbfounded Jeff. He listened to Henry's voice as if it were supernatural.

"I know you have sick friends in New York. But you're fuckin' frightened of your own shadow."

"So the answer is to do it without condoms?"

"Maybe. We may be okay. But that's not the point. You keep trying to make it all about that. It's about *us*. Either way, we'll face what's coming. Hey, it might be good times forever."

Henry had never talked about the future before. This was as close as he had ever come to saying he might have one with Jeff. For Jeff's part, he had to admit that he'd never thought about Henry in terms of a future either. He had learned not think about those things with other gay guys.

"What do you think I should do? *We* should do?" Jeff's little boy asked.

Henry raised one arm and rubbed his pectoral with the other. "There's what they call a worried-well group that meets at Mike's mom's house. No one's sick, they're all kinda just freaked out. You could join that. You'd fit right in."

"While you go to a meeting for addicts? My idea of a night out."

"I want us to do it," Henry said, lowering his arm to his side.

"Let me think about it."

"That always means no. I want a yes."

"It does not mean no."

"Then say yes. I need to know."

"Know what?"

"If you love me enough to do this."

Jeff thought that Henry's problem was much worse than his own, but he knew better than to say so. He went over to the chair and picked up the water glass from the floor. He took it back to the bed with him and lay down where he'd just been. Henry had used the word "love" with him for the first time, and now Jeff had to decide how to respond.

"I may love you enough for a lot of things," he finally said.

"Just enough for this will be fine. For now."

"Okay, baby."

They didn't hug, or kiss, or even squeeze each other's hand again. They just kept lying next to each other and stared into the space above. It was completely dark outside; clouds must have covered the moon. Still, they didn't move to turn on the lights. Something kept both of them motionless. Jeff and Henry were crossing a line in their Index hotel room. They were going to get better or they were going to go their separate ways. They might get better and still go their separate ways. As night in the Cascades grew darker still, they fell asleep on top of bed listening to a hard rain pummel the roof. They stayed that way until a lazy Northwest sun belatedly rose the following morning, its long bright rays penetrating their room like glowing rods of steel.

Two days later Henry and Jeff found the Yellow House. They were early and commandeered half of the living room sofa. It was an open meeting with no Big Book stuff. Neither Henry nor Jeff thought they would be into that.

"Will anyone with a year or more of sobriety please raise his hand?" said the guy running the group, raising his own hand.

"A month?" More hands went up, but not Henry's or Jeff's.

The first story they heard was from someone in his forties who had recently relapsed but was back in group again. The guy he was seeing had dumped him and he used that as an excuse to go off on a series of binges.

"You know what I really want now? I just want to be in a room full of naked men."

"No, you don't," corrected another forty-something. "You want a drink but you're calling it a room full of naked men."

Henry and Jeff stayed until the end. They stood, held hands and recited the Serenity Prayer as best they could for newcomers. The guy to Henry's right said it in Spanish under his breath. He glanced at Henry and seemed to expect him to do so as well.

"You didn't talk."

"Neither did you."

They stood in the living room while everyone else was slowly or quickly leaving the house.

"Let's go to another one."

"Now? Tonight?"

"Yes. Look at the blackboard over there. There's another meeting in an hour." Henry raised his arm to point at the notice for an NA group.

They killed time by squatting on the front steps. When a new crop of gay men began to walk by them to go inside, they stood and joined them in the living room. This time they didn't sit together on the sofa, but across from each other cross-legged on the floor. When hands went up again at the start of meeting, but not theirs, Henry and Jeff looked at each with eyes that did all the talking for them. That night in Henry's bed in the Tenth Avenue house, they convinced each other they were off to a good start.

The next day Henry showed up late for his next meeting at the Yellow House. He went alone. It wasn't his regular group but he decided to attend anyway, just to see what it was like. He was a little surprised to see Vinnie running the meeting. It had been about half a year since they had seen each other, around the time that Henry's boyfriend died. Vinnie had stopped by their place and asked if there was anything he could do for Henry. At the time, there was nothing.

After the meeting Henry and Vinnie stayed in the living room to catch up. Henry told Vinnie about Starbucks, and Vinnie told Henry how things were going down at city hall.

"I've started seeing someone new. Another Jeff."

"Is it working out for you?"

"Sort of." Henry shifted his position. "We both have issues. We're both coming here for meetings."

Vinnie saw the young man smile weakly. "Well, be careful. You know what it's like when both guys are using."

Henry changed the topic. "How's Ryan?"

"Shit if I know. Haven't been by his place in a very long time. He's big in the business."

"Yeah, right." Henry stood up to go. "Well, I'm living in a house on Tenth Avenue now. Just down the hill. With some other guys."

"In the program?"

"No, just me. And I'm not sure I'm in the program, either. Maybe just around it."

This time it was Vinnie who smiled a half-smile. "Be careful, Henry. It hasn't been that long since Jeff died. You're vulnerable."

"One of the guys is Mike. Straight. He says his mother owns this house."

"Nan?"

"I don't know her name."

As Henry walked down John Street to Tenth Avenue, he thought about Vinnie, Ryan, and his two Jeffs. Ryan and the first Jeff were lost to him now, but he, Vinnie and the new Jeff had a chance at making it. They'd have to want it, though. And for the first time in a while, Henry felt like he really did. When he got home he called Jeff at home and they talked for a very long time about their respective days. But he did not tell him about seeing Vinnie, because he knew that if Vinnie and Jeff ever met face-to-face, there would be a price for Henry to pay.

"Nan," Vinnie said, plopping down on the sofa in front of her as she was on her hands and knees, sweeping out the fireplace, "you've been great."

Nan sat back on her heels and brushed a strand of her hair out of her face. "I have?" She didn't feel pretty at the moment, but somehow Vinnie's compliment made her think she might be.

"We've taken over your house, I know. I'm sorry."

"Don't be. You know I like it this way."

Vinnie's eyes rested on Nan's. "You do?"

"I do," she said, putting the hand broom on top of the dustpan.

"Nan, are you sure? I mean, you've been looking tired."

Nan stood up. She scanned the mantel for the pack of cigarettes and matches she was sure she'd left there.

"When you're my age, you'll look tired too." She found the cigarettes but no matches. She reached down to the coffee table where she spied some.

"Nan, I have an idea."

She offered Vinnie one of her Salems. He waved no with one of his hands.

"How about some help?"

"What? You need help?"

"No, Nan. You. You need help." Vinnie leaned over the coffee table and played with a ballpoint pen. "Your house is not a house anymore. Yeah, you live here, but in a tiny corner of it. Most of the time it's filled with people you don't know, I mean, you nod hello after you've seen them around, but you don't know them. Hell, I don't know many of them either. How many guys' names do you know besides mine?"

Nan motioned to Vinnie to make room on the sofa for her. She sat down next to him and dragged the dirty ashtray on the table closer to her.

"So? I don't mind," Nan said. "I talked with two nice boys the other day. Stevie and Jack from Tacoma."

"You should mind. Actually, Nan, things are falling apart. Last week you had two meetings scheduled for the same time here in the living room. You leave the front door locked when it should be unlocked. Sometimes there's no coffee and you know alcoholics need coffee. Won't you let me help?"

Nan was surprised to be having this conversation. "Are you saying you're going to help me find a new place to meet?" she asked, a slightly sour feeling spreading in her stomach.

"Well, no, that's not what I was thinking. Your place is big and, look, it's in the perfect location."

Nan extinguished the rest of her cigarette in the ashtray. She looked at the fireplace and wondered when she'd be able to resume cleaning it.

"Let me move someone in here. To help out. You've got plenty of room. There are bedrooms upstairs you never go into, right?"

Nan wanted another cigarette. "*Move someone in here?* What? To take care of *me?* I'm the mother substitute for everyone who *needs* help."

"No, Nan. You just take care of yourself," Vinnie said in a calm voice. "I was thinking of someone who could work as a manager. Help with the cleaning, the scheduling, stuff like that. There are guys to do it, if you let them live here for free."

"*Them?* Just how many downstairs staff are you thinking of, if I may ask?" Nan realized Vinnie was going to win this argument.

"Oh, calm down, Nan. One! Actually, I have someone in mind."

"Jesus, you've arranged all this already?"

"Not at all, Nan," Vinnie reassured, pressing his hand onto his knee. "You're the first person I've talked to about this."

"Well, how thoughtful." Nan regretted she'd snuffed out that half-smoked Salem.

She heard a beeping sound. Vinnie reached into his front pants pocket and pulled out a gadget, looked at it for a moment and then shoved it back into the same pocket. "His name is Henry."

"Henry?" Nan said, louder than she needed to be heard.

"Yes, his lover died of something. We guess it was AIDS, almost a year ago. He's started coming to a couple of the groups here. You'd probably recognize him if you saw him. Dark hair. Good-looking. He's trying to keep sober and I think living here full-time would be good for both you and him."

No, Nan didn't know him. Dozens of young men looked like that.

"Just how do you know this Henry, anyway?"

"Our paths have crossed," Vinnie responded. "He knows—knew—Ryan. He's living nearby right now, in a house down the hill. Nan, it's the house that your son lives in too."

"Mike?" Nan was momentarily stunned. What had her son gotten himself into? It was fine for her to hang out with addicts, but she didn't want Mike to.

"Well, what do you think, Nan?"

"Jesus, Vinnie, I can't have a stranger living in my house. What are you thinking? What would *everyone* think?"

"I'm thinking of you, Nan. I can vouch for him. And there are already plenty of strangers in the house. If that's what you want to call us. Me."

Nan dismissed the thought that was trying to make itself plain inside her head: Why don't *you* move in here, Vinnie?

"I owe Greg money."

"For what?" Jeff asked.

"Stuff. From before I met you. A long time ago."

Jeff could guess it had to do with drugs, but he knew better than to comment on the obvious. He looked at Henry as he finished the last of the orange juice he'd poured into a coffee mug.

"How much do you owe?"

124

"Dunno. Maybe a thousand."

"Maybe more?"

"Yeah, maybe more."

Jeff wished he could help Henry, but he couldn't.

"I need to find some more work."

"So, what kind of work? An extra shift at Starbucks?"

"I thought of that. For a nanosecond. No."

Jeff was worried Henry might be tempted to pick up some extra cash doing something illegal. But he couldn't work at Starbucks sixteen hours a day either. For some reason Jeff now felt he wanted to talk about something else that was on his own mind. "I'm thinking of something myself, Henry," he said as he wiped his greasy fingers off on a dish towel lying on the counter. "Something I've been meaning to talk to you about. Not easy."

"Uh-oh."

"No, you won't be surprised, we've talked about it before. Kind of." Jeff exhaled deeply. "My glands are swollen. Were swollen. They're okay now, it was probably nothing, but I was freaked out. Too many things happen to my body for me not to be worried."

"Yeah," Henry said slowly, not looking at Jeff directly. "We have talked about it before. I'm sorry you're freaked, but you know, you freak easily." Henry looked up and blinked. "This is not new news. Everyone's sick now and then. That's life." Jeff realized that the whole time he had known him, Henry hadn't come down with so much as a sniffle.

After a long silence, Jeff told Henry, "I'm pretty sure I'm infected. I think I'm getting *arf*."

"Why do you call it that?" Henry snapped. "Stop it. It's called AIDS. A-I-D-S."

I call it *arf*, Jeff wanted to say, because that's what my friends in New York and I called it. But he didn't, because he knew how that sounded. Plus, it wasn't the whole story. It was a way of making it small and go away. Jeff was ashamed. "It's like a little pet dog, that you can take everywhere," Jeff finally said, "like a poodle in a purse."

Henry frowned. "If that's a joke, it's not funny, and why are we having this conversation anyway?"

Jeff didn't know what the answer to that question was, except that he needed to talk to somebody, anybody. And here was Henry, next to him. He really wanted to talk to Henry about this, but as usual he was finding it hard to confess his fears, especially to someone much younger than he. His anxieties ran deep, and he didn't want to alarm Henry and certainly not scare him away. All over America, Jeff told himself, gay guys were having this talk and getting past it. But he was paralyzed.

"There's going to be a test soon," Henry said firmly. "Someone told me they were working on it."

"Yeah, there'll be a test. And then what? There's no cure and I bet you end up losing your insurance. I don't see you lining up for it."

"I don't have insurance anyway," Henry said, raising his voice. "I don't work enough hours. But I'd take it, sure."

"I'm not talking about your insurance," Jeff barked. "I'm not talking about you at all, in fact. I'm the topic here."

"As usual," Henry said. Then he lowered his voice. "So, you're weirded out."

"Yes, that's one way to put it."

Henry took two steps forward and extended his arms to put both his hands on Jeff's shoulders. Then he grinned.

"Things are going good for us."

Jeff returned the smile. *Maybe Henry does love me.* "Yeah, I've been thinking the same thing."

"So let's not fuck it up." Jeff wasn't quite sure what Henry meant, but he let it go.

That night Jeff and Henry got out of their groups at the usual time and were talking to some other people on the Yellow House's front porch when a guy with a beard came up to them.

126

"Hey, Henry, good to see you again."

"Hey, Vinnie," Henry said. "This is Jeff."

Vinnie froze. The man in front of him was a dead ringer for Ryan. The same thin face, the same build, the same slight slouch, the same everything, down to way they both slipped their hands into their pockets. *Was* he Ryan? The Yellow House was the last place he'd expect to see him. Ryan, to whom Vinnie had given his wings way back when, now dealt big in Snohomish. This guy didn't seem to blink at him. Vinnie was confused for a moment before recovering enough to continue.

"Hey, how you doing. Vinnie." Vinnie kept his eyes locked on Jeff as he extended his right hand. "Listen, Henry, I've got something to propose to you. Can we sit down someplace for a bit?"

Henry and Vinnie disappeared into the house. Jeff sat down on the steps and watched the remaining men and a few women leave the Yellow House as their respective meetings ended too.

Henry came back about fifteen minutes later.

"Guess what."

"What?"

"That guy Vinnie asked me if I wanted to live here in this house, as a kind of administrative assistant to Mike's mother."

"Huh? Why? Why you? Why is he asking you now?"

Henry sniffed. "He must have heard I was strapped. Maybe he thinks I might like the rent-free part."

"So," Jeff asked warily, "do you?"

"Sure, it would help a lot. Maybe I wouldn't have to find a second job."

"That's because you'd *have* one. Crazy idea."

Henry sniffed in the air a second time. "Actually, I don't think so. And you know what?"

"There's more?"

"Maybe you could move in too."

Jeff couldn't believe what he was hearing. Three nights a week at the Yellow House were quite enough, thank you. Who wants to *live* here? But he also realized that Henry was proposing they be together.

"Vinnie said he'd ask Nan," Henry explained. "Actually, it was Vinnie's idea in the first place."

"And your job is to ask me?" Jeff was puzzled how he had become part of the deal.

"Let's do it. I could save the dough, and you could leave Fremont."

"Who says I want to leave Fremont?"

"You don't know anyone there."

"I don't know anyone here."

Henry frowned. "Okay, be that way. You think about it. I'm going to talk to Vinnie again about this tomorrow." He flashed his smile at Jeff and took one step down the steps to be at the same eye level.

"It's a way for us to be with each other."

"You can move into my apartment, if that's what you want," Jeff said. "And I won't charge you rent either."

"No good. I gotta earn my keep somehow."

They walked down John Street to Tenth. By the time they reached Jeff's car, which was parked in front of Henry's house, Jeff had made up his mind to go along with whatever Henry wanted, even if it meant they'd both be living in the middle of a freak show. Henry and he were at a fork in the road, and they were going to get closer to each other or they weren't. Maybe a stint at the Yellow House could give them the incentive to really quit the drugs and the booze. Jeff would keep the Fremont place as a backup—the university didn't need to learn he was camped out in some queer rehab frat house. Jeff was less than halfway back to Fremont that night when he found himself hoping that this Nan would meet with him and say yes to the both of them.

A week later Vinnie and two other men showed up in a van. Nan was waiting for them. She had been relieved at Jeff's good manners and reluctantly agreed. The three men carried their boxes up to the spare bedrooms on the second floor. Jeff had to be at the university that evening, so Henry walked to the store and came back with the groceries for beef stew, which he assembled in the kitchen while making Nan, sitting on a stool by the counter, laugh at his stories. Nan was sipping wine from a bottle she had uncorked for herself, after checking with Henry that that was okay with him. Sufficiently fortified, she asked the questions she'd wanted to all day.

"Tell me about him."

"Him?"

"Your partner who passed away."

"He didn't pass away," Henry replied sharply. "He died." He realized Nan was going to ask him questions that Jeff Number Two never had. "He got a bad cold, then he went from worse to worst and two weeks later was dead. Lungs filled up. He drowned in the middle of night."

"At home?"

"No. Harborview," Henry said in a quiet voice. "In the hospital, middle of the night, alone because I'd gone down to the coffee machine in the lobby, goddamn it. He had a big fat plastic tube stuck down his throat and was all by himself, just him and that tube."

Henry told Nan about how Jeff had grown up all over the country in a military family, but had lived in Seattle since getting out of the army himself five years before.

"He dealt drugs. The hard stuff. That's how I got messed up. Well, really messed up—I started in junior high. But he also worked at the Salvation Army store downtown, repairing things people donated before they were put on the floor for sale. Funny, no one could fix him when he needed fixing."

"Did he have family?" Nan asked.

"A mother and a sister. They didn't like me. When they came to our apartment for his things, they didn't say a word to me. They wouldn't even look at me. I guess they blame me."

Nan saw that Henry was tired, so she suggested they turn in for the night.

"Is there anything you need?" Nan asked. "I have more towels in the hall closet upstairs."

The two of them walked up the staircase toward Henry's new bedroom. Nan asked if he wanted any help unpacking more of his boxes. This was the first time she'd shared a house with a man since the last night she and her ex-husband were together. And now she had two men living with her.

"Thanks," Henry said to her at the top of the stairs. "Tomorrow we should talk about how I'm going to help you. With the meetings. And the house."

Nan smiled as she nodded.

"Sure, Henry. There's plenty of time."

CHAPTER EIGHT

Henry's room overlooked the driveway. Nan assigned Jeff the one across the hall, once she had moved the things she had stored there to the basement with the two men's help. Their first night at the Yellow House Jeff crawled into Henry's narrow bed to be with him.

"Well, we're here," Jeff said into the back of Henry's neck.

"It's quiet," Henry whispered a moment later.

"The groups are all gone for the night."

"That's not what I meant," Henry said. "There's no traffic."

"It's an old house, the walls are thick." Jeff wrapped his arms tight around Henry and felt the young man's breathing slow as he approached sleep and his first dream in the Yellow House. He wanted a dream where they are in a house with many rooms, each one different, and they explore them together to discover what people here before us. Jeff knew everyone leaves messy touches of their lives behind; it's not impossible to figure out. There'll be things they forgot under their beds, in the back of dresser drawers, on the top shelves of closets. In advance of his own sleep Jeff considered how little pieces of them are already here, some of them his and some of them Henry's, all lying now atop the telling traces of others.

The next morning Henry and Jeff were up by the time Nan made it up to the kitchen.

"Coffee?" she asked, tying her long hair into a ponytail with a band, and then she saw they had made some.

"So," she asked after taking a sip from the mug she poured herself. "Did we go over everything yesterday? Any questions?"

"No," Henry said. "Seems simple enough." He hesitated a moment before continuing. "Between the two of us"—he nodded at Jeff—"we'll keep the groups scheduled and out of each other's way."

"Look," Nan said, careful to readjust the tone of her voice, "I know you guys have full-time jobs." She didn't have any job at all, she almost added.

"Not me," Henry piped in. "I'm part-time."

"Right, that's what you said. At Starbucks. But look, I can be here almost all the time. No one expects that of you fellows. I'm here to do things."

Jeff almost shot Henry a glance, but thought better of it. He got the message. Nan hadn't a clue what to do with herself.

Henry left to go back to the Tenth Avenue house and finish cleaning out his room, but Jeff hung back a minute.

"Do you need something?" Nan asked.

"Ah, actually, I just wanted to say something," Jeff replied as he walked toward her. "Without Henry here."

Nan gripped her mug more tightly. "Go ahead."

"I feel a bit uncomfortable living in your house," he started. "But I'm happy if Henry is happy." He worried aloud that three might be a crowd.

Nan laughed and said, "That should be my line. Do you want more coffee? There's some left."

"Oh no," he said, "I really need to catch my bus." But Jeff made no move from where he stood, an awkward ten feet from Nan.

"There's something else you want to say, isn't there?" Nan said softly.

"I love Henry."

"I'm glad. Everyone should be loved."

"That's not what I meant." What he should have said was, I'm worried. It's hard enough for two without a third. I'm worried about this Greg, whom I still haven't met, and now there's you.

"But I do mean it." Nan guessed what was going on. "I know you'll do what's right. For him and for you. Whether you stay or go. I had difficult decisions to make when my husband and I broke up."

What Nan should have said was, Don't get too comfortable here. Vinnie may have been wrong about all of this. I sense there is something not right with you. At the same time Jeff was realizing that Nan's divorce was not unlike his own decision to leave Raul and New York. They both thought they needed a change but the fact was they were equally traumatized by the prospect. The two of them were similar in other ways, he suspected, and under this same roof they might well be trains racing towards a head-on collision.

"Nan, I'm sorry to do this to you so early in the morning." Jeff was under the mistaken impression he had actually said to Nan what he was thinking.

Nan was not quite sure what Jeff thought he'd done to her. She made her nervous gesture of brushing her loose strands of blonde hair back.

Jeff continued in a more settled voice. "Look, let's talk later. You around today?"

Nan nodded, relieved this odd early-morning conversation was coming to an end. She looked hard and closely at Jeff for the first time. He was on the cusp of turning early middle-aged, but his shiny brown hair and deep blue eyes still suggested an adolescent within. He had a narrow face and a weak chin, but there was still something attractive about him, if nothing special. The intelligence in his face won't fade, though he won't keep his looks much longer, Nan observed. It happened to me, and it will happen to him. I hope Henry loves him, too, and loves him more than Richard did me.

There was also something off-putting about Jeff as well, something hard and cold. Maybe something had made him that way, in which case she wanted to know more, or maybe he just didn't like women, in which case she didn't. Nan felt a shudder go down her spine. It was going to be different, here in the Yellow House, than when she had it to herself. She needed to learn to be on her own, she knew that, and now the presence of Jeff and Henry might cut the lesson short. Something could go wrong. She made herself stop thinking about that—she had doubts, but she thought she should try trusting Vinnie's judgment in people. And he had vouched for both men.

"I'll be around. I usually am. In my room, if nowhere else."

Jeff looked at Nan and realized that, since leaving New York, he hadn't really spent much time with women. There weren't many at work outside of class, and none in his Seattle social life. He hadn't grown up with girls and his interests sexually were limited entirely to men. He wasn't frightened of them as much as simply indifferent. But now Nan was making him curious. He wondered if there was something especially kindred between them, a connection Henry would be oblivious to. Something had hit her hard in life, for sure. Suddenly he wanted to know what she thought of him, and whether she had the same sense of a threatening congruence between them.

"I'm off now, Nan. This time for real. I'll see you later. I'll be back for the seven o'clock group, no later."

Jeff hoisted his backpack's straps higher up on his shoulders and turned to go. Jeff was uneasy by nature but today the anxiety was worse. By the time he reached his bus stop his stomach felt queasy. He had moved into Nan's house more to be near Henry than to help with anyone's twelve-step groups. But he hadn't figured on Nan's presence being a reminder of his own guilty pain at having abandoned Raul and other friends in New York, just as

134

her husband had left her. His fear, finally, was of *arf* and of death. Hers was a fear of being alive but alone.

Henry and Jeff came out of their meetings around the same time the following evening.

"Wanna go out?"

"Where to? It can't be a bar," Henry chuckled. "We just got out of group."

They walked down Fifteenth but everything was already closed for the day. Jeff still had trouble getting used to Seattle's early hours. The weather wasn't bad, so they sat on the wooden steps leading up to the entrance of the old house that was Horizon Books and decided to talk there.

"They warned us this would be tough."

"What?" Jeff asked, momentarily distracted.

"Trying to stay in a relationship when you're trying to quit."

Jeff thought things were going well between them. He made a play for time. "I thought they say it's tougher when one guy is in the program, and the other guy is still using."

"I dunno. Maybe." Now it was Henry's turn to drift off. He bent over to tie one of his sneakers.

Jeff looked up at the dark sky, which for a change was letting stars shine through. He watched two young women have a quiet argument with each other on the opposite sidewalk in front of Red & Black Books. Nothing but bookstores in Seattle, Jeff observed. "What's wrong, Henry?"

Henry sat up straight. "Too much is going on. I'm living in a new place. I go to these meetings every day. I spend a lot of time with you and I don't know how it adds up."

"Think we should take some time off?" Jeff dreaded the answer.

"From each other? No."

Jeff heard the arguing women's voices grow louder. He waited for the young man to say more.

"Greg says..."

"I don't care what Greg says."

"Greg says you're not a good influence on me."

Jeff let out a needlessly loud laugh that he instantly regretted. Greg, that paragon of virtue, was probably right. Sure, he was here in the Yellow House with Henry, and they were encouraging each other to stay with the program. But that wasn't the point. Deep down, the lives they were leading here with Nan felt dishonest, and Jeff was threatened. He was determined not to lose Henry, and his aggressive instincts surged.

That night, after they'd made love, Jeff let his fingers lightly run up and down the treasure trail that ran from Henry's navel to his crotch as they spooned together. Henry, as usual, had fallen asleep right away. Just like a baby. How does he do that? Jeff wondered. He was wide awake and unable to stop thinking that this could just as easily be the last time they ever sleep together. Henry might never be in this bed again, if he decides to take his brother's advice and split.

Jeff wanted to remember every detail of Henry's body and store it away for the future. He'd take photographs if he could get away with it. But soon Jeff fell asleep too. He didn't have any dreams that night, and when he woke up in the morning Henry had already gone to work.

On Saturday Jeff and Henry were invited to the Tenth Avenue house for Clark's annual Easter egg hunt.

The lawn in front of the house was still soggy with dew when they arrived late morning. Clark was inside, standing at the window to the right of the door. He waved when he saw them. Once indoors, Jeff handed Clark a dozen bagels he and Henry had picked up on Fifteenth before heading down the hill. In the old days, not so old actually, he might have brought Clark vodka and some Bloody Mary mix.

"Henry, Jeff, glad you made it."

They stood around the kitchen crowded with other guests and drank Clark's coffee out of his collection of cow mugs. Jeff didn't know many of the people here for what was, he learned, an annual gay event. There was no sign of either Mike or Tim. Out of the corner of one eye he caught sight of Henry, who had moved to the refrigerator and was talking to some blonde cherub. Jeff thought he recognized him. He seized the opportunity of a clear path through the crowd to make an exit outdoors.

Jeff walked around to the back of the house. "Sally," one muscular young woman squealed to another. "Look, they've got croquet set up. Let's start a game. No rules. It will be nasty fun." No one asked Jeff to join. He went back into the house through the back door for more coffee.

Henry was still talking to the cherub, who had been joined by another who could have been his twin. They're breeding, Jeff thought to himself. Jeff went over once the twins had drifted away from Henry.

"What happened to Cupcake?" Jeff asked.

"Who?"

"Cupcake. That child you were talking to."

"I dunno. But his name isn't Cupcake."

"Then it's Ding-dong. Cupcake and Ding-dong." Jeff waved one of his arms. "There are a million of them here. Does Clark raise them on a ranch somewhere?" Jeff remembered where he had seen the one Henry spoke with first. He was the boy Clark had been with at the Monastery the night of the White Party.

More people arrived and the kitchen was packed. It was mostly men with a few women. From what Jeff could tell, they were all gay. "Everyone find something to eat and drink?" Clark shouted above the clamor. He clapped his hands loudly to attract his guests' attention. "Let's go outside and I'll explain what's next."

Eventually everyone assembled on the sidewalk, except for the women playing croquet in the back. "Well," Jeff said after telling Henry about the game going on, "That's just more Easter eggs for us." Henry stood behind Jeff with his arms wrapped around his waist. He murmured coquettishly into Jeff's ear that he had no idea what he was talking about.

"Okay, people, we've hidden Easter eggs all over the yard, not just inside the house. They're green and red and blue, but three of them are yellow."

Cupcake and two of his friends were handing out straw baskets with fake grass in them and fancy ribbons tied to their handles. Jeff and Henry each took one.

"Do we need two?" Jeff said to Henry.

"Sure we do. I'm not playing with you. I'm here to win! You're on your own."

Clark continued. "Anyone who finds one of the yellow eggs gets a special prize. Ready? Okay, start!" Ding-dong blew a whistle.

Jeff and Henry looked at each other. "You look ridiculous with that sissy frou-frou basket," Jeff teased.

"So do you."

"I'm gonna win."

"We'll just see about that."

Henry shot off like a rocket toward the detached garage, leaving Jeff standing alone where there had been a crowd seconds earlier. Jeff found himself thinking about Henry when he should have been hunting for eggs. Henry, he realized, had a real life. Somehow the part-time job at Starbucks, combined with his late adolescence habits, had kept Jeff from seeing the big picture that Henry had a community of friends and felt he belonged in Seattle. It was Jeff's own life that needed something more in it. He watched his boyfriend off in the near distance scrounging for Clark's eggs in the weeds growing along one side of the garage. Jeff realized that it was more likely that Henry would walk out on him and not the other way around. Jeff knew he was hard to be with, and that was more of a liability than any of Henry's faults. Henry was what Jeff needed to make his life feel whole. He wasn't, Jeff realized, much different from alcohol.

Jeff peered down into his empty basket. Most people had gone inside to look for eggs. He let out a sigh and walked slowly toward the row of shrubs along the front of the house. Maybe he'd find an egg over there. If he were lucky enough to stumble across one of the yellow ones, he'd give it to Henry.

The woman who organized the croquet game found most of the eggs, despite her late start. Most of the guests, Henry aside, hadn't looked very hard.

"Marshelle takes all three prizes!" Clark announced to his guests re-assembled inside the kitchen. "A gift certificate to the bookstore," he started, handing her a white envelope. "A bottle of Oregon's best pinot noir," he continued, pointing to a festooned wine-in-a-box on his dining room table. "And—top prize!—dinner for two at the top of the Space Needle!" Jeff wasn't disappointed to lose.

"Where are your eggs?" Jeff asked Henry when they were standing next to each other again. This time it was Jeff with his arms wrapped tight around Henry's waist, his empty straw basket grasped tight between his hands atop Henry's belt buckle. Jeff thought: *I'll* take him to the Space Needle for dinner. He didn't do enough for Henry. He never showed him how he felt, outside of the sack. Jeff slid one hand into Henry's front pants pocket and squeezed his thigh.

The party was dwindling so they went out to the front stoop to sit.

"Haven't been to an Easter egg hunt since I was a kid," Jeff said.

"I've never been to one," Henry said, pretending to pout. "Not since I was invited to the White House."

"Wanna do something?" Jeff asked.

"Like what?"

"I don't know," Jeff said. "We're near Broadway. Take a walk?"

Henry stretched his arms up over his head. "Let's go back to the Yellow House," he suggested. "I'm sure Nan has something she wants us to do." He lowered his right arm and rubbed the back of Jeff's neck with his hand. Jeff turned his head and tried to give Henry a smile to say both the things he loved about Henry, and the things he worried about. They stood and with long, exaggerated strides, climbed the hill back to Fifteenth Avenue and the Yellow House, where Nan was standing on the front porch, smoking a cigarette and looking as if she had been expecting them just that moment.

Greg lay on the bare floor next to his brother's bed while Henry finished talking on the extension phone he had in his room. When Henry finally grunted goodbye and hung up, Greg yawned and resumed the conversation they had been having.

"You go how many times a week?"

"A lot. It depends." Henry stifled a yawn inspired by his brother's.

"Three? Four? More?"

"More." He yawned anyway.

"And you've really gone straight?"

Henry took a step toward the ironing board he had set up in the middle of the room, and touched the iron to see if it was hot enough to start on his shirts for work.

"You don't believe it, do you?" Henry said, moving the ironing board a bit closer to where the iron was plugged into the wall. He had to kick his brother to make room.

"It just doesn't sound like you. I've known you a long time. You don't like to give things up."

Henry put the first of the white shirts on the board. His brother's commentary on his character had him thinking.

"You don't know me as well as you think you do. You left home way before I did."

"I'm older. I knew plenty by the time I left." Greg lifted his black T-shirt to scratch his stomach. "I knew you were a fairy. Even before Mom did, even before you did."

When Henry was done with his first shirt, he took it to the closet and hung it on a wire hanger.

"Jeff. It's Jeff, right? It's always Jeff. What are you doing, hanging out with an old guy like that."

"Shut up. You're an old guy too. Mind your damn business."

Greg rolled over onto his side and cupped his head in his right arm. "You *are* my business, *Hank*. Speaking of which, you owe me money. And I hear you owe other people money too."

Henry put a second shirt on the ironing board. "For fuckin' what now?"

"The blow I got you in Spokane. To begin with."

Henry thought for a second. "I've started to pay you back."

"I need it all. Now."

Henry finished ironing the back of the shirt. He turned it over to work on the sleeves. "You're a bad influence on me."

"More than that prick boyfriend of yours?"

Henry wasn't sure how to answer. His brother was definitely spoiling for a fight, probably the result of coming down off of something. He loved his brother, if for reasons he couldn't fathom. It was funny. When he looked at Greg, he saw their deadbeat father in him; when he looked at Jeff, sometimes he saw a bit of the brother he loved. It was a funny family he'd made for himself. Henry felt like he weighed a million pounds and might crash through the floor of his second-story bedroom and land somewhere below. He didn't have anyone in his life he could really say *everything* to. He stared down at the white cotton shirt he was ironing and focused his thoughts on driving every single wrinkle out of it.

Greg's cough brought Henry back to reality. "I hear about my prick boyfriend all the time, thank you," Henry said, "I don't need to be reminded by you."

Greg went to the window. He rolled up the old venetian blinds and looked at the house next door. "I think I know the people who live there."

"Customers, probably." Henry looked around the room to see if there was anything else to iron.

"No, but close. They're people who know my real mother. Not yours." Greg pulled a joint and a book of matches out of the pocket of his denim jacket.

Henry realized that Greg didn't have anyone to open up to either. They were both bastards. One straight, one gay, both bastards.

"You hear anything from Mom?" Henry asked, not sure he wanted to know.

"Not since she needed money. That's how it works, right?"

Henry felt an unstoppable anger rising inside of him. Everything looked clear to him and it was all unfair. Neither Greg nor he was headed anywhere good. They'd been born that way. It wasn't going to turn out well. Jeff, Henry thought with envy, might get away with it. He'd pull himself together, make it past thirty— Christ, he was there already. Henry watched Greg fumble with the matches and saw no happy ending for either of them. For the first time he was angry about the hand they had been dealt, and then how they had played it.

What he did with that anger did not help things, and Henry would regret it. He picked up a wooden hanger he had left at the foot of his bed, thinking there was another shirt to iron. He held it in his right hand and stared at it listening to his brother suck noisily on his joint. He turned the hanger over in his hand, examining it as if it were some rare artifact he'd just come into possession of. What a fucking loud noise his brother was making. Henry raised his arm. The hanger left his line of vision as it glided through the air above his head and went flying across the room, like a bird or a soundless drone, aimed for Greg's head. Henry saw it all happen in slow motion as the hanger winged its way toward a brother he'd just as soon be dead and might have been, had the speeding object struck its target just right. The slow motion ended when the hanger hit the glass in the window Greg was peering out of again. The sound was sharp and loud, though the glass did not break. Henry would remember lowering his arm and formed fists with both hands, prepared for what was next.

Greg spun around toward Henry with a look on his face that matched the way Henry felt inside. "What the fuck, you little..."

Before Greg could finish, Henry bolted out the bedroom door, knocking the ironing board over with the still-hot iron perched on it. Henry heard a thud but did not look back. And before he was out the front door of the house, he knew he wouldn't be back until he'd scored and was sure Greg was long gone from the scene of their brotherly love.

Greg went looking for Henry downtown, and he knew where to go. First he visited the vacant lot under the Viaduct off of Western Avenue, but none of the heads there had seen his brother. Then he tried the corner of First Avenue and Washington Street. He immediately recognized one of the two guys dealing there. The man didn't seem to know who Greg was at first, but then his surprised face registered that he did. Greg explained to Ryan that he'd been living in Eastern Washington.

"Did time?" Ryan asked.

"What?"

"Walla Walla? Prison?"

"No! Did you hear something?"

"Nah, just that you say you were in Eastern Washington."

The three men, all roughly the same age but looking older than their years, sat together on the sidewalk against an old brick building at the corner of an alleyway. They shared a cigarette.

"And I heard you were set up real comfortable these days in Everett. What are you doing down here, selling on the street?"

"Always fun to visit the old neighborhood," Ryan answered. "Look, I ran into you, didn't I?"

Greg cleared his throat. "Do you remember my brother, Henry?"

"Henry, sure. Your kid brother. Spanish guy. Of course I do. Don't you remember, he lived with me for a while. It was nice to have him around in those days." Ryan snickered and grinned at the fellow dealer next to him. Greg figured that Ryan's business associate was a cocksucker too.

"Ever see him around?"

"Here? Naw. You lookin' for him?" Ryan's partner ground the cigarette butt out with the heel of his boot.

Greg wondered where Henry was scoring his shit. He didn't believe the rehab crap, he knew his brother was still using. He had the look. Henry used the way he used to use, and it wasn't going to stop. He just didn't want to be his brother's connection. Still, he was curious whom he was hooking up with. He was going to make sure that his little brother scored the good stuff, not the garbage he sometimes sold. Not the shit that could kill him.

"I'm worried about him. You know him. You know him real well, if I remember."

"Like I said." Ryan gave Greg a menacing look. It was just the look Greg expected after saying that. Ryan was the one that started his brother on the stuff, and maybe started him on other things too. Fucking faggots everywhere.

"But you know, there was a time I really had it in for him. I groomed him for the business but he fucked customers over. People go missing for that, you know."

Greg knew a threat when he heard one. But he let it pass, thinking Ryan was showing off in front of the other guy with them.

"If he comes by, don't say I was here. You just take care of him, got it? "

"Man, we take care of everyone."

Greg needed to move on. "Don't mess with him."

"Naw, we won't mess with him," Ryan said. "Any more than he already is messed with." This time Greg wondered if the threat might be real. "He owes people money and they don't tend to forget. *I* don't forget."

Greg stood up and brushed the dirt off his pants. He was going to keep Ryan close to him for a while, make a buddy of him again the best he could, just to make sure he wasn't up to anything. Sometimes he wished Henry harmed himself because some part of Greg was so much like his queer brother, and he had wanted the resemblance gone. The drugs they shared were just a way of being like each other in a macho way Greg could deal with. He'd known that but did nothing about it. And now, he realized, it might too late.

Greg started up First Avenue and passed two parked police cars, which must have been watching him talk to Ryan and the third guy. The police looked straight ahead, as still as mannequins, and didn't glance in Greg's direction. Greg deliberately looked across the street to avoid meeting the cops' eyes if they decided to check him out at close range.

There, across the street, standing alone on the sidewalk and staring at Greg, was someone who looked just like Ryan. He might have been surprised at the coincidence, but hallucinations were common when coming down off the junk. He turned and left, his mind now focused on the promise to himself that if something were to happen to Henry, he would be the one to do it and it would be a fucking act of mercy, like putting a crippled old dog out of its misery; and out of brotherly love.

"Let's get out of town today," Jeff said to Henry one weekend. "Or do you have to work today?"

"No." Henry was distracted playing with a Rubik's Cube someone had left on the counter in Nan's kitchen. "How about Mount Rainier?"

"It's a ways, isn't it?" Like driving from New York to New Haven, Jeff calculated.

"Mount Saint Helens is even further away," Henry said, proposing and rejecting the idea at the same time.

"Oh, Mount Saint Helens. Cool. See what's left of it. Where is it exactly?"

"Closer to Portland than to here. Like a hundred miles. Maybe more."

"Can we get close to it? I mean, it's not really a dead volcano or anything."

"No volcanoes are dead," Henry said. "They don't erupt, except when they do. Mount Baker smokes sometimes."

It was a gray day, but it didn't look like rain. Jeff leaned back on the stool and stretched both arms in the air.

"Okay, sure. Let's do it. Let's see if we can make it to Mount Saint Helens and back in one day."

The heater in Jeff's car wasn't working right. It was April but still cold enough to need it. It only worked full-blast, so all the way down I-5 they had their windows open partway. When they stopped for gas near Olympia, Henry said he wanted to drive. As Jeff handed him the keys he let his middle finger rub against Henry's palm.

Back in the car and on the highway again, they talked about Seattle, the very place they were escaping for the day.

"I don't know why I'm still the fuck here," Henry complained. "I could go anywhere. Two of my best buddies from high school are in L.A. They love it. I've had it here."

"Had it with what?" Jeff asked, instantly thinking he never wanted to be asked the same question about New York.

"I grew up here. My mother's here, somewhere. It's small." Henry turned to Jeff in the passenger seat and flashed him a big smile. "And I'm not."

"You have to decide what you want to be when you grow up."

146

"Jesus, now you sound like my fucking father." Henry had never mentioned his father before, other than to say he had one.

They turned off the highway to go east on Route 505. They were the only car on the road. So far the drive had been easy. Jeff tried to find something on the radio, but it was Sunday, and the stations were all broadcasting Christian music.

"Wind up your window some. It's cold in here."

As they rose in elevation they saw a sign for the volcano's visitor center.

"Let's go up to the observatory. That's as close as we can get."

"May be closed this time of year."

Just as Jeff figured they'd be there soon, they found themselves behind a big logging truck carrying a load of timber. Henry tried to pass him a couple of times, but the road had too many curves in it.

"No rush. It's not like there's a whole lot to do once we're there."

They went higher and the weather became foggier. Henry fumbled around the car trying to find the headlights. "Great," he mumbled. "We should have gone to Mount Rainier."

Jeff wondered what he could do to save the day. Giving Henry a blowjob might be fun, but he didn't quite trust Henry's driving as it was. There were a few forks in the road where Henry and Jeff weren't quite sure which way to go. Henry fumbled again at the controls of the unfamiliar car, finally realizing that the switch for the high beams was on the floor under his left foot. The extra light did not help much in the fog. They made it to the visitor center entrance as if by accident.

Jeff and Henry looked at each other for a moment, as if to ask why they'd done this trip. They wanted to go out of town, Jeff reminded himself, and he still had an important errand to complete on this excursion, one he had been postponing.

"Pull over there."

"Where?"

"There. By the railing."

Henry did as he was told and parked the car.

"I guess the mountain is over there."

"Are you sure we're not on it?"

"Might be. I dunno."

They left the car and tried the massive cedar and glass doors at the visitor center. Closed for the season. Jeff asked Henry why they kept the drive open if they were closed; Henry shrugged. They walked around the parking lot and eventually found an information sign. Another sign said "Scenic View." The mountain, what was left of it, was indeed in front of them. But in the fog they couldn't see anything.

"Well, this was a wasted trip."

"Yeah, guess so. At least we can say we've been here."

"Why would we say that?"

They went back to the car, where it was warmer.

"This place blew up and killed people."

Jeff, back in the driver's seat, looked out his window at the damp pavement.

"I saw a documentary on public TV about it. It could have killed a lot more."

"Fifty-seven. That's how many died."

Not so many, Jeff thought. Just a lousy way to go. Or maybe not. "Did you hear the explosion?" Jeff asked Henry, turning in his seat to face him.

"Ah, I was in the shower. My mom heard it, though. At first she thought it was something in Seattle, a cannon or something."

"There are no cannons in Seattle."

"How do you know so much? Anyway, we watched the news on the TV. We were worried that the wind might blow all the ash to Seattle. Portland sweated it out even more."

Jeff thought about Seattle as a modern-day Pompeii. Everyone caught unaware where they were, in their homes or on the streets, fleeing the city or huddled in churches, as lovely hot pumice encased them for eternity. He looked at Henry again. "Did you think of leaving town?"

"Leave Seattle? Naw, didn't occur to us."

Everyone thinks they'll survive, Jeff thought to himself. No one thinks he'd better pack the car and get the hell out of Dodge, not until it's too late. Except for him, of course.

"Someday Rainier's gonna blow," Henry added, almost cheerfully.

"And then?"

"And then Tacoma's a goner for sure. It's right in the path of the lava flowing down to Commencement Bay. I've seen a 3-D map of where it will go."

"You'd like it to happen, wouldn't you?"

They sat silently in the car for what seemed a long time.

"Wanna head back?" Henry eventually asked.

"Still got time," Jeff replied. He searched for courage to talk.

Henry squirmed in his seat, like a child might.

"Henry, I saw Greg."

Henry leaned forward and put his hand across his forehead and looked at Jeff as if the sun, of which there was none, might be in his eyes.

"I heard you and Greg fighting in your room. I was across the hall, the door was shut but I could hear you. You threw something at him, didn't you? Anyway, I heard you run out of the room, and I heard Greg swearing at you. When he left your room, I followed him."

"You *followed* him?"

"Yes. He ran down the hill, jumped on a bus. So did I. He went downtown to a couple of places. He was looking for something. Maybe a fix. Maybe he was looking for you."

"Maybe he was just going for a walk. You think of that?"

"He was not going for a walk. He was in Pioneer Square, at that corner with all the dealing. He talked with some guys, then left. I didn't follow him anymore."

"That's it? That's what you wanted to talk to about? I wish we had a joint."

"A joint? Why do you want a joint?"

"To relax me. You're making me nervous."

"Is that why you shoot up sometimes? To relax?"

Henry gave Jeff a look full of contempt. "You don't know shit."

"I don't know shit? Okay, educate me."

"I use when I have to use. It's not to adjust. It's to avoid *not* using. Think about that, why don't you."

Jeff looked ahead through the windshield at the fog. "I don't know what you mean. Anyway, there's more."

"You don't drink because you *want* a drink. You drink because you drink. It's just what you do. It's who you are." Henry sighed. "Alright, go on."

Jeff didn't take the bait, and continued with what he had to say. "Your brother Greg was talking to someone who looks just like me. And I mean *just*. Is this the guy they call 'Ryan'? The one everybody mistakes me for? Do you know who I'm talking about?"

Henry let out another sigh, a much longer one this time. "Yeah, I bet that was Ryan. He's a drug dealer, too. I used to know him."

"*Used* to?"

"Yeah, long ago. When I was in high school. He's older. Your age."

"Does he still sell you shit?"

"No," Henry snapped. "He doesn't sell me *shit*." He turned and looked at Jeff. "Don't you know I'm trying to go straight?"

"Yes, I know that, and I also know I saw you at the Monastery shooting up."

"That was before," Henry murmured. "That was before the Yellow House."

"Where were you when I was following Greg?" Jeff asked, and when Henry didn't answer, he asked again. *"Where were you when I was following Greg?"*

Henry played with his passenger-side window, winding it up and down. "I was looking for a score. Got it? A score. And you know what, Sherlock Holmes? I found it. Now shut up."

Jeff stepped on the clutch and turned the key. He shifted into reverse and pulled out of the parking space. He thought: This is never going to work out. A wall stood between him and Henry, and it wasn't just age. It was the accumulation of stories each of them had, which neither was much disposed to share, and even if they did tell might not make any sense to the other.

Henry seemed to brighten up when they reached the city limits. He fidgeted in his seat, and played with his seatbelt strap. "Wanna do something?"

Jeff didn't know what to make of Henry's offer. "Let's go back to the house, maybe talk some more?" He exited at Olive Way and wove their way to the top of the Hill. It was late and they decided just to hang on the second floor. They watched the TV in Jeff's room and did not talk anymore. Finally, when the national weather forecast came on, Jeff complained they didn't report anything about Seattle. "They never do," Henry said. "They always skip this part of the country." Those were the only words they exchanged. That night, after Henry had fallen asleep, Jeff sketched a picture of Henry's face on the back on an envelope and went down stairs to put it up on the refrigerator door, but Nan had no magnets to share. Henry had wanted a joint earlier in the day, and now, in the dark of the Yellow House, Jeff would have given anything for a drink.

Henry had a scowl on his face the next morning, as if something not quite right was on his mind as well.

"Everything okay?" Jeff asked as he joined him on the sofa, pushing his leg out of the way.

"Actually, no." Henry reached for the previous day's *Seattle Post-Intelligencer* on the coffee table and made a show of reading it.

"Did I do something?"

"You? No." Henry noisily turned the pages of the paper.

Just what will it take, Jeff wondered, to pry it out of him. He and Henry sat without saying anything. Then Henry threw the paper onto the floor and crossed his arms. Jeff knew something was coming.

"Why am I here?"

"Huh?"

"Here. The Yellow House. The groups. The fuckin' *steps*. And especially the fuckin' sponsors. Bad idea. Is it too late to change our minds?"

Jeff fetched himself a can of soda out of the refrigerator. "Want a Coke?" he yelled from the kitchen, but Henry didn't reply. Jeff could have lectured him, but he bit his tongue. What did he know? The fact was that Jeff felt the same way himself. Neither of them was in the program, just around it.

"Well, go ahead and take a break. Why not?" he shouted. But both he and Henry knew why not. Jeff's sponsor had told him you were always either moving away from a drink or closer to one. There was no in-between.

Jeff put his can of Coke down and felt again for the swelling under his jaw with both his hands, one of which was cold from having held the soda.

Jeff stepped away from the counter and went into the dining room. He could see Henry rummage through his backpack in the living room. Henry pulled out a magazine and started reading. Jeff was not sure what to do. A chasm was opening between them, or maybe it had been there all the time. He had thought it was due to drugs and liquor. Or *arf*. Or the difference in their ages, about which Jeff could do nothing. But now he wondered if the worlds they inhabited were impossibly distant from each other.

In the silence there was only the low electric buzz of the refrigerator, punctuated by the angry, defiant sound of a man turning the pages of a magazine in which he had no interest. Something jarred Jeff's memory, and what he retrieved was the scene of a similar tableau, when it wasn't Henry who was making his frustration with him plain, but Raul. Jeff had been making plans to leave New York but said nothing to Raul about them until confronted by the very first boyfriend he ever had. Raul's rage had filled his apartment and could have become violent in lieu of the words that neither found easy to say. Now it was only a matter of time before Jeff's second boyfriend caught on to his habit of furtive betrayals.

Jeff couldn't sleep that night, but lying in bed he could tell from the absence of traffic noise that it was too early to start his day. Still, he edged himself out of bed carefully, so as not to wake Henry. He put on a T-shirt and sweatpants and went down to the kitchen.

The unfinished can of Coke he'd opened hours ago was still on the kitchen counter. Jeff picked it up and downed the warm, bubbleless sweet liquid. He wasn't thirsty, but it seemed a waste to pour it down the sink.

Out of sorts, Jeff distracted himself by putting away the plates left to dry next to the sink. There weren't many, but he took his time doing it, in part because he didn't want to make any unnecessary noise.

Jeff pulled the silverware drawer out so far it almost fell to the floor. Fortunately something caught and stopped it. But this was the first time Jeff could see everything in it. At the back he saw the steak knives Brandon in New York had mailed him. He had completely forgotten about them since he had moved into the Yellow House and put them there. They were bound tightly with the thick rubber band Brandon had used to pack them. He'd never undone the bundle or thanked Brandon. Jeff found himself wondering how his old friends and friends of friends were doing.

He lifted the knives out of the drawer and placed them on the counter. He would never use them. He didn't eat steak, and he never made it for anyone else. Also, there was something used about them. Where had they been, what had they done? They weren't really Brandon's or Brandon's ex's anyway, were they? Maybe neither of them had used them. Maybe no one had ever used them, like rare stamps that collectors never stick on envelopes. Sam was probably down to the baby food by this point, if that. Jeff's right hand floated up to the swollen spot under his jaw, though he had ordered his hand not to.

Jeff picked up the knives. He probably should just throw them away, but something told him that was bad luck, like not forwarding a chain letter. He placed them on the counter out of the way and went back upstairs, but to his own room and not Henry's.

CHAPTER NINE

It was after work but before dinner, and every aisle at the QFC on Broadway was packed. Jeff was stuck behind three lesbians blocking him with their carts. He looked around and realized, Yes, everyone here *was* queer. Lots of clones. And the body-builder types Raul used to call bionic sissies. Older women in comfortable shoes, younger ones with nose rings and tattoos. Jeff put broccoli, hamburger, two cans of frozen orange juice, and a lemon in his hand basket and navigated his way to a checkout line that looked like it might move fast. He stood behind two men around his own age and listened to them gossip about Fistful of Crinolines, their gay male square-dancing club.

Jeff handed a twenty-dollar bill to the cashier, pocketed his change, and walked back to his car. As he slid behind the wheel of his car, he felt himself in familiar danger. He was falling into that place in his head where he knew he'd soon contemplate things he would regret later but were about to be irresistible. Sometimes this state of mind led to a bender, but right now it felt headed somewhere else—though it was always the same loneliness. Jeff thought about leaving his car and nipping across the street for a drink at Ernie Steele's, the old geezer bar, but he knew it would never be just one drink. And besides, he had another idea in mind.

He sat and made himself think carefully for a moment, just to be sure.

He pulled out of the supermarket parking lot onto Broadway but didn't turn left at John to head home to the Yellow House. He went straight through the light and headed another block, knowing he'd turn right onto Pike and end up at Summit Avenue where the bathhouse was. It was ridiculously early, he told himself as he rapped his fingers against the steering wheel. Stopped again by traffic, he thought about the frozen orange juice in his trunk. It will thaw. It will go bad. But he did not doubt what he was going to do.

He spotted an empty space on Summit Avenue almost directly in front of the bathhouse. God meant this to happen, Jeff assured himself. The rain had stopped, but the temperature was dropping and Jeff, who decided to leave his coat in the car, hurried into the baths. The old smells seemed so comforting: disinfectant, a little pot in the air and the whiff of amyl. He paid his money to the bored guy behind the glass window, took a towel from the pile at the bottom of the staircase and darted up to the locker rooms on the second floor.

He found his locker, took his clothes off, wrapped the thin towel around his waist and put the elastic key strap around one of his ankles. Okay, let's go. First he did a quick tour of the hot tub area and the steam room: no one. Either he'd picked a bad time, or the stories he'd heard that guys were avoiding the wet areas were true. At the far end of the bank of showers he spotted a tall, thin black man, hands clasped together under his chin as if in prayer, swaying under a spray of steaming hot water to the beat of some imaginary music in his head.

Jeff entered the labyrinth of identical cubicles. It took a moment for his eyes to adjust to the dim lighting. Gray walls, gray ceiling, gray carpet, gray doors. Everything was designed to suck light out of the world. Even the sounds were gray, as monotonous electronic music seeped out of hidden speakers.

Jeff thought, I've made a mistake. Why am I here? Who in the world goes to the baths at six thirty p.m. on a weekday? In a small city? Maybe he'd just find the room where they showed nonstop porn on a small TV screen. He'd sit on a shelf with stained carpeting and jerk off. Better than nothing. He headed off in the right direction, which he vaguely recalled from the time he came here to explore his first week in Seattle. But as he hurried, he approached two doors open to cubicles even darker than the hallway.

In the first of the cells he could make out the outlines of a man slowly dressing. Mid-thirties, paunchy and balding. Jeff knew who he was, if not really: some married guy who'd stopped off on his way from downtown back to Renton, hoping for something quick. Jeff rushed by.

The second open door was next to the first. Jeff tried to peer inside. Lying on the thinly padded platform bed was a young man who at first looked something like Henry. Same age, same thick black hair. This person did not have a trim goatee like Henry's, but the smile he flashed was so similar it startled Jeff. The brightness of his white teeth filled the cubicle.

He waited for a sign either to come closer or move on. He thought he could see the young man nod his head slightly, so he moved two steps forward. Jeff used his right arm to stroke the calf of one of the guy's outstretched legs, and he nodded again. Jeff stood up straight, turned slightly around and closed the door to the room. He loosened the towel around his waist and let it drop to the floor. His penis was slightly engorged, and he could see the young man looking at it.

The man raised his arms and put his hands behind his head, exposing two small, soft patches of dark hair under his armpits on an otherwise smooth body. He smiled again, and seemed to whisper something. Jeff took a last step forward to close what short distance between them remained, and lay down half on top, half beside. He extended his own body, much longer than the stranger's, its full length.

They kissed. He tasted of cigarettes, but the mouth was warm and wet. Jeff readjusted himself to be fully atop the young man, whose legs rose to wrap themselves around Jeff's buttocks. As they continued to kiss and Jeff got harder, he suddenly realized that the man beneath him had already reached down, wrapped his greased hand around Jeff's penis and guided it to his buttocks, which felt loose and practiced. Jeff's penis, pulsing and fully hard now, went inside, joining their bodies. Jeff knew there was no condom but felt no terror. The young man's feet moved up and down Jeff's lower back and ass, inviting him to come in farther. Jeff obliged, and the man's ass bucked up and down as much as it could under Jeff's weight to help with the coupling. It was all so quick. Soon his semen was inside the man, with whom he had yet to exchange a single word.

Jeff went soft quickly as he realized what he had done, and his penis slipped out of the man panting underneath him. Jeff rolled off and faced him side by side.

He flashed his beautiful smile a third time. "Nice."

"Thanks. I'm Jeff."

"Stavros." It wasn't just the name, but it was the lilting accent that gave Jeff the clue his host this evening was not American.

"Where are you from?"

"Hoquiam."

"No, before that."

"Greece."

Jeff ran his index finger down the Greek's smooth, lean chest until he reached the place his pubic hair should have been. The man was lightly damp all over. Jeff wondered how many guys he'd had today. Your money got you twenty-four hours here.

"All the way from Hoquiam?" Jeff wasn't sure where that was, but he suspected it was far.

"I just moved here. To Seattle."

"Where?"

"I have a cousin in White Center."

"Many Greeks there?" Stavros did not answer. Another immigrant, Jeff thought. Just like me. He moved his body slightly so he could fondle Stavros's penis, which struck Jeff as small for a Greek's. It was slightly stiff but declined Jeff's admittedly halfhearted efforts to make it any harder.

"You like it here?" Jeff asked, though he knew the question wasn't clear.

Stavros giggled but did not reply. "I should take a shower," he eventually said.

"Oh, not yet. I'll go with you later. Just lie here with me for a moment."

Jeff's hand moved from Stavros's little-boy dick and moved down to the warm orifice he had just entered, and thought about what they'd done. Bits of him were swimming around inside this man now, something he hadn't done to Henry, ever.

"I'm new here, too," Jeff whispered. "Well, not so new."

Stavros frowned, not out of displeasure but from surprise. He probably thought of all Americans as having always been here. From his point of view, all Americans must be natives. But we're not, Jeff wanted to say.

"I should go," Jeff said, now thinking their business together was done.

"You just said you wanted to lie here."

"I did say that," Jeff said, rubbing the side of Stavros's torso with his hand. "But now I think I should go."

Jeff made no move to get up. They just lay there saying and doing nothing. Despite the music, Jeff could hear the floor creaking outside the cubicle as other barefoot men walked past looking for open doors.

"Greece?"

"Yes, Greece. Delphi. Have you been to Greece?"

No, never, Jeff thought. "Do you miss it?"

Once more, Stavros laughed but said nothing. Aren't oracles supposed to speak? Jeff wondered.

The floor creaked again. They were all going to be strangers at home with others, those men in the corridor making those sounds. Jeff could hear someone down the hall moaning as someone took his pleasure with him. Hurried intimacies for sure, he thought. Here in the far upper-left corner of the nation, Jeff and Stavros, two men with no further place to go, decided to be motionless as long as they could.

"Henry," Nan began one morning in the kitchen, "does it seem half the city comes here now?"

"Here? Then I wonder what the other half is up to then," Henry shot back. He stirred his lukewarm coffee with a finger and continued. "A lot of them are new. From California. Oregon. Montana." Why were gay guys moving to Seattle? he wondered, when he was so eager to leave sometimes. Nan seemed happy the Yellow House was so popular, but Henry took it as a warning that the big town he grew up in was now becoming a small city full of strangers. Jeff was one.

"You know, Henry, I was thinking of moving myself." It was if Nan had read his mind.

"Right after my divorce. I had this idea I'd make a new life for myself in Laguna Beach. But instead I bought this house."

Henry had heard of Laguna Beach, but he wasn't exactly sure where it was. He guessed Hawaii. It sounded nice. Sort of tropical. Henry hadn't been outside of Washington State often. There were those couple of long plane rides to Chile, when he sat alone in a seat, surrounded by strangers, with a piece of paper pinned to his shirt with his name and destination on it. His school band had been invited to march in Jimmy Carter's inauguration in Washington, D.C., but they didn't raise enough money to go. Henry really didn't know much about the rest of the world. Sometimes he thought he should have enlisted after high school like his friends.

160

Nan noisily drained the last of her coffee and disappeared. Henry put both their mugs in the sink and found himself momentarily at a loss what to do next. He went downstairs for no particular reason, and was sitting at his desk when he noticed, in the corner of the dark, damp basement where Nan's unpacked boxes were piled up out of the way, an old globe of the world. With the wooden stand that supported it, it was over three feet high. The globe itself had to be almost two and a half feet across. He hadn't seen anything like that for years. He wondered why Nan had one.

He went over to it. It was covered with thick gray dust. He went upstairs to the kitchen closet and came back down with some spray cleaner and a couple of paper towels to clean it off. Dragging the whole thing over to his desk, he put it near the gooseneck lamp to manage a better look at it. It was really old, Henry realized. Most of Africa seemed to be part of England or France. America looked pretty much the way it should. Henry leaned over and looked closely at Hawaii. He saw two colored dots, for Honolulu and Hilo, but no Laguna Beach. Looking at the mainland, he saw Houston, where the guy in the NA group with the herpes infection on his upper lip that never healed said he'd come from. His finger traced a straight line to Saint Paul, where his first Jeff had spent a couple of years in the service but they'd never had a chance to visit. Then he found Los Angeles, where several of the Yellow House guys had come from. Chile was a long red streak, like a thin wound oozing blood.

Henry tried to spin the globe on its stand, but it was gummed up. It didn't budge. He put it back in the corner of the basement, went upstairs and washed his hands in the sink. While running his hands under the water and looking out the window, he felt depressed. It was still early in the day and while he had things to do, he went upstairs to his room and lay on top of the bedspread. Assuming the fetal position, he wondered where in the cosmos Jeff Number One was, and what he was up to.

161

One day Jeff dropped in at Starbucks during Henry's shift.

"Jeff," Henry said in a low voice, "look, I can't talk now. There are customers."

Jeff took a seat on a metal stool along a shallow counter built into one of the walls, designed for discomfort to keep the crowds moving. He extracted a stack of student papers and a red felt pen out of his backpack and started to correct them, making sure Henry could see what he was doing and realize he was not leaving until the two of them talked.

It wasn't long before Henry, wiping his hands on an apron festooned with the chain's brown mermaid logo, came over.

"Customers are supposed to buy something."

"Then I'm not a customer," Jeff said, not looking up from the paper he was reading.

"Okay, I could pretend I'm just a barista making nice to a stranger, but everyone who works here knows who you are."

"A what?"

"A what what?"

"What you are? A bah…"

"Barista. Bah-ree-stah. It's Italian."

Jeff put the student papers down on the narrow counter not meant for anything but coffee cups. He watched them perch precariously on the edge.

"What are you doing tonight?" Jeff asked.

"Same as you. Groups. Friday night groups"

"Skip yours, I'll skip mine. Let's do something together."

Henry glanced back over his shoulder at the busy counter, then at Jeff again.

"Like what?"

"I dunno. A movie. A burger. Gay bingo, for crissake."

Henry wiped his hands on his apron again, right where the mermaid's big breasts were.

"Okay. Maybe around ten. Let's meet up back at the house."

Jeff noticed Henry's big dark eyes dart back and forth. "Sure, ten." Jeff picked up the papers, which hadn't fallen off the counter, and shoved them into his backpack. He nodded so long to Henry and left.

By nine-thirty Jeff was back at the Yellow House and in his room while a Big Book meeting was going on in the living room. He heard the sound of Henry's heavy Doc Martens come up the stairs. Henry came into his room, leaned over to kiss him and lay down alongside him on the narrow bed.

"How was the rest of work?"

"Work was work. Some asshole got upset because he thought we charged too much for a latte. Which we do. You?"

"Read some books, took some notes. The usual."

Henry yawned. "You're lucky you don't have a boss ridin' your ass." He turned to Jeff and flashed him his incandescent white smile, reminding Jeff of another.

"You've got something between your teeth. Lettuce or something." Jeff cursed himself for pointing out every fault. Henry fished out whatever was green with his middle finger and swallowed it.

They decided to see what was on the TV in Jeff's room and fell into watching an old *That Girl* rerun. Henry didn't know who Marlo Thomas was, and when Jeff explained that she was Danny Thomas's daughter, he didn't know who that was, either. When it was over Henry insisted on choosing what they watched next. He spun the dial and found a Sonics game in its last minute of play.

Jeff didn't want to interrupt with a question, so he waited until a commercial. "Henry?"

"Yeah?"

"How are we doing?"

"Huh?" Henry grunted, his eyes glued to a TV commercial.

"How do you feel about me?"

Henry pulled his red baseball cap low over his forehead and chewed his lower lip.

163

"I like you, Jeff. More than like. You know that, right? But we're really different people."

Jeff let that hang in the air before saying, "Can't that be a good thing?"

"Don't be defensive," Henry snapped. "You know it's true."

"I didn't say it wasn't true. I just wonder how much it matters. My parents were really different people."

Henry stared at the television as the game went into overtime. "Were they happy? Mine weren't."

Jeff felt his heart race a bit. "We're not our parents," he said, realizing how circular his argument was.

"Sure we are," Henry snorted, finally turning his head toward Jeff and lifting his cap's visor. "I have an idea," Henry offered. "There's a Chinese restaurant downtown, a real dump on Second Avenue. I've never eaten there—no one has, I think—but on weekends it turns into a drag club at midnight. They put on a show. I hear it's pretty good."

Drag wasn't Jeff's thing ordinarily, but he felt like pleasing Henry tonight and going along with whatever he suggested.

"There's a cover, but it's like only five bucks. And you get a drink," Henry said.

"Okay, sure, let's do it," Jeff agreed, both disappointed and relieved they had blown their chance to talk more about their relationship.

They found a parking space on Second Avenue. It looked like a wait to get in, but the line at the door was gone by the time they had locked the car and walked over.

"The Jade Pavilion. The original."

"There's more than one?" Jeff asked without sarcasm.

A young, pimply guy sitting behind a dining table moved toward the door, took their money, and mumbled that they could sit anywhere. The restaurant was small, but only a quarter full, so they took one of the larger tables for themselves. The restaurant had no windows, and Jeff smelled old cooking oil. The flowers on their table were plastic; the vinyl chairs, a tired plum color. A beaded curtain had been strung across the metal door to the kitchen. An Asian man came out through the curtain and, after waiting on a table of boisterous men he seemed to know, came over and asked them what they'd like to drink.

"Water," Jeff said, offering the waiter his drink ticket.

"Coke for me," Henry said.

"You can have anything you want, you know. Mai Tais?"

"No, we can't," Henry said with a snigger. The waiter shrugged his shoulders and went to the compact bar to the left of the kitchen door to fill their orders. Jeff saw that the area directly in front of the kitchen door had been cleared to be a makeshift stage.

The white guy at the door eventually brought Henry and him their Coke and water. Meanwhile, music began to play from the two big speakers set out on the floor on either side of the temporary stage, old disco alternating with some kind of Asian pop. By half past midnight the Jade Pavilion was packed. Jeff wanted a refill of his water, but he knew he'd never get it.

The music stopped and the white guy dragged a microphone stand to the middle of the stage. He was the master of ceremonies as well as the sole waiter, the Asian guy having disappeared long ago. He leaned into the microphone and breathlessly introduced the drag queen, Nora Tacky. He stepped to pull the beaded curtain back with a flourish as the gray metal door opened wide and Nora swept in, speakers bellowing out a song Jeff recognized from *Flower Drum Song*. It was the same Asian guy, now transformed. He wore a tight red dress with a slit up the leg and had a huge flower behind one ear, stuck in a black wig as shiny as lacquer.

Jeff watched Henry out of the corner of his eye. He was clearly enjoying the act, laughing repeatedly to himself as Nora lip-synched one camp oldie after another. Maybe drag queens were Henry's thing, Jeff noted, filing that bit of information away.

Nora soon took her first break and disappeared back into the kitchen. Jeff used the men's room, and when he came back Henry was standing beside another table with three heavyset women. When he saw Jeff heading back to their own table, he motioned goodbye to them and rejoined Jeff. The second set started. Jeff dragged his chair closer to Henry's and cupped his hand around Henry's ear to say something.

"Still enjoying this?"

Henry looked straight ahead at the stage and said, "Not really," loud enough for Jeff to hear it. They stood up to go just as the waiter emerged from behind the bar with a tray loaded with glasses and beer bottles. Jeff threw a couple of bucks onto the table.

Second Avenue was deserted when they emerged from the restaurant, which Henry was now referring to as the Jaded Pavilion. The wind off Elliott Bay had picked up. Jeff saw that Henry was shivering.

"January or July, July or January. Could be either," Henry remarked.

They drove up to Kerry Park near the top of Queen Anne. Their parking spot had a good view of the Space Needle and the downtown skyline. They walked to the edge of the park, where they could see the last ferry headed to Winslow.

"Well, it started out okay."

It took Jeff a second to realize Henry was talking about the drag show.

"I'm glad we went," Jeff offered. "It was something to do."

Back in the car, Henry fished the last cigarette out of a pack he'd stored away in Jeff's glove compartment. He played with it in his left hand rather than light it.

"Roll down the window if you're going to smoke," Jeff admonished. But Henry made no move to do so.

"It's a funny thing about gay guys," Henry abruptly announced.

"What's that?" Jeff asked, already imagining a number of potential answers to his question.

"It's not like chicks and guys."

"As if you know." Jeff wondered what Henry's point was. He rubbed both sides of the steering wheel. "What are we? Just best friends?"

"Oh no, not by a long shot." Henry turned and faced Jeff directly. He sighed. "I've got lots of friends. I'm not looking for any more. I want something else." He turned his head toward Jeff. "I want you."

A van too big for the narrow side street tried to drive by them. Jeff made eye contact with its driver, a woman with long stringy blonde hair and a bewildered look on her face. Jeff guessed that she was completely lost. Her vehicle had Minnesota plates.

"I want you, too," Jeff said. "Can we just say it? We love each other."

Henry finally struck a match and lit the cigarette he had been playing with. He rolled the window down.

"I guess my best friend is Greg. I've known him the longest. I know you don't like Greg. He doesn't like you either. So you're equal."

"I know you're close to your brother," Jeff said carefully. "But does everyone in your life have to deal drugs? And can we get back to the part where we were saying we want each other?"

"Sure. Brothers can't be lovers, right?" Henry stuck his cigarette out the open window to tap the ashes at the end of it. "By the way, last time I checked, you don't deal drugs."

"Just why doesn't Greg like me?"

"Don't know. You're from Yale. You have a PhD. Too good for us trailer trash. Or maybe you remind him of someone I used to know."

Jeff turned the key in the ignition and edged carefully out of the parking space. Henry hadn't said the name "Ryan," but he might as well have. He noticed the bright headlights of the Minnesota van just behind him. That woman, he thought, needs to figure out which way she wants to go. He picked up speed as they headed back to Capitol Hill.

Nan came in through the front door, weighed down with a full bag of groceries, to find a woman rummaging around her kitchen. The two women were roughly the same age. They eyed each other closely. They recognized each other, of course, but had never really talked and certainly had never been alone together.

"Nancy, hi, I'm Doris…"

"Nan. The name's Nan."

"Sorry, Nan. I'm with Virginia Mason's chemical dependency program and they asked me to come to group tonight. I've spoken with Henry, but he doesn't seem to be here today. I was early, so I thought I'd get the coffee going. Can't seem to find any in the kitchen, though. Sorry. I was looking for Henry, thought he'd be here."

"Henry is definitely the one to talk to, if you looked in the refrigerator and there wasn't any. But I doubt it, he's good about replacing things." Nan said, hoisting the bag awkwardly higher in her arms. "Henry is good about those things. Look, let me put these groceries down. Did you look upstairs?"

"Upstairs?"

"Yes. He's either there or in the basement. I'd check his room. Up those stairs."

Doris didn't move.

Nan continued, "Last door on the right." She started to put the groceries away.

Doris had trouble finding Henry's room, since the hallway was dark and she didn't see a light switch. She knocked on the door she hoped was his and was surprised when the force of her fist made the door swing open.

It was a small room, something you'd expect to find a child in. A tall dresser had atop it a framed photograph of a young man holding an oar. The one window had a cheap, old-fashioned venetian blind pulled nearly all the way down, but the remaining light of the day seeped in around its edges and made the interior of the room visible. A scruffy backpack lay on the rugless floor.

The only other object in the room was a narrow bed. It was covered with a chocolate-colored bedspread that reminded Doris of the 1950s home she had grown up in. Henry lay on the bedspread on his side with knees drawn up halfway to his hips, arms folded across his chest and head tilted down. This is the position, it occurred to Doris, that he had been in for nine months before joining the world. He looked so peaceful, Doris hated to disturb him.

"Henry? Sorry. It's Doris. Are you asleep?" Doris felt embarrassed to be there, intruding on this man's nap. "Henry, are you awake?" She moved slightly closer to the bed. "I'm sorry to bother you." She felt stupid as well as sorry. "Could you tell me where you keep the coffee?"

Henry did not answer, nor did he move. He didn't seem to be breathing. He is either a sound sleeper, Doris decided, or something else. Should she go get Nan?

Instead she stepped cautiously to the edge of the bed. After hesitating she extended her right hand and let her fingers lightly touch one of Henry's pants legs. She touched Henry's shin again but he did not stir. Now she used her entire arm to shake him. He still did not move. Doris imagined the worst, and her professional instincts took over. She stood up and scanned the room. She didn't see any amber vials lying about, but she knew that didn't necessarily mean anything. This is still what an overdose looks like. She took two steps toward the head of the bed and used her right hand to feel Henry's wrist for a pulse, where he had none.

Oh god, she swore. She trained for this and now it was happening. But her social-worker self disappeared as quickly as it had come, and she panicked. Get a grip, Doris told herself. Is there a phone in the room? She didn't see one. Rushing into the hallway, she shouted for Nancy.

Down in the basement Nan thought she heard a noise upstairs, but she couldn't figure out what it was. Henry will take care of it, she reassured herself while taking clothes out of the dryer.

Doris turned back to the inert Henry and realized she had to call an ambulance right away. She ran out of the bedroom again and flew down the stairs, almost tripping at the bottom. Where do these damned people keep their telephone? The kitchen, she thought, there's always a phone in the kitchen.

Henry woke up from his dream. He'd been in an old wooden canoe, paddling through the thick marshes that hugged the shore of Lake Washington. He was in the front of the canoe and Jeff was at the back, but he couldn't tell which of his two Jeffs it was. It was a beautiful day with no sound other than that of their paddles slicing in and out of the calm waters. Jeff was in charge of steering the canoe. Henry had a bright orange life preserver on, but Jeff's was lying at the bottom of the canoe near its middle.

They saw no other boats on the lake. It was all theirs. Henry was turning around to face Jeff to say something to him when he saw an eagle flying in the distance above Jeff's head. He could see it but Jeff couldn't. That's not fair, Henry remembered thinking to himself. He wanted Jeff to see it, too.

When the dream abruptly ended and Henry woke up from his nap someone was shouting. He stretched his bent legs out straight, swung them around and put his feet on the floor. Sitting up now, he stretched his arms over his head and yawned. His feet searched for his slippers and found them. He went downstairs to find out what was going on. He wondered how long he'd been asleep.

He saw Doris in the kitchen. She had the phone in her hand. Nan was standing almost on top of her, shouting something either to Doris or into the phone. Nan's back was to Henry, so it was Doris who saw him first. She let out a cry and dropped the phone, making another loud noise as it hit the floor.

Nan turned around and now saw Henry as well. Her face twisted into a contortion Henry hadn't thought a face capable of, and it frightened him. Nan started to lunge toward Henry, but when he instinctively recoiled, she stopped herself.

"You're alive!" she shouted. "Are you all right?"

Henry thought: This could still be my dream.

Nan pivoted around and snapped at Doris, saying something that ended in "stupid bitch." Doris cradled her head in her hands and started to cry. What the holy fuck is going on, Henry said to himself. Something big has happened at the Yellow House, he realized, and he had slept all the way through it. The story of my life. Next time he took a nap during the day, he swore, it would be without the help of any junk first.

CHAPTER TEN

One day Jeff was fidgeting with the old floor lamp in the living room. "I put a new bulb in it, so I know it's not that. It was okay for the four p.m. group, but they didn't really need it anyway. Nan, does the cord look frayed to you?"

Nan held the lamp upright by its glass shade while Jeff wrapped black electrical tape where the plug met the cord.

"Vinnie stopped by," he added. "He had something to check with you about."

"What's that?" she asked.

"He wants to have a party. Here."

Nan looked down at Jeff's head as he wound the tape, and thought she saw the signs of a small bald spot in the middle of his crown. "What kind of party? When? Why?"

"Um, a party for everyone. All the groups. Clean and sober, the AIDS folks. Boys, girls. Everyone. Could you hand me the scissors? They're on the mantel."

Christ, Nan thought. This place is big but not that big. She let go of the lamp in order to retrieve the scissors.

"Next month. When it's Pride week. Friday, June twenty second."

She handed the scissors to him. "Groups meet here Friday nights."

"I thought about that. They can use the basement, then come upstairs to the party when they're through. Should work."

Suddenly a bright light filled the room.

"You put a bigger bulb in there than before."

Jeff ignored Nan's comment and righted the lamp in the corner where it belonged.

"I think it's a good idea," Jeff asserted with authority. "I like parties." Nothing was further from the truth. Jeff flashed back to his encounter with Charles.

"You guys will have to handle the details," Nan said with equal force. "I'm not sure I'll be around." Nan didn't have anywhere to go that weekend—or any other weekend, for that matter.

"Oh, Vinnie will help. We'll charge everyone at the door. Five bucks? Vinnie thinks maybe Mike and his band will play. Could you ask him?"

"I just said you're in charge of the details."

"Can't pay much, but maybe he'll think it's good publicity."

"Okay, I'll talk to him. But to get my son to do anything, it's not a good idea to go through his mother." Nan took two steps toward the lamp and turned it off.

"Got it. I'll tell Vinnie to talk to him instead."

Nan wondered just how Vinnie knew Mike. She couldn't imagine their paths crossed easily, but then they did both live on the Hill. The possibility there was a story she didn't know about bothered her for a split second—out of a maternal concern perhaps, but maybe out of jealousy, too. She didn't want to think about it.

Nan went upstairs to her bedroom when Jeff retreated to the basement to spend some time in the makeshift office. She was about to start a mystery novel when she heard a loud crashing sound somewhere in the house. Someone was breaking in, she thought at first. Unsure if Jeff heard it, she ran down the stairs, but once in the living room it took no more than a moment to realize that the floor lamp, just repaired, had fallen over. Jeff had heard it,

173

too, and he ran upstairs from the basement. He stood where the dining room ended and the living room began, staring at the fallen lamp just as Nan was. Neither of them said anything. Jeff made the first move to clean up the sharp shards of glass scattered all over the floor.

Vinnie stood up and tossed his empty latte cup halfway across the B&O café, making a perfect basket in the trash bin. But before leaving he asked Henry if he ever saw Ryan.

Henry scribbled in his notebook. He liked to keep things organized, though in real life he'd learned it was hard. He closed the notebook, wrapped his red rubber band around it and slipped it into his backpack. He gulped and answered. "Once. A while ago. He came into the store."

"Your Jeff looks just like him. It's friggin' weird."

"I could say it's a coincidence, but probably not."

"Probably? Not many of those in life. What's going on?"

"You know, when I first saw Jeff, my heart stopped. We were in an elevator, just the two of us. I mean, I knew it wasn't Ryan, but looking just like him made me miss him somehow. Yeah, weird. The guy who started me on drugs, and I missed him. I know why, I think. Ryan was my older brother, the real one I never had. Greg was never around. Ryan was somehow good for me. I always wanted someone to help me, and at least Ryan really loved me, at first anyhow. All that stuff, the good and the bad, came rushing back in my head. I got a hard-on in that elevator, Vinnie. I knew right away I was going to repeat the whole cycle over again. Funny, isn't it, the new Jeff has his issues, too. Like attracts like."

Vinnie left it at that. He rose from his chair before Henry had a chance to do the same. Henry watched Vinnie's back recede as he walked out of the B&O and headed for the Tenth Avenue house, where Mike had told Vinnie he'd be waiting.

The next day Nan came home from the dry cleaners to find Vinnie on her couch.

"Someone let you in?"

"I have a key, Nan." She hung her dry cleaning on one of the hooks of the coat rack near the front door. Something told her not to keep Vinnie waiting by going upstairs to put her clothes away. When did she ever give him a key?

"We have to talk."

"So I gather." Nan went and stood by the fireplace mantel and faced him.

"Look, I don't know how much you know, or how much you don't know."

"About *what?!*" Nan erupted.

"Down, down. If you start yelling, I don't know how we'll get through this."

Nan's stomach felt nauseous. The last time a man spoke to her like this was when her ex-husband-to-be dumped the news of his girlfriend and his "need" for a separation on her. This time, Nan told herself, she wasn't going to cry.

"Deals are going down in your house."

"Deals?"

"Drugs, Nan. People are showing up here without them and they go home with them."

"Who? You know these people?"

Vinnie waved his hand dismissively. "I could guess. Yes, I do know some of them. So do you, probably. But that's not the point. I'm not the cops and neither are you."

"Well," Nan said sharply, "get them to stop." These are your people, she thought, not mine.

"Actually, the real cops know. That's who I heard it from."

Nan's blank expression turned into a frown. "You're telling me this now? How long has this been going on?"

Vinnie sighed. "It always goes on. Always has. Some people, whether they come intending to or not, join these groups—

175

especially the NA ones—and find fellow addicts. Some have dealt, probably most have. It's just a matter of degree. Anyway, the temptation is there. People exchange phone numbers. They pick up where they left off. End of story."

"Not the end. So you knew this was going to happen? When you first agreed to use my house?"

"Nan," Vinnie said, shrugging his shoulders. "Just how naïve are you?" He looked at her with his penetrating blue eyes. "You don't look like someone born yesterday."

Nan was not going to let this be about her. This had to be about what was happening under her roof and what Vinnie meant to do about it.

"What do you mean, the cops know?"

Vinnie grimaced slightly. "What I said. Someone I know in the precinct called me. He told me to put a lid on it, that if things got any more out of hand they'd have to do something about it."

Nan raised her hand to cover her mouth as she coughed. "What do they do, when they do something about 'it'?"

Vinnie waved his hand again. "Let's not get ahead of ourselves. That won't happen. I've got friends. I'm here to talk to you about this." They looked at each other and said nothing.

"All right then," Nan resumed. "What do *you* do about it, when you do something?" She felt anger rising in her. It was the first time she took notice of any emotion that fierce toward Vinnie. She knew at once the intensity was there to take the place of other emotions she might have. Vinnie, sitting in front of her, was now the target for things he knew nothing about.

"I'll talk to some of the facilitators," Vinnie said in a low voice. "I'll talk to all of them, in fact. I'll come up with a list of the likely culprits. Then the boys and I will talk to them."

"Talk?"

"Tell. Tell them it's not cool. To stop and go elsewhere."

Nan began to soften, thinking: Aren't we in the business of trying to help people? Then she thought more about what Vinnie

176

had just said. "The boys? You and the boys will talk to them? Henry and Jeff? Oh, great. A drunk, a junkie and you. That will really do the trick!"

"Nan," Vinnie pleaded. "Why are you so upset? I told you, this crap happens. We'll deal with it. Get the word out."

"The word out," Nan repeated as she folded her arms. "Hmm. Maybe I want you and all your buddies out. Get my house back, before I'm arrested."

Vinnie flashed Nan a pained look. "Nan, now I'm really worried. Something else, something beside this, is eating at you. You want to tell me what it is?" Vinnie rested his palms on his knees.

Nan put her left arm on the mantel. She made a fist with her hand, as if she meant to hang on to something tightly, but there was nothing to grasp.

"Vinnie, Vinnie. I thought getting involved in the Yellow House would give me something useful and good to do. But it doesn't feel like it's working out that way."

Vinnie squeezed his kneecaps with his large hands. "Just how unhappy are you, Nan?"

"Jesus, don't talk to me like I'm in one of your fucking groups, excuse my language. I'm not."

Nan knew she was having a tantrum, and the best thing to do was just to let it run its course. She thought: I'm still not over Richard, and that's why I want Vinnie to be like him and fix everything in my life and make it right. But now the men I wanted to help are doing drugs in my house. Maybe this was a bad idea. But if I give this up, I'll be alone again.

They looked at each other, searching each other's face for something. Nan released her tight, empty grip. Vinnie raised one hand off a knee and ran it through his thinning hair.

"So, you'll talk to everyone," Nan said, breaking the silence. "You know who they are?"

"Yes, I said I did." Vinnie put his hand back on his knee.

"There's something else," Nan said stiffly. "Do you have anything to tell me about my son, Mike?"

Vinnie swallowed. "He's not one of the people doing the deals here, if that's what you mean."

"That's not what I mean," Nan snapped. "He's not in any of the groups here. You're talking about the people in the groups, right?"

"Yeah, people in groups." Vinnie paused. "Why are you asking me about your son, Nan?"

Nan thought carefully before responding. "I'm worried about him."

"That's natural."

"Should I be?" Nan was almost certain that Vinnie could tell her more.

"Nan, I'm asking you again. What's going on?"

At that moment, from a place Nan hadn't known existed inside of her, a new wave of fury crested. Nan panicked—this wasn't her, she'd never had feelings this raw, even at her angriest with Richard. These things belonged to other people, people capable of pointless anger but not her.

"Vinnie, you need to be straight with me." She fixed her gaze on him. "What have you been up to all this time? Coming into my house, my life?"

"Your *life*? Whoa, Nan. All we do is borrow your space for—"

"You do more than that, and you know it."

"I do not know it. What the hell are you accusing me of?"

"Forget it," she snapped back. She could have said: You filled my house with people, and I am still alone. She could have added: There is Henry, there is Jeff. You brought them to me. But they belong to each other and not to me. I want someone who belongs to me, and will not hurt me either.

Henry was sitting on his bed, trying to thread his new shoelaces through his old running shoes, when he heard Nan and Vinnie speaking in raised voices in the living room. At first he thought something was wrong and they might need his help. He instinctively stood up to go downstairs, but then he heard more and realized they were arguing.

The voices became louder. Henry fell back on the bed, rolled over onto his side and curled into a ball, drawing his knees all the way up to his chest and wrapping his arms around his head, covering his ears with the shoes he was still holding to block out whatever Vinnie was saying to Nan. So, this was now another house where people fought, just like the one he grew up in. That's okay, Henry said to himself, I wasn't planning on staying here forever anyway. He'd been thinking a lot about going somewhere far away. He'd never really been away. Maybe Jeff would take the both of them to some place new.

He looked up at the chest of drawers in his room and fixed on the framed photograph of his first Jeff holding that oar. Henry really wanted to talk to him for advice, but didn't know how to reach a dead person, or exactly what it was he'd say if he could. He closed his eyes and moved his hands holding the running shoes to his chest, and thought really hard about getting a canoe, all by himself this time, and paddling wherever the water led.

Jeff walked carefully down the stairs to the basement because he didn't quite trust the old wood. He had his hands full with the laundry basket. The steps creaked and groaned as if they might give way at any moment. The only illumination came from the kitchen behind him and the single bare bulb in the basement. When he was sure he had made it safely to the bottom of the stairs, he put the laundry basket down on the dirty concrete floor, stood up straight and found the string that turned on another bare bulb.

He put the dirty clothes in the washing machine, got it going and asked himself what to do next. He walked over to the school chair and desk that he and Henry used as an office. He fumbled for the switch on the gooseneck lamp on the desk. Once he found it, he finally had some real light.

On the desk was Henry's notebook, the same kind that his students used in class. Thinking he would stay down here until the clothes were done, Jeff sat down in the chair and leafed through the notebook. Half-legible markings were scrawled in a rushed hand. "NA not Tuesday Thursday." "Nan says no." "Need new markers." But then there were also doodles that rose to the level of real drawings. A unicorn here, some kind of alien spacecraft there. One of them took Jeff a moment to recognize. It looked at first like a mess of lines going this way and that, the kind of thing you might draw without thinking while talking on the phone. But the lines gradually took on a recognizable form: a human heart, strikingly detailed. Where did Henry learn to do this?

The washing machine started making loud noises, as if it had a rock bouncing around in it. Jeff went over and lifted the lid to stop it spinning. Once he thought he had re-balanced everything, he closed the lid and pressed a button to start it churning again. Now it was quieter. As Jeff went back to the little school desk to wait out the rest of the machine's cycle, he noticed a big globe of the world on a wooden pedestal next to a pile of boxes in the corner. He thought: How the hell did Nan end up with something like that in her basement?

Jeff was feeling restless, so he went to Henry's room across the hall. The door was open as usual. He stretched out on the bed after throwing the sheets and the blanket in place and waited for Henry to get home from Starbucks.

He hadn't ever been in Henry's room without Henry. It was a real pigsty, but so had Jeff's room when he was Henry's age. In a corner, partly obscured by a pile of dirty or just out-of-the-dryer clothes, was a hockey stick. When did Henry play hockey?

There was a lot Jeff didn't know about Henry. They were busy during the day, and much of their time at night was spent apart, though that often just meant different groups at the Yellow House. But Jeff was making an effort that every day should count for them. He was focused on trying to live in the present, not in any uncertain future. That swelling under his jaw had gone away and he felt great, but he knew something was amiss. His fears would return eventually. Most of the guys in his group at the Yellow House felt the same way, though some had a better way of dealing with it than Jeff. They'd all realized that in their worried-well group, no one was really well. But Jeff had his worries about Henry on top of his hypochondria.

Henry was going to the NA group for guys who weren't "youth" anymore, though technically he was. He felt more comfortable with guys older than himself, he'd told Jeff. He thought the group was cool, and he'd cut back on using, but Jeff assumed he sometimes still got high. He and Henry had managed to compartmentalize their lives: good behavior when they were with each other, but no questions asked about what either of them did when they were off on their own. It wasn't a quiet understanding; it was a completely unspoken one.

Jeff heard Henry's heavy footsteps coming up the stairs. When he appeared in the door, he could tell Henry was tired.

"Long day?"

"Nothing special," Henry said blowing air out his mouth. "How long have you been here?"

"Not long."

"Let me take a shower." Henry took all his clothes off slowly, as if it was hard work, threw them into the pile on the floor in front of the hockey stick and then marched naked out of the room and down the hall to the bathroom. Jeff watched a perfect ass walk out the door.

Jeff looked up at the ceiling and thought more about him and Henry as he listened to the water run in the shower. So, what if he got really sick, or Henry seriously relapsed? Henry was already more important to Jeff than Raul ever was. Jeff played with his navel in the space that had opened up between his pants and his sweatshirt. Henry returned with a towel wrapped around him but dripping water everywhere.

"So, your day good?" Henry asked while searching for clean clothes in one of his dresser's drawers.

"Same as always. No classes, but a lot of other stuff to do."

"Like what? I've never figured out what it is you do."

"I read. I write. I think." Henry had teased him about his job before.

"Jeez, and you get paid for that. I'd pay to be able to do it."

"Well, I teach, too. You could come watch me one day."

Henry found a pair of white briefs in the drawer, turned to Jeff and smiled at him as he put one leg through them, then the other. The wet towel made its own new pile on the floor.

"Sweet of you to invite me. And it won't happen," he said with a laugh.

"What would you read or write, if you had a job like mine?"

"And think about? I dunno. But I *would*. No PhD here," Henry said, using an index finger to point to his head, "but there are things I wonder about." He gave Jeff a long, but not unfriendly, dirty look.

Jeff sat up on the edge of the bed as Henry put on more clothes, a pair of long shorts and a T-shirt with the name of his high school on it.

"You know," Jeff said, "I had jobs like yours."

"At Starbucks? They don't have them on the East Coast."

"No, not at a coffee shop. I worked at a bar."

"Huh-uh," Henry chortled. "I should have known. Perfect."

"The money was good. But the hours were terrible."

"The opposite of my job, then." Henry stood in front of the mirror above his dresser and ran a black comb through his damp hair.

"So, what do you want to do?"

"I thought we were going to eat, then hang out in the groups. We're the hired help, you know."

"Yeah, that's right." Henry put the comb down on the dresser and turned around. "Sounds like a plan."

Jeff was amazed to find an entire half of a roast chicken in the refrigerator. He and Henry ate it with their hands, pulling the meat away from the carcass like jackals. They decided to both go to Vinnie's late-night meeting. It was always huge. They drifted into the living room, where some guys had already occupied the sofa. Part of Henry and Jeff's job was to see if anyone was showing up drunk or high, which was frequent. Jeff had done it a couple of times himself, but no one said anything to him. He didn't know if Henry had ever been buzzed at a meeting, but it was hard to imagine he hadn't. Tonight they were the cops.

Vinnie came out of the kitchen and sat down on one of the folding chairs near Jeff and Henry. At about ten after eleven, the room full, he called the meeting to order and asked if there was anyone present who had a year or more of sobriety. Six hands went up, including Vinnie's.

Vinnie spoke. "I thought I'd get the ball rolling by telling a story of my own."

Vinnie told a story about being a bartender and waiter at the Deluxe. It was there that he began to use heavily. All the waiters and kitchen staff would chip in at the start of their shift and buy enough cocaine to keep their energy up until closing. They'd run back to the kitchen now and then and snort a line of All-American, then go back to the customers. After closing they'd sit around the bar and buy one another shots to bring themselves down.

"I never went home until I was good and completely drunk, and still buzzed from the coke on top of it. That was life in the restaurant business. I was dating, on and off, another of the bartenders, and we'd go to his place or mine and make an attempt to screw—never worked too well. Then one night I really lost it."

Vinnie shifted in his chair and resumed. He said he got to his then boyfriend's apartment and didn't feel quite high or drunk enough. He asked for a drink and wondered what kind of drugs there might be in the house. When the guy said there was nothing on hand just now, Vinnie went berserk. He flung open all the cabinets and drawers. He pulled up all the cushions on the sofa. He went into the bathroom and searched the medicine cabinet, nearly pulling it off its hinges. Finally, screaming at the boyfriend, he demanded he go out and get him some dope and vodka to go with it, or else.

"So, I lost it, and by the way, that was the end of *that* boyfriend."

Jeff thought: I haven't had a scene like that. Maybe I haven't really hit rock bottom yet. Or maybe it's because there *is* always something to drink in my house. Even here in the Yellow House, he kept an emergency bottle in an old shoe box in his closet. Jeff cast a sideway look at Henry, who was staring back at him.

The front door opened and a young man came in. He was carrying a baby in his arms.

"Frankie, my man, welcome," Vinnie said. "What have you brought us?"

"My friends," Frankie said with a big grin. "Meet my new son!"

"Frankie, who have you been fucking to make babies?" someone asked.

"Frankie's always liked pussy, too," another said. "You've got a girlfriend, don't you, Frankie?"

"Aw, the best chica in the world. My Angelina." Frankie continued to beam. Later, one of the guys told Jeff and Henry that Angelina was another Puerto Rican addict, and who turned tricks to support the two, now three, of them. She lived mostly on the streets in Pioneer Square and was totally devoted to Frankie, as well as to her pimp, a guy from up north who supplied her with both johns and drugs.

"He's fine, you all. Fuck, nothing wrong with my boy, is there?" Frankie said, now sitting on the floor himself and bouncing the baby up and down in his lap. "Look at him! Hey, clean and sober from birth, my friends. Clean and sober."

Frankie passed the baby around for all the men to hold. When he was handed to Henry, he held the baby out at arm's length and gently shook him, making the baby gurgle happily. "Frankie, you haven't told us his name," Henry said.

"The kid? Angelina and me fought about that. I said he had to be Frankie Junior. But Angelina said, 'Fuck that, how do you know you're the daddy!'"

"Ryan," Frankie finally replied. "Can you believe it? As P.R. as this kid is, his fucking name is Ryan."

Jeff could tell he was headed towards trouble, and that next Saturday he went to find it. He ferreted out an after-hours party in a private home by badgering a couple of guys at the Rebar. Henry was out elsewhere with old high school buddies. Jeff wasn't drunk when he arrived, but he was blotto by the time he left. He'd gone there knowing that would happen but he went anyway. The process of intoxication hadn't taken much time, no more than an hour to go from sober to barely able to stand. He stood to one side of the table in the hallway where the bottles the host had assembled stood. Jeff was never more than an arm's-length away from refilling his plastic cup. He worried that Henry might have friends there and he'd find out. But that didn't stop him from refilling that cup. When Jeff drank he became one person again, which felt good at first but which also meant he lost any ability to see himself plainly. Plastered, though, all there was was *him*. Jeff became perfectly and exquisitely alone—a singularity that filled the room and, after a couple more belts, went on to fill the house, the world and lastly the universe. Not the smallest place left for anyone else to enter. I'm thirty years old now, Jeff thought. I'm omnipotent when I'm sloshed. I don't need anyone. I don't need anything but this. This moment, this place. I'm thirty years old, Jeff's last minimally sober thought told him, and I don't care what comes next. Even if it's *arf*. Jeff walked home to the Yellow House and went directly to his room to sleep it off.

Later Henry would confess to Jeff that he, too, had shown up late for that party after leaving his friends, but made sure that Jeff didn't notice him. Unlike Jeff, Henry had shown up at the party already buzzed. After Jeff stumbled out the door and was gone, Henry copped a couple of pills from a buddy and sat on some stranger's lap on a futon on the upstairs hallway while the bennies took effect. Jeff might have confessed his own shame to Henry, but he chose instead to take Henry in his arms and hold him tight, as if that sufficed for making the dishonesty between them plain, and thus somehow safe.

Jeff found Henry in the living room playing with his Green Hornet Pez candy dispenser, making a snapping sound over and over again with its spring-loaded head. For some reason this irritated Jeff more than usual. He wanted Henry to grow up.

"Is your Barbie doll down with women's problems today?"

The next thing he knew, the Pez dispenser was whizzing past his left ear and hit the wall with a loud, sharp crack. It fell to the floor in two pieces. Jeff turned to face Henry and saw him looking as if he were about to cry, or maybe curse. Jeff bent over and picked up the broken pieces and put them in his pocket. A few of the little tablets had scattered on the carpet but Jeff left them there because they looked like drugs and not candy. He might have gone over to the couch and held his boyfriend, but he was filled with contempt and did not move. He looked at Henry and considered humiliating him further.

Henry rubbed both eyes with his fists. He glared at Jeff. "What an excuse of a faggot you are. Is there *anything* I do right?" Jeff could have used the opportunity to tell Henry several things he never did right, in fact. But instead he went out for a long walk to cool off, and when he came back he found Henry in his room. He decided to try to make amends. "Where do you want to go, if you could go anywhere?" Jeff asked him, hoping it would be a place he actually could take Henry one day.

186

Henry rested his chin on his chest and pondered. "My father said he'd take me to Easter Island sometime."

"Easter Island? The place with those statues?" Jeff had expected Henry to say London or Paris.

"Yeah, the *moai*. Awesome. I read about them in an old *National Geographic*, and my father said we'd go. Hasn't happened yet. You know, everyone died on that island. Well, almost everyone. They chopped all the trees down to drag the statues on them, and then they ate each other when the food was gone. Maybe I'm descended from the survivors."

"Why the hell do you want to go *there*?"

"Well," replied Henry, his chin still on his chest, "why the hell did you want to go live on *Man-hat-tan*? Same difference. The statues are tall, like skyscrapers. And they don't face the sea, like people think. They face inland, staring at each other." Henry turned and grinned at Jeff. "You know why they carved those statues? It was to keep busy building things instead of fucking and dropping babies. Not enough food on the island for any more people. Bad case of blue balls, wouldn't you say? My dad said Dutch sailors discovered the island, on an Easter Sunday, and the fuckers gave the natives the clap in about three hours flat, that's what finally killed them. Eventually anyway. They must have been pretty horny, huh?"

That afternoon the make-up sex was athletic. After their nap Jeff looked down at Henry's beautiful, olive skin. His eyes moved towards the hollows and beacons of Henry's armpits and his chest, his blemishes, his one small mole, the rib cage of a boy with none of the redundant flesh of an adult. The smell of sex was rising from his body. Jeff wanted to lower his torso and press his lips into Henry's painterly shadows and silhouettes. But he'd wait until Henry woke to make it count. So Jeff just stood there and looked down at Henry imagining himself loving this person for a very long time.

Jeff was reading a thick hardcover book on the back porch when Nan approached. She sat down in the other Adirondack chair next to him and lit a Salem. The lawn looked like it needed mowing, but they hadn't had a dry day in some time.

"What's the book, Jeff?"

Jeff lowered it into his lap and pinched the bridge of his nose. "*Civil War*. It's a memoir written by a Confederate soldier who was at Fort Sumter."

"Oh, so he survived. That's good."

"He didn't die," Jeff said. "No one died at Fort Sumter. All that came later. But I wouldn't say he exactly survived." Jeff didn't bother to explain further.

"Work? Pleasure?" Nan felt the word "pleasure" hang unpleasantly in the air.

"It's for work."

"Well, I hope it's interesting. How did you get into that stuff, anyway?"

Jeff sniffed. "Not sure. Curiosity, maybe? I had a great-great-grandfather who died in Andersonville."

"So you're not from the South?"

"No. Connecticut."

"I guess I should have known that by now." Nan tapped her cigarette to make the ash fall, but it wasn't quite long enough. "You haven't told me much about yourself. Henry's more chatty."

Jeff closed his library book. "Don't take this the wrong way, Nan, but I don't know much about you."

"I guess you're right. Not much to say in my case. Married just before I graduated from college. Was an okay wife and mother for nearly thirty years, I think. Then divorced. Now here." She smiled weakly at Jeff.

"His name is Richard, right? Your ex."

Now the ash fell of its own accord. Nan crossed her legs at the ankles.

"Yes, Richard." She paused. "Anyone in your life before Henry?"

No one in Seattle had ever asked Jeff that question. Not even Henry. "Before I left New York, I was with a guy named Raul. A Cuban raised in New Jersey."

"Richard's mother was originally from New Jersey."

Jeff caught sight of a blackbird foraging in the overgrown lawn out of the corner of his eye.

"Did you love him?" she asked.

"Raul? Funny. That was never on the menu. Seems a long time ago." What was probably an obvious question to Nan was unexpected by Jeff. He asked his own question to prevent Nan from asking a follow-up. "You must have loved Richard, Nan."

"Of course I did," Nan answered defensively.

"Sorry. Didn't mean to imply otherwise."

"I still love him."

"Is that good?"

"Better than hating, don't you think? He left me for another woman. A much younger one. His secretary. A story as old as they come."

Jeff turned slightly in his chair and let the book slide off his lap. "I left Raul."

"But you didn't love him."

"He didn't love me. And even if he had, I would have left him anyway."

"Afraid of commitment, Jeff?"

"What do you mean? Marriage, kids? We were two men." Jeff paused. "No, let me tell you the truth. Actually, I left him because I didn't want to be around him anymore."

"Why?"

"He'd had his whorella years, if you know what I mean. Lots of them. I was afraid he had what we called the 'gay cancer'."

"Does he?"

"No. I guess I was worried that I might have to take care of him if he did. I was a coward."

"Are you still in touch with him?"

Jeff said no again.

"I talk to Richard every week or so. I pretend it's to discuss Mike, but actually it's just to hear his voice."

"Because you still love him?"

"Or just miss him. Hard to tell the difference."

Really? Jeff wondered. If Henry were to leave me at this point, would I make up reasons to call him? No, probably not.

"I've never been on my own, Jeff. Ever. I'm not really alone now, am I? You and Henry are here. But I don't think I could ever live totally by myself. It's not anything I was programmed for."

Jeff looked at Nan. His problem was the opposite. He doubted he could ever live *with* anyone. Even growing up at home, he felt he inhabited some parallel universe all by himself. In his head he loved Henry but it was hard to translate that into occupying the same close space together.

"If you could marry Henry, would you?"

It was Jeff's turn to be defensive. "Don't be ridiculous. Nan, let me explain something. I get the impression that you think all the gay guys that come through your house are nice boys who just have a little problem. Well, problems aside, we are not nice boys. We don't walk up the matrimonial aisle. I'll put it this way. We are very different from straight people. We do nasty things, Nan. Things that would *disgust* you. We always have been perverts and always will be, no matter how much we are tolerated by breeders, excuse my language. Our whole lives we've looked at the world through X-ray glasses, seeing things you don't see. Your lives are so drenched in heterosexuality it's invisible to you. Dick and Jane, Ozzie and Harriet, Popeye and Olive Oyl. We've only got Felix and Oscar.

"Look, Henry and Vinnie and I were born into families that were the enemy from the get-go. Who wants a queer kid? Sure, some gay guys think they are 'almost normal' but they're fooling themselves. They can vote Republican and join the Rotary Club but they're still fruits. Sometimes I think the nineteenth century got it right and we really are a third sex. Not male or female but something else. I don't want to be rude, Nan, but there are a million miles between you and me."

He made a show of warning Nan off with his little speech, intended to convince the both of them they were so different that their fates could not possibly be the same. But behind Jeff's bravura was the secret suspicion about how similar he and Nan might be, with her desperate emotional need for men and his carnal one. No matter what happened, he was not going to allow their private competition to spill over to include Henry. Jeff hoped he had cautioned Nan from any intrusions into their lives.

Both he and Nan went back to staring at the lawn. The bird was gone. Nan ground her cigarette out in the dirty ashtray she kept on the right arm of the chair. She used the same hand to brush a strand of hair back behind her ear. "Don't mind me, just being silly."

What would Henry feel, Jeff speculated, if he were to desert him the way he had Raul? Would he just "miss" him? Henry had never lived on his own either. He'd find someone else fast, or someone would find him. Why was Jeff even rehearsing the scene in his mind? Was he preparing himself should he lose Henry to drugs? To disease? To another man? To Nan and the almost normal world, with all its irresistible incentives for gay men so at risk in their own?

That evening Jeff took his bicycle upstairs. He was keeping it in his room so it wouldn't disappear on him. When he got to the end of the hall and was about to wheel it in, he looked to his right and saw through the open door that Henry was lying atop his bed, in boxer shorts, writing in his notebook.

"Hey," Jeff said.

"Hey. Where you been?"

"Went to the Canterbury for a burger."

"Alone?"

"Yeah, alone." Jeff didn't add that two vodkas on the rocks had kept him company.

He left the bike leaning against the wall and went into Henry's room. Henry shifted to make room on the bed for him as Jeff removed his helmet and dropped it to the floor. Jeff sat down on the edge of the mattress.

They didn't speak. The silence between the two men was how they chose to love. It was often this way between them. When they spoke, words often brought them into dangerous contact, a proximity that could, Jeff supposed, be love but just as well what puts obstacles in its way. Neither Jeff nor Henry suffered under the illusion that love between two men could be all that profound, and their disbelief suppressed any talk that might prove the contrary true.

Jeff shoved Henry closer to the wall, grabbed the notebook and pen out of his hands and tossed them onto the floor, where they landed close to the helmet. He forced Henry's arms behind his head and used his weight to pin his entire body down on the bed.

"Oh, you want to wrestle, do you?" Henry said with a grin.

Jeff grinned as well but used his strength to press Henry down harder. "Why not?"

"Because you'll lose. I did this in high school. What were you?"

"Track. The broad jump."

"Fuckin' pussy!" Henry exclaimed, this time laughing.

"What kind of wrestling?" Jeff countered. "Wait, let me guess. Greco-Roman, emphasis on the Greco."

There were no more words after that. The contest was on and it would be silent. They'd never fought before, and so they had never had that closeness, or the perfect high that follows battle. Now it would happen. Jeff held his boyfriend tight and rolled over until both of them fell with a thud onto the floor. He kicked the helmet out of the way and nodded to Henry they were ready. The two men entwined and wrestled each other, Jeff fully clothed, Henry barely. They rolled together. Jeff flushed red where Henry pushed his face back. Jeff could feel every muscle in Henry's body become tense. His boyfriend seemed on the verge of penetrating his older, softer bulk. Henry seemed to want his body to fill Jeff's own, to subdue and master it. Henry knew Jeff's body and just how it would react to each of his forays. He played upon Jeff's limbs and chest like some hard wind. It was as if Henry's whole being joined with Jeff's, as if his energy could enter into the flesh of the older man, using his muscles to imprison Jeff in his own, weaker body.

So they wrestled swiftly, rapturously, intent and mindless at last, two gay men working into a tighter close oneness of struggle, with a strange, octopus-like knotting and flashing of limbs in the subdued light of the room; a tense knot of flesh gripped in silence between the walls of the Yellow House. Now and again came a sharp gasp of breath, or a sound like a sigh, then the rapid thudding of movement on the hard wood floor, then the strange sound of skin escaping under skin. Often there was no head to be seen, only the swift, tight limbs, the solid white of Henry's back and the checker pattern of Jeff's flannel shirt, the physical junction of two bodies clinched together. Then there was the ruffled head of Jeff, as the struggle changed; in the next moment, the darker head of Henry lifting up from the conflict, eyes wide and seeing everything.

"Uncle?" Henry demanded, giggling and panting at the same time.

"Uncle!" Jeff shouted back with a grin. He felt something warm on his lip, and when he took his hand away where he touched it, he saw his fingers were carrying blood from his battered nose.

"I'll get some toilet paper."

Left alone in Henry's room for a moment, and sprawled on his back on the floor, Jeff stared at the ceiling. He felt closer to Henry after they had tested each other's strength, but farther away as well. Like the first time they made love, another milestone had passed and was not ever going to return, no matter how often it might be imitated or remembered. Life, Jeff reflected, was a series of firsts, until one day there were no more.

After Jeff wiped his nose and his fingers clean with the toilet paper Henry brought him, he shoved it into his pocket, well out of the way, worried that Henry might inadvertently touch it later.

Henry looked down at Jeff on the floor. "Not a fair fight, Jeff," he said in a low voice. "You've been drinking. It's all over you. You better stay up here tonight and not go down to group." Jeff felt relief at not having to pretend any more tonight in front of Henry.

Henry had a new dream that night as he lay next to Jeff. The Greyhound bus had stopped outside of Boise to let the passengers buy some dinner at a large roadside diner. Henry wasn't hungry. He sat on a parking lot fence while everyone else was inside.

The land was flat, dry, dusty. Scrub bush here and there, some planted trees that didn't look like they belonged here. It was hot but cooling off fast as the sun set in the direction the bus had come from.

He held his knapsack tightly in his lap. The old suitcase he'd thrown his less valuable things into was safely stowed under the bus. His ticket to Salt Lake City was stuck halfway in one of his knapsack pockets. He found himself looking down frequently to make sure it was still there.

Next to the diner, whose neon lights had just flickered on, was a Chevron gas station. A sign said there was a sale on for their winter oil, but it was summer. That was either planning ahead, or someone forgot to change the sign.

A big pickup truck pulled off the road into the station, taking up one side of the old-fashioned gas pumps. A woman with two small children jumped out and ran into the office. Only later did a tall cowboy emerge from the truck to put fuel in the tank.

Henry looked at the big canoe loaded into the back of the truck, its bow at a forty-five degree angle resting on the roof of the cab. It was long and green, and had a short series of numbers and letters painted in white at one end. The twin set of ropes that held the canoe in place looked flimsy. Henry wondered just how far they were going. He remembered that great day he and his first Jeff had had paddling around in the canoe they'd rented to go around the marshes in Lake Washington. Henry wished they'd done it more than once. As the woman and her children scrambled back into the pickup, Henry looked back at the Greyhound bus and saw in his dream it was a big boat instead, with sails and a handsome captain at the helm who knew where they were going and would guide everyone there safely. They'd be like the Pilgrims headed for the New World, or maybe the animals in Noah's ark, except there were two of everyone and Henry was alone in his dream. Neither of his Jeffs was with him. He stood up, hoisted his knapsack onto one of his shoulders, and stood in line to board again. He waited behind a Mexican family eager to get back on the hot, dirty bus. Just as he was about to take the first big step to climb in, he heard the pickup race its engine, determined to beat the Greyhound back to the highway.

CHAPTER ELEVEN

"Dealing?" Jeff said, repeating Vinnie's news. The three men were in the living room after the last group had left for the night.

"Yes, not just the NA people, but AA, too."

"Vinnie," Henry said as if speaking to a child, "people don't deal booze. News flash. It's legal."

"Yeah, sure, well, how many of the guys in the AA groups also use? Don't be stupid." Henry looked down at the candy bar wrapper he was idly folding and unfolding in his lap.

"And the cops told you this?" Jeff asked, confirming what he had just heard.

"Yes. A closet case I know. He says the precinct is keeping an eye on the house." Vinnie looked at Jeff as he answered, though it was still unnerving to face someone who reminded him so much of his old lover.

"So," Henry asked, "what is it you promised Nan we'd do?"

"Talk to folks. Get them to stop. She's freaked out."

"Okay then, go talk to folks. I wouldn't know where to begin."

"C'mon, Henry, you and I go to the NA groups. Jeff here doesn't. You must know what's going on."

Henry looked up from his lap at the two older men, one sitting beside him on the Yellow House sofa, the other standing a few feet away.

"Yeah, I'll tell you what's going on." He stared at Vinnie looming over him. "Mystery solved, Vinnie. Your cop friend who's dropping his hairpins must like watching Jeff here come and go from the house. Every day, all day probably."

"What?" Jeff said. "Me? The police think I'm dealing drugs?"

"Relax," Henry said. His eyes stayed riveted on Vinnie. "They think Ryan is. Vinnie, do you want to explain, or should I?"

Vinnie glared at Henry but did not answer. He would have preferred some things to remain unspoken, but that was apparently not going to happen, and so he was determined that everything said was true.

"Okay, Jeff, listen up," Henry ordered. "That day you followed my brother? Down to Pioneer Square? You saw him talking to someone who looked just like you, right? Well, that's Ryan. The guy everyone mistakes you for. Apparently some clueless cop included.

"Ryan's a big dealer. Among the biggest around. Kinda famous. So someone's saying that Ryan's in and out of this house. But he hasn't been. It's you. Sorry, Jeff, but it's you."

"Tell him the rest, Henry. Go on and tell him everything." Vinnie leaned closer to pressure Henry into continuing with the truth.

"Sure." Henry stopped playing with the wrapper. "See, Ryan was Vinnie's boyfriend. Their place was party central. Then Vinnie split to sober up, and here he is today, Mr. Fucking Clean. The Police Auxiliary."

"What Henry hasn't told you," Vinnie said, "is that it was Ryan who got your Henry on the stuff, way back when. It's a small world, Jeff, or should I say, a small Seattle. By the way, Ryan used to do Henry. When I wasn't around, of course. Ryan was a real scout leader, wasn't he, Henry?"

Jeff was connecting the dots. "Henry, you never told me any of this."

"Jeff, how much about your life have you told me?"

Jeff raised his voice. "So, it's not just that your last boyfriend had the same name as me, but that your first boyfriend *looks* just like me."

"You saw him, Jeff. You tell me. And he was no boyfriend."

"What am I to you?" Jeff asked in exasperation. "Jeff Number One back from the dead, but with the added bonus of looking like the dude who sold you your first shit and took your cherry to boot?"

"No, Jeff, he gave it to me, actually. The shit, that is." Henry threw the wrapper onto the floor and stood up. "The cherry was just my way of saying thanks.

"I'm going upstairs. You two guys figure out what to tell Nan and the fairy fuzz. No one's dealing drugs here, Vinnie. It's a goddamn clean-living paradise." When Henry reached the foot of the staircase he turned around as if to say something more. He wanted to break the rules and really talk to Jeff for once. But he changed his mind and went up to his room.

The night of the party, the front door of the Yellow House was jammed with guys trying to pay the cover charge at the card table set up by two volunteers. The weather was unseasonably warm and the inside of the house was already hot. Jeff fidgeted with the soft drinks lined up on the kitchen counter. Someone gently moved him aside to reach for a big plastic bottle of Fanta. He turned slightly to the side to let the guy in and was caught by the man's broad smile. Jeff forgot his shyness and took the initiative to introduce himself. The man quickly introduced himself as well, as did the guy he was with. In the din Jeff had trouble catching their names.

"Hey. How's it going? Where are you from?" one of them asked Jeff.

"I've got a place in Fremont." Jeff thought it best not to tell strangers he lived upstairs.

"Oh! The Bay Area. Us, too. Oakland."

"No," Jeff said. "Fremont here. Not Fremont there. Seattle."

The Californians explained they were on a road trip through the Northwest, and had planned it to be in Seattle during Pride weekend.

"I don't know how impressed you'll be."

"There's a gay cruise tomorrow," the Smile friend volunteered. "Tacky Tourists. Have I got that right? We got tickets for it!"

Jeff had no idea what they were talking about. If Henry were here, he'd be a much better local guide. Henry was late. "You guys in the program?" Jeff asked, changing the topic of conversation.

"Oh yeah, sure, that's why we're here! Me, two years. Theo nearly three."

Theo. Okay, one name down. One more to go. "Where are you staying?" he asked next.

"We've got friends in Columbia City," the newly identified Theo answered, sucking on his Fanta through a straw he'd found somewhere. Theo's friend was cute.

Jeff stopped flirting when a huge drag queen muscled his way into the now crowded kitchen. Already a tall man, he was made taller by spike-heeled boots and an immense, teased-out platinum wig. He nodded hello breathlessly to everyone around him, tugged on one of his dangly earrings and bellowed in a deep voice, "Who's gonna get the girl a drink?" Oh, okay, Jeff thought, a sober drag queen at a sober party. It had to happen sometime. He overheard one guy say to another that was Crystal Lane. "She's on every week at the Brass Connection."

"The Ass Infection."

"The what?"

"Ass Infection. That's what everyone calls it."

"Just like everyone calls you and the missus 'Chubby and Tubby'?" The joke was lost on Jeff.

Theo was the first to reach the diva with a plastic cup full of Coke and ice. She pulled out a little pink paper umbrella from her bodice, made a show of opening it and putting it in the cup, pinkie raised. "Just like the old days, boys. At the Copa. *Before* it went all disco hell."

The house fell almost silent as Mike's band was between numbers. Jeff could peer over the drag queen's shoulders and see that the dining room and beyond were packed. Glancing at his watch, he saw that it was just nine. Henry should be here.

Jeff wiped some sweat off his forehead with a party napkin. "It's crowded in here," he said to the Californians. "Wanna go out back?"

They were the only ones out on the porch. The air was much cooler.

"You have a boyfriend?" the Smile asked.

"Yes," Jeff said, deciding that he did. "He's coming. He finished work a while ago."

After a moment Jeff announced, "Think I'll take a walk around." He realized that his new friends from Oakland might think it strange he wanted to go back into a house he'd just left, but he was feeling antsy about Henry. Jeff snaked his way through the packed interior and made it to the living room, where someone told him he thought he'd seen Henry go out to the backyard. Jeff turned around and tousled with the crowd to retrace his steps exactly the way he had come.

He found Henry sitting in one of the chairs on the back deck and smoking a cigarette. Jeff stood behind him and rubbed his shoulders.

"Big crowd."

"Yeah," Henry agreed. "Lots of folks. People brought friends, I guess."

"Where were you? I thought you'd be here earlier to help set up."

Henry took a long drag on his cigarette and turned his head towards Jeff. "Did a few lines, then got fucked by a busload of hot big-dicked strangers. What the hell do you expect me to say? Arrest me, for crissake, I was late."

"Let's not fight, okay? It's a party."

"That's right, it's a party. Lighten up." Henry took one of Jeff's hands off his shoulders and held it in his own. He squeezed hard. Jeff was struck by how often it was Henry who made the move to defuse the tension between them.

"Jeff," Henry said. "Let's go upstairs. The party can take care of itself. I want to get naked with you."

Mike's band finished their break and started up again. It was too loud for Jeff and Henry to talk to each other anymore. They made their way through the crammed first floor and went up to Jeff's room, where Henry got his wish. He took advantage of the noisy house below and shouted rather than murmur his favorite, filthy commands. Jeff played daddy and Henry was a bad boy with attitude. The real fight they had been on the verge of having was postponed, but not indefinitely.

After going to the movies Nan drove up her driveway after moving the two orange traffic cones the boys had placed there. Nan walked to the back thinking she'd enter through the French doors to the dining room. But the rear of the house was as crowded as the front. Not quite sure what to do, she roamed her pitch-black backyard. As she wandered this way and that, her eyes grew accustomed to the night and she could see herself, faintly illuminated by the lights from the house, casting a long shadow on the grass. A moment or two later she heard voices closer toward the house. She tried to listen more closely to what was being said, but without moving closer to the source of the noises it was impossible to hear.

Another car rolled down the driveway. Its headlights illuminated the thick greenery where two shapes stood. Nan could see the back of the head of a man who faced away from her and toward the man he was holding tight. Nan's heart stopped for an instant. She would recognize the back of her son's head anywhere.

Nan felt dizzy. *What will I say to him?* As the parked car turned off its headlights, everything in Nan's backyard went black again. But in the split second before it did, Nan willed herself to imagine what she was seeing was not the head of her boy but a head so like it: not Mike at all, but his father. Nan closed her eyes and searched the fading image projected against her eyelids for confirmation of treason. What she really had seen was neither Richard nor Mike, or any of the men in her life, but two ex-drunks from California on a road trip through the Pacific Northwest and in love with each other.

A week later Henry stood over the kitchen sink looking at dirty dishes as he drank his morning coffee. Jeff stumbled in and said, "Okay, out of the way. I'm on it!" He took one step toward the sink.

Henry sighed and turned around. He looked out the window.

"We're out of dishwashing liquid," Jeff said slowly.

"Go fucking get some. Jesus, you're helpless. PhD-grade helpless."

Jeff had to get to the bottom of what was going on. They hadn't when they argued last night, but this morning they might. The fight started over nothing and went on to be about everything: Ryan, Greg, drugs, someone Henry learned was named Raul, Jeff's drinking, *arf*, the Yellow House and that night at the Monastery. But somehow they avoided the real thing they should have fought about, which was whether they should surrender to each other and a precarious future.

"C'mon, we've fought before. What's up?" Jeff asked, drying his wet hands on his khakis.

Henry glared at Jeff but didn't say anything until asking: "Why the fuck are we here?"

Jeff took his time answering, since he knew this conversation could disintegrate into another shouting match. But Jeff gave in to his impulse, never far from the surface, to handicap his opponent.

"We're here, if you remember, because you wanted to be."

Henry shifted his weight from one leg to the other, the way an elephant sways before charging.

"Yeah, and the reason was, was because I thought it would help me *and you* stay—correction, *get*—sober if we were in the damn house all the time. We've been here three months now and nothing's changed. Summertime and the living is definitely *not* easy."

Jeff saw where this was going and realized it was going to be a conversation he wouldn't emerge unscathed from. "And it's not helping," he said, stalling for time.

"And it's not helping. Big-time. You're drinking, I'm using, and worse, we've gotten real good at hiding it. From group, from Nan, from each other."

"We both have sponsors," Jeff said defensively.

"Don't make me laugh. Mine's trying to get into my pants and you think yours is an idiot." Henry continued, "This isn't working."

So what do you want to do about it? Jeff thought. But rather than ask the question out loud, he cut to the chase.

"Is this what is really bothering you? It's not like you to play the drug and alcohol counselor." Jeff paused. "Something else is going on."

"We should go our separate ways." As Henry heard his own words he wondered if he meant them. I've told Jeff that I love him. We lay on a hotel bed in Index and I told him. We sat in his car on Queen Anne in the middle of the night and I told him. But he wasn't saying it now. He was scared they were breaking up and something inside him wanted to beat Jeff to the punch, just so it might hurt less.

Jeff felt a pool of acid in the pit of his stomach. Those were Henry's words he'd heard and not his own. Usurped, he was at a loss how to respond. He realized that getting straight was not the problem Henry meant to talk about right now. Is now the time to tell Henry again how much I love him? No, it wouldn't sound sincere. It would sound like yet another excuse not to talk it out. But he needed time to organize just how he felt about Henry and his fears for them. Was he always going to need time? Jeff felt ashamed of his cowardice, and of how he always seemed to disappoint the young man in front of him.

"I want to think about it," Jeff finally said.

"I don't," Henry quickly replied. "I've made up my mind." Henry thought: Yes, I've made up my mind that I won't be abandoned by any Jeff a second time.

I don't understand, Jeff wanted to say. Made up your mind about what? But before Jeff could respond, both of them heard footsteps upstairs.

"Look, Jeff," Henry said. "Before Nan comes down, let's just agree to take a break. That's all. Boyfriends do it all the time. That's what we'll tell Nan we're doing. That's what we'll tell everyone."

Jeff seized on the ambiguity of the word "break." Maybe it would be good for them to spend some time apart. Jeff knew he could use a breather from the Yellow House. It didn't mean they were breaking up, just that they were taking some time. "Okay, fine, I'll tell Nan I've got a work project and I'll be spending my nights at the Fremont place for a while. I'll break the news to her."

"I'll tell her," Henry said firmly. "You do the dishes." Henry walked out of the kitchen. Jeff turned to the sink and looked at the coffee mug Henry had added to the pile. Jeff picked it up and rubbed it against his cheek, hoping it was still warm.

Vinnie asked Mike to turn down the volume.

Mike rolled over in the narrow bed and reached out with his long arm toward the boom box on the floor. His fingers grappled for the right control, fumbled with it, and then just turned it off with a grunt.

"I better get back," Vinnie said, pulling Mike toward him to make maximum skin contact between the young man's back and his own naked chest.

"Back where?" Mike asked in a voice muffled because he had buried his head in one of the pillows. "Oh yeah. You work. I forgot."

Vinnie ran one of his hands up and down Mike's smooth chest. When he reached his navel he played with the fine hairs growing out of it. Vinnie's penis rose slowly back to life against the young man's buttocks.

"What are you doing with the rest of your day?" Vinnie asked, not really interested in the answer.

"Steph's coming over."

Vinnie's hard-on softened.

"Practice?"

Mike laughed. "We're past the practice stage."

"I meant *band* practice."

Vinnie thought of getting up but at the moment it seemed like too much work to climb over Mike's large, inert frame. Big boy, he noted. Nan's ex must be a giant. Both of them lay there without saying anything. Vinnie's hand, still on Mike's chest, registered the lazy rise and fall of his breathing. Nan's son wasn't gay, Vinnie knew that now, but he enjoyed being the one Mike had decided to experiment with. He heard a siren, faint enough to mean it was an ambulance going down Broadway. Vinnie remembered the time he was in an ambulance racing to Harborview.

"I really gotta go," Vinnie said, nudging Mike to move.

A few minutes later, Vinnie was walking from the Tenth Avenue house toward downtown. Vinnie thought about Nan and her family. Now he had a secret to keep from her. She thought he was a good person and he wanted to keep it that way. He waited for the light to change as he thought: Sometimes I wish I could talk to Ryan about my secrets, if only I had the courage to be alone with him once more. Vinnie was not just worried about his sobriety, he was worried about his occasional thoughts of wanting to hurt Ryan for all he had done.

A day after the argument Jeff worked himself into an ugly fit and impulsively decided that Fremont was not going to be enough distance between him and Henry for a while. He was angry with himself and with Henry for painting them into a corner, and he wanted to punish the both of them for it. He knew it was more self-destructive behavior, probably a side-effect of trying to go sober by harming himself in ways the booze wasn't anymore, but he called Brandon to say he was coming to New York for a visit. He had the impression that his old friend didn't recognize his voice at first. He could have called Raul instead, but he was too intimidated. Raul would have said, Yes, stay with me, but it would have been awkward after this much time. Raul, Jeff had heard, had moved on. He was living with someone new, someone with money, and was installed in the boyfriend's huge apartment at One Fifth Avenue with no intention of slumming with the old crowd. Brandon knew that Jeff knew all this, but he said what was on his mind nonetheless.

"You should call Raul."

"I will," Jeff said. Then he added, "Why did you say that?"

"Because it's good manners, that's why," Brandon snapped, the tone of his voice letting Jeff know that manners had nothing to do with it.

Jeff went first to One Fifth Avenue after arriving in New York two days later. He'd head uptown to Brandon's place later that night. He stepped aside on the sidewalk for someone walking four dogs, but then went back to the same spot to stare up at the whole twenty-seven stories of the apartment building.

He was still looking at the building when a short, broad man with a toupee and a uniform came out of the building's lobby and approached him with large strides. Raul has a doorman now, Jeff thought. What a difference a year makes.

"Can I help you?" the short man asked in a tone Jeff remembered as New York brusque.

"Ah, I'm here to see…Raul."

"Mr. Alarcon?"

"Yes, Raul Alarcon."

"Is he expecting you?"

"I called," Jeff replied.

"You are?"

"Jeff. From Seattle."

"Come into the lobby," the doorman said with a shrug. "I'll telephone up."

Jeff sat in a chair and waited.

"Please go up. Apartment 17D. The elevators are on your left." The doorman raised his arm and pointed.

Jeff shared the elevator with an ancient woman holding a small, pure white dog. She smiled at Jeff but said nothing.

At first Jeff headed down the hallway in the wrong direction, but then he heard a familiar voice. He turned around and at the other end of the corridor Raul had stuck his head out a door and was calling his name.

"Hi, Jeff!"

Jeff gave Raul a bear hug.

The apartment had marble floors and antique furniture. In the middle of the day it would be filled with sun. Once Jeff lowered his knapsack to the floor in the foyer, Raul put his arms around him again, kissed him and took him over to a small sitting area. Raul was wearing navy blue sweatpants, a green cashmere sweater and some kind of headband around his forehead that looked like it might have started life as a necktie. He looked older than the last time they had seen each other, but perhaps Jeff looked older as well. Raul was tan, which added to his gaunt look. His high cheekbones seemed higher, and Jeff was sure he had lost weight. It was a toss-up in Jeff's mind whether this made Raul more handsome or less, but he had certainly lost a measure of his lingering boyishness.

"Air-conditioning. You've come up in the world." No wonder he was wearing a cashmere sweater in late July. Jeff thought he'd freeze in here.

Raul sat on an ornate settee across from the big chair Jeff had taken. Raul crossed his legs and spread his long arms in either direction along the top edge of the settee.

"Hal's not here. Too bad. You could have met him."

"Hal? The boyfriend?" Jeff understood from the way Raul put it that he would never meet Hal.

"Yes," Raul replied with a slight hiss. "This is all his."

Jeff made a show of looking around. "Lucky him. Lucky you."

Raul disappeared into another room and returned with two Perriers. He assumed his earlier position on the settee. The fizzing green bottles sat on the glass coffee table, untouched by either of them.

"I guess you've heard I'm on the wagon," Jeff said, knowing from Brandon that the two of them had talked.

"I know you're trying. I've pretty much stopped myself."

Jeff saw a bar cart in a corner of the sitting room behind the settee. Jeff guessed that Hal was the one who drank. Either that or Raul, like himself, was not telling the truth.

They were silent for a moment. Both of them picked up their waters at the same time, perhaps out of a shared awkwardness.

"Tell me about Hal," Jeff said.

"Oh," Raul said, revolving his head at the end of his long neck. "You can guess. Older, late forties, came into the family money early. Knows everyone, has a house in the Grove, likes us Cuban boys *a lot*. And this," Raul concluded, waving one of his arms in the air, "I get in return."

"Is it serious?"

"Baby," Raul laughed, "I'm living here, aren't I?" It dawned on Jeff that Raul was unlikely to ask him a single question about his own life after New York. Jeff gulped the rest of his Perrier down quickly, and Raul did not offer him another.

"So, how long are you in town?"

"Not sure, Raul. Maybe awhile."

"Great, there'll be time for you to see everyone. And meet Hal." Jeff realized he was being hurried through this reunion with his old lover.

"I've got work to do," Jeff said somewhat defensively.

"You always work," Raul commented accusingly, as if that were the reason they were no longer together. The real reason, they both knew, was that Jeff wanted to leave New York and was glad Raul did not.

"I'm sorry, Raul. I could have been better explaining things to you."

Raul shrugged his shoulders and cocked his head. Jeff decided that aging had improved his old boyfriend's looks after all. But whatever he once saw in Raul he didn't see anymore. There was a kind of residual warmth between them, but in not too much time Jeff guessed it would be gone completely.

The Perrier had run through him. Jeff asked where the bathroom was.

"Use mine," he was told. "It's at the end of the hallway on the right."

The bathroom had marble floors, too, and a bidet to boot. As Jeff stood over the toilet and pissed, he looked at himself askance in the mirror over the sink. He shook the last drops from his penis, stuffed it back into his pants and, noticing his hair was mussed, took two steps to the left to stand squarely before the mirror.

Not only was his hair a rat's nest, but his entire face was covered with a greasy sheen from having traveled across the country. Jeff turned the coldwater faucet, leaned over the sink and used his hands to splash his face. When he looked into the mirror again, he realized that Raul had lost fat in his face but he himself had gained some.

He looked around for a towel and found one. As he wiped his face dry, he noticed the mirror was hinged. His left hand reached up of its own accord to the lower edge to pry the cabinet open.

The door swung easily, and in front of Jeff's eyes were several rows of white enamel shelves evenly spaced from top to bottom. The cabinet was shallow, not meant to store anything large. But each shelf—except the lowest, which had the usual paraphernalia of nail clippers, dental floss, an emery board, a couple of Band-Aids and half-squeezed tubes of whatever—was crammed with plastic amber prescription drug vials, maybe dozens of them, some tall and narrow, and others short and wide, but all with the same unvarying white round tops. There must be just one factory in the world that makes all of these. The labels had instructions and ALARCON, RAUL typed neatly on them, in a variety of typefaces. Some of the vials were full, others half empty. He stood there and thought: I *could* read the labels, but I won't understand what these drugs are for. But I do understand how my world and Raul's are connected. These drugs aren't just his, they're all of ours.

Jeff closed the cabinet door slowly so as not to make a sound. He wiped his hands off on his pants and walked out of the bathroom into the living room, where Raul had not stirred an inch. His long arms were still stretched along the top of the settee, and there was a warm smile on his face. Jeff noticed that Raul was wearing a gold chain with a crucifix dangling from it, an expensive version of Henry's own.

Nan locked the front door after the last of the evening's group had left, but she felt too agitated to go to bed yet. She felt like a cigarette outdoors to calm down. The French doors stuck a bit when she went to close them behind her. She faced the yard and lit her Salem. When Nan's gaze wandered down the steps to the lawn, she saw that some of the ground was darker than the rest. Instinctively she moved toward it, expecting to find someone's forgotten sweatshirt or jacket, but she was startled when the pile seemed to look back. A glassy eye stared up at her, its iris reflecting the light from the porch fixture. Nan almost cried out but realized the animal was dead.

The creature had four paws and a tail. It had to be the raccoon. Nan felt nauseous. She spun around and rushed into the house, cigarette clenched between her lips but now forgotten. She raced to the second floor and went into her bedroom. She pulled open the top drawer of her dresser and looked frantically. Jesus Christ, where is it? She'd wrapped it in her purple scarf, easy to find if she ever needed it. Maybe she should call someone. Richard? No, Mike. Just calm down, she told herself. It's only a dead animal and there must be dead animals everywhere. I'm not in danger, she reassured herself. But where is that goddamn gun.

Nan closed the drawer and stood up straight. She saw her reflection in the mirror above the dresser. She still had the cigarette in her mouth. Its smoldering tip glowed orange in the semidarkness of her room. Her face looked so old and lined, the face of a witch. She never looked so ugly, she thought.

Henry stared at the sheet of paper he had filled just short of halfway. He was lying on his bed, one leg crossed against the other to support the pad of paper secured to an old clipboard he'd found in the basement. His first pen had run dry, but he found another under the bed. He missed Jeff badly and was so desperate to take his mind off it he was attempting to write his father.

Henry was having trouble finding enough news to share. He'd told his father about his job at Starbucks and his reunion with Greg the last time, so unless he was going to tell him about moving into the Yellow House, or something about Jeff, there wasn't much to say now. He tapped the second pen against the edge of the clipboard.

He was nearly at the point of making up things, things not true but that might make his father proud of his son—when there was a sharp knock on his half-open bedroom door. Before Henry could say anything, Greg walked in. Another guy hung back in the door frame behind Greg. Henry stretched his neck to get a better look.

For an instant he might have thought it was Jeff, but Henry could tell the difference between him and Ryan, even if others couldn't.

"Hey, Henry," Greg said in a gravelly voice. "Long time. Look who I brought."

Henry scurried to sit up straight on the bed. He dropped the clipboard and pen onto the bedspread. "Greg, what's up?" he asked warily, watching the other visitor out of the corner of one eye. "Ryan. Man. You, too."

Henry was alarmed. Seeing Greg and Ryan together was already a surprise, and his instincts told him they both meant to do him harm. His brother detested him because he was gay, and he knew Ryan was still pissed he had betrayed him as a dealer in training, and then for having left him for the first Jeff.

"Aw, nothing's up, little bro. Nothing. Just in the vicinity, thought I'd drop by with an old friend of yours."

Henry stared at his brother, and then at Ryan lurking behind him. They both had loved him, if in different ways; and they both hated him, if for different reasons. That they were both here together put Henry on guard and wishing for the second Jeff.

"I didn't think you liked my friends," he said, his chin nodding in the direction of the doorframe. "Even the old ones."

"Ryan, come on in. You remember Henry, I'm sure. You too shared so much together."

Ryan took a step forward and grinned. He did look like the new Jeff, but had deep creases around his eyes. "Henry, it's been a while. You been avoiding me? Guess I know why."

"What are you guys up to?" Henry asked, still staring at Greg to avoid looking at Ryan directly.

"Not much," Greg said, turning his head to the right as if he was looking for something. "Ryan, this is the place where people get straight. Bet you didn't know that. Your old piece of pussy is off the junk. Or so he says."

Henry nodded without glancing at Ryan and said, "That's the idea." Greg turned his head toward Ryan now, said something to him Henry didn't catch. They laughed. Then both Greg and Ryan looked at Henry as if they expected him to say something.

"Straight. As in clean. Sober," Henry said.

"Homework?" Greg asked, gesturing toward the clipboard on the bed.

Henry crossed his arms across his chest. "I'm not in school anymore, Greg," he said. "You know that."

"So," Greg continued, "we were just in the neighborhood."

"Cool."

"Front door was unlocked, Ryan was surprised."

Henry explained that people came and went from the Yellow House all day long. He stared harder at his brother. "So, what's up?" he asked again. "Ryan, don't you talk?" Henry harbored the slim hope that if Ryan spoke, he would be less of a threat.

Greg flashed a smile. "Can't I just stop by and check in on my little brother?"

"That's not your style, Greg."

Greg smiled again. "I was saying, check in on my brother." Henry noticed Ryan looking around his room now. What was he looking for? He didn't have any money.

Greg leaned toward Henry and looked as if he was going to take another step forward. "Wanna get high?" he asked Henry in his once more gravelly voice.

Henry half-expected this. The only thing his brother might like more than scoring was scoring in the Yellow House. It appealed to his sense of irony.

Henry snorted. "Greg, c'mon, there's no shit here. Anywhere. And you know I'm working the program. Why are you fucking with me? Why's Ryan here? I don't like being ganged up on."

Ryan moved past Greg, walked past the bed, and stood looking out the window. Henry couldn't see his face anymore. He concentrated on his brother's leer.

"Hey, Henry, we're not here to bum off of you. We're holding. It's holy fucking Christmas."

213

Several times in group they'd talked about this. About how if you were serious about sobriety, you'd need new friends, new lovers, maybe even a new family. And now, leaning over him, was Greg. Half of Henry, half something else. One of these two halves was going to make the next few minutes make-or-break for Henry.

"Greg, forget it. Come back some other time. And," Henry added, "come back by yourself."

"Gee, I thought you used to like Ryan," Greg teased. "Isn't that why you went out of your way to find an exact copy of him? Yeah, I told him about your new Jeffie-boy. I don't think he likes him much, either."

Greg took a step backward and closed the door to the bedroom. It didn't latch, and Henry watched it slowly swing open again about halfway. His brother sat down on the bed and didn't seem to notice. He told Ryan to stop looking out the window and come over.

"Ryan, show Henry what we brought." Ryan fumbled with the left front pocket of his loose army-surplus camouflage pants.

"Where is he?" Ryan asked as he dug into his pocket.

"Out of town."

"Oh, out of town." Greg turned toward Ryan, who was still struggling with his pants pocket. "Out of town, out of mind, you know what they say."

Henry frowned. Ryan now had a syringe, a bag, a cotton swab and a spoon in his left hand.

"Matches?" Ryan finally said.

"What?"

"Matches. I need matches." Ryan opened the top drawer to Henry's dresser and started to fish around. Henry was momentarily frightened he'd find the old Jeff's pistol, which he kept hidden under his socks.

Henry hated himself when he thought: Jeff, you did this to me. You left me here alone. None of this will be my fault. Why did you go? Why did we fight? Now I'm here with a brother who is disgusted I'm a cocksucker, teamed up with my first connection who thinks I messed with the count. This was not to going to end well. "You fuckers in business together now?"

"Let's just say I keep Ryan near me these days. For your own good. I wouldn't want him to be alone with you, would I? I think his feelings are hurt. Hah hah."

Henry stared at his brother some more, the look now more pleading than dismissive. Ryan found a book of matches under Henry's pack of Marlboros on his dresser. Henry knew the next step was preparing the fix.

A voice not quite his own came out of Henry's throat and told Greg to get the hell out. "Ryan, you too."

Greg went over to Ryan, who was heating the white powder in the spoon. Greg reached into Ryan's right pocket and extracted a length of flexible yellow tubing.

"Who's first?"

Henry didn't say a thing. He saw Jeff's face in front of him, but Jeff was not in the room. Greg and Ryan were. His brother plus his first pusher. A family reunion all around. The old familiar scent of hot heroin filled his nostrils and, with that, Henry knew there would be no more halfhearted protests. "Close the door," he quietly ordered no one in particular. No one moved.

"Baby brother goes first." Greg sat down on the bed. He grabbed Henry's right arm and wrapped the rubber hose around the lower part of his bicep.

"Make it nice and big," Greg purred.

Ryan had filled the syringe. He tapped it a couple times and handed it to Greg. Henry closed his eyes and made a fist. He wasn't thinking of Jeff just then. He was thinking of his father and the unfinished letter, still waiting for some good lie to fill it. "Okay, drop the hose," he told his brother.

"Good boy. Here it comes." Greg slipped the hypodermic needle into the blue vein on Henry's smooth forearm. "What a good, good boy," Greg kept murmuring. Greg's voice seemed to become his father's voice in Henry's mind, but saying the nice things to him his father never did. Henry's thoughts drifted off into space, into a quiet place that was alternately cold and hot, looming ominously above everything. Henry felt Ryan put his hand on his shin and massage him gently, and he liked it. Whatever he and Greg wanted to do to him, it would be okay.

Nan was trying to remember what errand she'd left her bedroom for when she heard the door to Henry's room start to close, guided by some invisible hand or maybe a breeze from an open window. It didn't shut all the way and she could hear two low, male voices talking on the other side of the door. She impulsively turned and peered into Henry's room. She caught sight of what she assumed were Henry's legs stretched out across his bed. He was leaning forward with his shoulders hunched and his head bowed low. The memory of two men in her backyard, hidden by darkness, seized her.

Nan could see the seated man's arms were moving, doing something to Henry. She took two steps closer to the door. It was definitely Henry on the bed. His right arm was stretched across the man's lap with a hand resting palm up on the man's thigh. Then she noticed something tied around Henry's bicep, a yellow ribbon of some sort.

The man gave what looked like a syringe to a third person in the room, until now hidden by the door. Nan recoiled, stepped backward, but then moved forward again, drawn to what was going on. Whatever had been in the needle was inside Henry. It was as if she was watching two people make love. Private and unstoppable, the primal scene. Nan was intruding on something she shouldn't. But she couldn't take her eyes away. Henry's arm stirred a bit, but then fell back onto the man's lap.

She had half expected what she was seeing. What bothered her was that it was Henry. Henry was going to help solve the problem, that's what Vinnie promised. Henry was not supposed to *be* the problem. Henry, her own son's age. Henry, the boy toward whom Nan had felt protective. Tiptoeing backward, Nan returned to her bedroom. She sat in the chair by the window and thought about how weak men could be. She should be angry, but that was not what she felt. Instead, Nan raised her right arm, bent it at the elbow and, using the index finger of her left hand, pressed hard into the soft flesh of her inner arm, at just the spot she had seen the thin silver needle leave Henry.

CHAPTER TWELVE

Two days later they found Henry on Jeff's bed. His body, apart from the small pieces forcibly detached and scattered around the room, was in the fetal position. He was fully clothed and still had his shoes on, as if he had meant to lie down only for a moment. His knees were drawn halfway up to his torso, but his right arm was twisted in an unnatural position. He might have shot himself, the police would say, or conceivably someone else did. Until they had more evidence they would investigate Henry's death as either a suicide or homicide. But no one said anything about the possibility it could have been both.

Nan had discovered Henry shortly after returning home. She passed Jeff's room glimpsing Henry and his blood everywhere, including what had collected in a large, half-dried pool on the floor where the remaining fraction of Henry's head rested on a dark, cherry-black pillow. Nan felt sick to her stomach. She raised her cupped hand to her mouth both to keep from screaming and to stop the vomit she felt rising in her throat. Her eyes were unable to focus. Everything in the small bedroom grew bleary. Only then did she register the bitter smell, which later she would learn was gunpowder.

Nan didn't run down the stairs. She took each step slowly and carefully, watching each foot move in front of the other as she gripped the railing to keep steady. Halfway down she looked up to see the Sex Anonymous group meeting in the brightly lit living room, some men sitting on the sofa or the folding chairs, others cross-legged on the floor. The cant of an older man talking about his obsessions was clear and loud.

Nan opened her mouth to say something but no words came out. Instead a low cry, something close to a growl, came from a creature inside her. It started softly but gradually rose in both pitch and volume. Her voice, if that is what it was, eventually assumed shape and acquired mass. It drifted from the empty space in the air above the members of the group to settle like a thick tarpaulin atop them. The older man, who had begun to sob at the pathos of his own story, became aware that another voice was competing with his own. Everyone who had been listening to him turned in their seats and looked at the woman standing on the stairs, ghostlike. Her groan turned from a bestial roar to the human scream it was, stretching with a horror that everyone in the Yellow House, save Henry, heard.

They sat in uncomfortable metal chairs with no cushions and cold hard backs. The fluorescent lights in the ceiling were bare and made everything in the room look fake and ugly. The linoleum floor had an old-fashioned checkerboard pattern of once evergreen squares alternating with off-white ones streaked with bits of black. Nan thought: This is a filthy floor no one has mopped in a long time.

The chairs faced a frayed poster on the wall, and next to it a sheet of paper held in place with short lengths of discolored tape. The print was too small for Nan to guess what it said, but the poster next to it was easy: it was a cartoon figure of a friendly policeman, telling us with a toothy grin the ten easy things we can to do to protect our homes against breaking and entering. Nan found it amusing. That had never been the Yellow House's problem.

The police wanted to know many things. Sometimes she knew the answers, but mostly she did not. It seemed to surprise the police that she knew so little about this young man living under her roof, and eventually their frustration showed. What drugs did he take? Had he ever overdosed? She delivered her answers in short, clipped sentences. They asked if she kept a gun in the house. She said yes, but unprompted added she didn't know where it was anymore. Once those words were out of her mouth, Nan realized that she'd be at police headquarters a long time.

Henry had been shot. A gun was found on the floor by the bed in his room, but the bullet that had shattered his skull was unrecovered so far. Once they extracted it from the wall, and the police lab ran ballistics on it, they would know if it was the weapon that killed him. There was a syringe on the floor, too, but well out of Henry's reach. The toxicology report on his blood would take two weeks. For the present, the police were beginning by questioning Nan as a person of interest. She wondered if she should ask for a lawyer. She wished Richard were here.

"There was no sign of a struggle, Mrs. Maxwell. Who were Henry's friends?"

Nan told them about Jeff, of whom she knew even less than she did of Henry. She said he was out of town—not sure where, maybe New York. Not upstate, the city. Henry had a brother, too, Nan seemed to recall, but she didn't know anything more than that. She was sure the police were exasperated with her and understandably wondering what kind of household she ran.

"Mrs. Maxwell, we are going to test your hands for gunpowder residue. It's standard procedure."

That was when she had asked if she could call a friend to come be with her. She reached Vinnie and the questioning resumed.

"Tell us more about the brother, Mrs. Maxwell."

"He's from Spokane. No, I don't have an address. No, he didn't have the same last name as Henry's, I know that. Half brother, I think. Older? Yes, he's older. I don't know if he has a job. He's been visiting Seattle, I think."

Vinnie appeared a little later. She caught a glimpse of him on the other side of the glass. His hair was wet and combed back. Nan hadn't noticed he was going bald before. She couldn't but think to herself, in the middle of all this, just how virile he was.

After asking her the same questions a second time, the police let Nan take a break but told her not to go anywhere.

"They've put yellow police tape all around the house," Vinnie told Nan as they sat next to each other in the small outer room.

Nan closed her eyes and imagined her house as she waited for the detectives to call her back into the larger and even cooler room where she'd already spent two hours. She saw in her mind a bright yellow tape, maybe five inches wide, with big black letters repeating the command Police Line Do Not Cross. It snaked its way across her front porch, turned right as it proceeded east, made contact with the brick of the chimney, stretched across the windows of the dining room, sped along the porch on the backside of the house and continued to the exterior of the kitchen until it finally reached the moldy north side of the house and returned to the front. My house must look like a badly wrapped birthday present, Nan thought. A yellow box with a yellow ribbon, minus a fancy bow.

Nan opened her eyes and turned to Vinnie. "You don't have to stay here. I'm fine," she said, even as she squeezed his hand.

"I know you are," Vinnie whispered. "I'll stay a while longer," he added after hesitating a moment.

"Nan, why do you think Henry was in Jeff's room? Jeff's away, right?"

Nan didn't know why Henry was in Jeff's room, but she could guess. Henry was on Jeff's mattress for the same reason that she still slept sometimes on Richard's side of her bed. That thought prompted a question. "Where will I sleep tonight, Vinnie?"

"You should go to a friend's. I'll drive you."

Nan shook her head. She'd get no rest at Joan's. She'd be pummeled by a thousand questions.

"I need to call Mike."

Vinnie didn't blink. "You've got his number?"

"Of course I do. He's my son."

Nan and Vinnie sat alone for over an hour after she'd used the pay phone in the hallway to call Mike's house. While waiting Nan remembered something important. "Vinnie, there's more. Henry was shot, but the police say there was a hypodermic needle on the floor near the bed."

"They said he overdosed?"

"No, they don't know yet. But they found a syringe." Nan hadn't told the officers, and she wasn't going to tell Vinnie, what she had seen Henry do in his room only two days earlier.

Someone in a uniform Nan hadn't seen before led her son into the waiting room. Vinnie stood up and said he was going outdoors for a smoke. Mike gave Vinnie an odd, quizzical look when he rushed out of the room. Mike sat down next to his mother in the chair Vinnie vacated.

"Sorry, Mom. The guys and I were at the studio cutting new music tapes all night."

"Oh, Richard Junior—" She stopped herself and started over. "Did you know Henry Sosa?"

"Sure I do," Mike replied. "He lived in my house, don't you remember? Until he moved in with you."

"I need a place to stay, Mike," Nan said. "No one's allowed back in the house for the time being."

She could have his bed, Mike offered. He'd take the sofa in the living room. The two of them sat there and said nothing.

"Steph's with me, Mom."

"What?"

"Steph's with me. My girlfriend. From the band. She's out in the car."

"Let her stay there," Nan snapped. "No more people right now, please. But where's Vinnie?"

Another hour passed, and no policeman asked Nan to do anything. The clock on the wall said 5:30 a.m. If there were a window, there'd be daylight now. Over the course of the night Nan had become aware of the nonstop buzzing of the overhead light fixtures. Vinnie never came back after his cigarette. Just as she was about to say something to her son, two officers came into the room and told Nan she was free to go but added that they would want to see her again. Mike stood up to mumble some kind of inappropriate thanks to the policemen. Nan noted how much taller he was than they.

She sat in the back of Mike's old Ford. Mike drove, and it was only after the car was moving that Steph, in the seat next to his, woke up. "It wasn't drugs?" she asked.

"He was shot. But they think there were drugs, too. I don't know." Nan leaned forward toward her son. "Mike, I had a gun. Your father gave it to me. And now I don't know where it is." Nan turned her head and looked out the window.

"Do the cops know?" he asked his mother.

"How could the police know where my gun is?"

"No. That you *had* a gun. *Have* a gun." He turned left to go up Tenth Avenue. "What the hell were you doing with a gun?"

"Your father was out of town on business trips a lot. He was worried about you and me in the house without him."

"Well, where did you put it?"

"I know I had it. I know I took it with me from the old house. I thought I'd put it away in a safe place in my bedroom, but then it disappeared."

"*Disappeared?*"

"Or maybe I misplaced it. Or maybe someone took it. Mike, there were all kinds of people coming and going. Someone might have wandered into my room and found it. Stolen it. I just don't know, Mike. I'm so confused. Do the police think I killed him?"

223

Steph turned in the front seat to face Nan. Nan imagined from the cold look on Steph's face that she was wondering if Nan had killed Henry.

"Do you think the gun on the floor was mine? What if it *was* mine, Mike?"

Steph turned back around and extracted a cigarette from an unseen handbag in her lap, but they reached Tenth Avenue before she could light it.

"Mike, there's a parking space. You better grab it," Nan barked.

Mike led his mother by the arm to the house. Inside, Nan asked if he had any Valium in the house. He did not. She waited silently with Steph in the living room as her son straightened up his room and put clean sheets on the bed. Once she went up to his room, she quickly took off her dress and slipped under the covers. She thought she'd fall asleep right away, but instead lay wide awake in the early morning light of her son's bedroom and listened to his and his girlfriend's voices in the living room. She looked around his room. It was filled with stacks of record albums and a number of electric guitars. She began to think Mike and Steph were arguing, but about what she couldn't tell. She tried to think about something else to avoid listening to what they were saying, but Henry popped up in her mind. He must be Mike's age, she thought, just a boy. Same as Mike, but so different. She wondered if Henry had ever been happy. Vinnie had found him somewhere, Nan realized, which meant he'd probably had a hard life, at least until he started showing up at the Yellow House. "Just where," as Nan thought her last thought before sleep, "does Vinnie find all these boys?"

Vinnie eased into the left lane and raced north on I-5. There was almost no traffic and he gunned it. After leaving Nan in the police station for a smoke, he had gone straight to his car and headed for Mukilteo and Ryan's place.

The news of the syringe by Henry's bed had startled Vinnie, though perhaps it shouldn't have. He didn't know anyone in his groups capable of shooting a gun, but plenty who had experience with a needle. He couldn't imagine the sequence of events that resulted in Henry's death, but when Nan mentioned the possibility of an overdose he was seized with the impulse to go see Ryan, who he knew was skilled at doing terrible things.

Vinnie passed Northgate and a disabled Toyota on the shoulder, flashing its yellow lights for assistance. He had done this manic drive before, hoping to have the courage to confess to Ryan the mistakes of his past and make amends, something Vinnie's sponsor had long demanded he do. But making amends to Ryan was beyond him. A part of him insisted Ryan begin with apologies of his own. That would never happen.

But Vinnie wasn't going to dodge the confrontation this time. He was sure Ryan was involved with Henry's death and that Henry's drugs had come from Ryan. He had no proof but he knew, just as he knew Ryan resented the new Jeff in Henry's life as much as he had the old. Ryan had a motive for hurting any one of them. Henry had a brother who dealt, too. Vinnie knew that. The kid was surrounded with trouble, and it had struck.

What *would* he say to Ryan, after forcing his way into his house? "Did you give Henry, your old piece of booty, drugs? Did you fucking *shoot* him?" At this point, what difference would any answer from Ryan, true or false, make? How could Vinnie make Ryan pay for what he did? He let up on the gas pedal and considered pulling over. This cannot end well. Where is Jeff? Why isn't *he* here? As his car came to a slow stop, Vinnie knew that once again, despite his years of staying clean, he still lacked the sobriety to make it all the way to Ryan's house. He had loved him, but the dope ruined everything for them and Vinnie worried that just seeing Ryan would trigger him. He sat in his car for a while and considered heading back to Seattle. Eventually he thought: I need to do this. For Henry and for me. He put the car in gear and pulled back out into traffic.

By the time Nan was falling asleep at her son's house, Greg had reached his destination. He hitched as far as Moses Lake and then called Crystal to come get him. They got to her house outside Spokane just as light broke. Crystal went ahead to bed. After Greg polished off the rest of a bottle of tequila he found atop her refrigerator, he crawled under the sheets next to her. Crystal had the covers pulled entirely over her head to block the sunlight that was leaking into the room through the fabric tacked over the windows. Greg turned onto his side and fell asleep.

He was alone when he woke up. The room was no longer bright. His watch said it was four in the afternoon, and the sun was now illuminating the other side of the house. Greg tried to sleep some more, but that wasn't going to happen. He went into the living room. There was no sign of Crystal. She was at work at the bottling plant, Greg realized. He peered into the refrigerator, hoping there was juice or something, but there wasn't. What he really wanted was some grass. He looked everywhere in the small kitchen: through all the jars in the spice rack, then each of the drawers crammed with utensils, coupons, elastic bands, unused chopsticks from takeaway Chinese restaurants, an old Yellow Pages, keys on a variety of rings and a few matchbooks. He returned to the bedroom and foraged. Nothing in her closet or in the nightstand drawer. Irritated, Greg went back into the main part of the house and was about to phone a friend in Spokane he knew delivered, when he heard someone fumbling with a key at the front door.

Crystal tossed her big jute shoulder bag onto the sofa by Greg's feet. She saw the empty Tequila bottle on the floor by the sofa.

"I see you made yourself at home." She was wearing a stained T-shirt, and in one of her hands was a rolled-up newspaper. She shuffled into the kitchen and dropped the paper on the counter, where it slowly unraveled to lie almost flat.

"Greg, what's your brother's name?"

Greg opened his eyes. "My brother? You mean Henry?"

226

"I mean his last name. What is it?"

"Sosa."

"*Sosa*," Crystal repeated slowly, as if to make sure she had it right. "Well, someone named Sosa's been shot dead. In Seattle. Page three of the newspaper, if you want to check." Greg didn't stir or say a word, but something inside him started to calculate.

"They're not sure yet it was, ah, foul play." Crystal opened the refrigerator door and looked inside.

Greg eventually left the sofa and stumbled back into the bedroom. The dog raised his head registering the move of a human in the room, then lowered it again onto the rug. He sank into the mattress as if a pile of heavy blankets were weighing him down. He lay on his back and looked up at the ceiling and saw water stains running in a long line perpendicular to him. Directly above his head the stains were especially dark, almost the color of red wine. No, more like blood, he thought. It looked to Greg like this section of the ceiling had just become wet, maybe since he'd shown up at the house. He squinted and tried to see the face of Jesus in the wet marks above him. Greg wondered if God would forgive him his sins.

A minute or two later Crystal came into the bedroom and sat down on the bed alongside Greg. The familiar scent preceded her, and he opened his eyes knowing she'd brought a joint in with her. She handed it to him without taking her eyes off of his. Just as he was about to put it between his lips, the phone in the living room began ringing. Neither Crystal nor Greg made any move to answer it, Crystal too stoned and tired to care and Greg too frightened. One less hooked homo in the world, he mulled while sucking on the reefer. But also one less brother, he thought, and I have no more to lose.

Vinnie pulled up slowly onto the gravel shoulder in front of Ryan's house. He didn't want to give him any advance warning of his arrival, but he didn't want to catch him completely off-guard either. He compromised by turning on the overhead light in his car so that Ryan could see who it was, if he was peeking out the window. Vinnie was startled when Ryan came out of nowhere to open the passenger door and sit down beside him.

"Turn off the light. I got curious neighbors." Vinnie did as he was told.

"Long time, Vinnie. If I didn't know better, I'd think you dropped by for a little grocery shopping."

Vinnie instantly realized that Ryan meant to spar with him before turning serious. But he knew how to short-circuit that. "Your old protégé Henry is dead, Ryan."

"What the fuck. Well, had to happen. Bad apple from day one."

"And you didn't have anything to do with that? Look, he got blown away but there was works near him when he bought the farm. Sorry, but somehow I thought of you. Don't know why. Do you?"

"Like I say, Vinnie, rotten fruit. Used too much of the merchandise himself, and when customers got shorted they were, well, displeased. Never understood why he hung around Seattle afterwards. Liked living dangerously, I guess."

Vinnie might have said that Henry had fallen in love with someone in Seattle who looked just like Ryan, but that would derail the conversation he'd come to have and start another. And as much as he detested Ryan, he didn't want to twist the knife deeper by telling him that Henry just might have found what Ryan never would.

"Okay, Vinnie, you got me. Me and the kid's brother Greg paid a visit on him a couple of days ago. In that house you're the fucking king of."

"And you guys shot up."

"Yeah, us guys shot up. Nice shit and not too much of it. End of story. No one OD'd. Left little Henry sleeping like a baby."

228

"Cops have a gun. Sure hope they don't decide it's one of yours."

Ryan raised his hands as if under arrest. "The kid had a piece of his own. I saw it when I was there. Maybe he shared it with playmates like he did that prize ass of his. You remember those days, don't you, Vinnie?"

"I never touched him."

"Then you get the medal of honor. But you missed out on the butt of the century. Too late now, apparently."

Vinnie, the bigger man, could have thrashed Ryan with his fists and dumped him here in front of his house to think about it for a long while. But he had more questions to ask, so he held his anger.

"Just tell me you didn't have anything to do with it."

"What difference would that make? No matter what happened, one way or another the fucker did himself in. Don't want to say he had it coming, but do the math, man."

Vinnie looked at Ryan in the dark of his car and compared his face to Jeff's. He thought: Jeff would never say such things, even if he and Ryan were otherwise perfect twins. Maybe Henry had been searching for a Ryan with the insides of a good person rather than a bad. But then Vinnie reminded himself that Jeff was not around now, that he had left Henry and Nan in the Yellow House and split for parts unknown, just the kind of thing a typical alcoholic running away from responsibility would do. It happened all the time. Vinnie predicted they would never see this Jeffrey again. Good riddance maybe. Poor Henry got dealt a bad hand every round, and now the fucker was dead. Vinnie had been so focused on AIDS suddenly threatening the gay men around him that he had trouble digesting what had just happened in the Yellow House.

"You know, Vinnie, you had a choice to make once. It was either going to be getting off the shit or staying with me. You chose getting off the shit. If you're so upset about this kid croaking, it may be because you're wondering now if you made the right decision."

Vinnie turned the key in his car's ignition to signal Ryan that their long delayed reunion was over. No more questions. Ryan slammed the door shut and disappeared.

Although Vinnie didn't realize it, he had just chosen to run away no less than Jeff had. Henry's death and seeing his old lover all in one day was more of a trigger than he needed. Two weeks later and his money gone, he would check into a VA hospital in Idaho to join other old soldiers whose surrender in wars they had lost delivered them, wet-brained, to detox and then the alkie ward. When the admitting nurse asked him the name of his closest living relative, he said Nan Maxwell because he wished it were so.

Stevie and Jack parked the car and walked toward the Yellow House for their meeting.

"Something's up," Stevie said.

"Shit, look at that," he said to Jack. The property was wrapped with lengths of police tape, its yellow color close to that of the siding. "Christ, what the fuck's happened," Jack said to Stevie. "Let's check it out."

"There were a lot of cops here a few days ago," a woman with a dog told them as they stood on the sidewalk in front of the house. "One of them told me somebody got shot."

"*Shot*?" Jack exclaimed. "Like with a gun? Who?"

"The paper said his name was Sosa."

Stevie and Jack looked at each other again. "That had to be one of the guys they said were living in the house helping the older woman run it," Stevie said to Jack. "You remember Nan. She sat with us at the start of group once."

No sooner had Stevie spoken than Nan pulled up in her Volvo and parked in front of them. She wasn't driving, a young man was. He stayed behind the wheel as Nan got out.

"Nan, hi. Remember us? Stevie and Jack. We chatted a while back."

Nan thought she remembered, but nothing came easily to her these past three days. She smiled weakly and nodded.

"We just heard the news, " Jack said. "Damn."

"Not the best time to talk, boys. I've just stopped by to pick up some of my clothes."

"What's gonna happen?" Stevie insisted on knowing.

Nan resigned herself to giving a brief report. "As soon as the police say I can, I'm putting the house on the market. No more Yellow House. Sorry, I'm not sure where the groups are moving to. Maybe they told me but I don't remember. No one can reach Vinnie. Check the gay paper." She turned and started to walk up the driveway to the back of the house. Not long later she returned with two armfuls of clothes on hangers.

"Take care, you fellows," Nan said, suddenly remembering that the white one had a lesion on his back. The young man driving her car leapt out and opened the trunk for her. "I may move out of state after this," she added loudly from a distance. "Be good!" She slammed the trunk shut. "Let's go, Mike."

The Volvo drove off but Jack and Stevie, at loose ends with no meeting to go to, stood idly on the sidewalk.

Jack grabbed Stevie by the elbow and whispered in his ear. "Let's go around to the back." They skirted the sawhorses at the foot of the driveway. No one was around to stop them. They turned the corner of the house and stopped where small steps went from the lawn up to the back door. Yellow tape prevented them from going any farther.

"Let's have a look inside." They jumped over the top of the tape.

"See anything?" Stevie asked, one step behind Jack.

"It's dark in there," Jack reported, his face pressed against the French doors. His hand reached out to the doorknob. Stevie watched him tighten his grasp and turn it.

"It's open. She left it unlocked."

"Jack, hold on. White boy with black boy, breaking and entering. Not smart."

"We're not breaking anything." Jack ignored Stevie and took a big step across the threshold. Stevie followed, just as he knew he would.

"Let's go upstairs."

"What's upstairs?" Stevie whispered. "We've never been there."

At the top of the staircase Jack found a light switch. Stevie could see more police tape strung along either side of the hallway against the walls and across all the doors. The room at the end of the hallway was open. It was bare except for a bed stripped of all its sheets, and a dresser against the wall. Leaning in over the tape, Stevie could see a bicycle leaning against a wall. Both of them stared at the blood splattered along the far end of the wall where the bed was wedged. There were two large splotches and many small ones.

"Jesus, that's where he got it," Jack said. "What a way to go," he added after a pause.

"What, with a gun? There are no good ways to go."

"I'd take pills."

"Sure you would, Marilyn," Jack said to Stevie. They knew someone in Tacoma who had used goofballs last year.

"I'm going in." Jack stared into the bedroom.

"*In?* You're fuckin' nuts."

Rather than squeeze under or hop over the tape, Jack simply pulled it down. He took a step into the room.

"Keep the light off," Jack murmured. "What are you waiting for?"

Jack had a strange look on his face, something halfway between a grin and a grimace. He wrapped his arms around Stevie, drew him close and kissed him hard on the lips. Stevie, flustered, would have backed away but Jack's arms were locked tightly around him. He felt Jack's tongue search the recesses of his mouth. This can't be happening, Stevie thought, even as he put his own arms around his boyfriend's waist and didn't back up when Jack began to grind his crotch into Stevie's own. Jack moved his large hands up and down the small of Stevie's back. Stevie's hands rested on the top of the back pockets of Jack's jeans. He moved his feet closer together, trying to be taller for Jack and accommodate his kisses better. Jack's hands moved from Stevie's back to his arms, which he squeezed hard, first the biceps and then the forearms. It hurt a little, and Stevie pulled his head away from Jack's. They moved from the edge of the bed where they had been sitting and lay down the length of the mattress. Stevie's head was where the pool of blood was the biggest. Jack pulled at Stevie's shirt and slid his hand underneath. He found one of Stevie's nipples and pinched it hard. Stevie had unbuckled Jack's belt and was at work on the buttons of his shirt. Once he had them loose, he ran his fingers through the small patch of hair between Jack's pectorals.

Jack put his hands through Stevie's short afro. Stevie rolled his eyes upward and saw the blood stains on the wall only a few inches above the mattress. He made himself look down to concentrate on his lover's body. Jack now had his back to him, and Stevie used his fingers to make little circles around the dark purple lesion between his shoulder blades. Jack must not have liked that, because he turned over at once with an exaggerated thump to face Stevie. Jack's smooth belly moved forward on the mattress to meet Stevie's own.

A few minutes later Stevie was stretched along the full length of the bed flat on his back and looking up at the ceiling. There were no bloodstains there, and he cursed himself for even wondering. Jack's torso moved over him and blocked his view of anything but Jack. Everything in the room was darker now. Jack pushed Stevie's knees to his chest and entered him. Stevie was not afraid of the room anymore. Stevie was grateful to Jack. Stevie moaned to let Jack know he wanted more of him. Jack thrust hard and ejaculated his warm sperm inside him. There were no condoms when they met in prison, and so there had never been any point to them afterwards.

He and Jack said nothing to each other after finishing. Eventually Stevie turned his head and saw a large pile of clothes in the closet. The door to the closet had been taken off its hinges and was leaning against the wall near the bike.

"Who did that, do you think?" Stevie asked, breaking the silence. His voice seemed so loud in the room.

"Did what?" Jack asked, suppressing a yawn. His hand was wrapped around his spent penis, a drop of clear cum gathered at its tip.

"Take the closet door down."

"Dunno. Cops maybe?"

Stevie extricated himself from Jack's legs and went to peek into the closet.

"Hey, don't fuck around in there. The cops might be coming back and then they'll find your prints or something." Stevie guffawed. Both of them knew how absurd Jack's warning was after what they'd just done on the mattress. But Stevie didn't care much at this point. He rummaged through the closet. He saw more clothes on the floor. What to wear, what to wear, he giggled. He could see there were a lot of things on the shelf in the closet, but he was too short to take a better look.

Stevie surprised Jack when he came back and stood at the edge of the mattress wearing a flannel shirt, buttoned all the way up to the neck.

"Look, it fits."

"Shit, man, that's the dead guy's clothes you're wearing."

A *perfect* fit, Stevie thought. He spun around on his heels in front of Jack, as if he were a runway model. "No, they're not. I think we're in the boyfriend's room."

"You're strange," Jack said, rolling onto his back and looking at the ceiling. "But then, maybe the dead guy was, too. Henry? That was his name?"

Yes, Henry, Stevie said to himself. "Call me Henry."

"Huh?"

"Henry. Call me Henry."

"Not my scene, baby," Jack said.

"I'm Henry."

"Yeah, sure you are."

"And you're Ryan."

"Christ, who's he now."

Stevie let out a sigh, thinking back to the time he and Ryan were seeing each other on the side. Stevie was buying from Ryan and they'd messed around a bit when Stevie was short on cash. Jack never knew a thing. Now he saw Ryan sometimes at meetings in the Yellow House. He heard someone call him "Jeff" once, so Stevie guessed he'd changed his name for some good reason. Like maybe he'd done time or needed to be scarce. Stevie never said anything to him, thinking Ryan might not want to talk with someone from the old days. Stevie never mentioned any of this to Jack, even if now he were tempted.

"We didn't come here to have sex," Stevie said.

"But we did. Think of it as the gay version of an Irish wake."

"But with no corpse laid out in the room." Stevie stretched out on the mattress next to Jack. Henry and Ryan must have had sex on this bed. You could feel it. Stevie commanded his imagination to picture himself dancing in the room, dressed in Ryan's flannel shirt and nothing else. In his mind he spun round in circles like a dervish, arms flaying and chanting nonsensical rhymes. Stevie could still feel Jack's warm sperm inside him. He was dancing his magical dance to beckon the spirits of the men who used to live and screw in this room. Stevie looked at Jack next to him on the stained mattress and thought for a moment he saw someone else lying there with a sly, mischievous look on his handsome face. Stevie wasn't frightened, he was glad Henry had come back. Maybe his dance had summoned Henry back from wherever he was to finish what was unfinished between him and his boyfriend.

Stevie grabbed Jack's hand, placed it over his own, and pressed down hard. His grandmother had told him that people who are killed don't depart the earth immediately. They linger around a bit, just to see what happens. Sometimes they are needed to do things, good things as well as vengeful things. Stevie's grandmother told him that one of his great uncles, murdered by a gang of white boys for talking to one of their sisters, had never left for the afterlife but was still hovering over Huntsville decades later, patiently waiting for his chance to set things right. Can I see the ghosts? Stevie asked. Oh no, they are not really ghosts, his grandmother replied. They are still people, just people who can come and go in our world as they please. When they are with us it's like it was, you can even touch and hold them, but when they go missing there is no way for us to follow. It's up to the dead to decide when and where to appear to the living.

CHAPTER THIRTEEN

It was almost chilly when the sun began to crawl above the ragged horizon of flat-topped buildings. Jeff had left Brandon's apartment before Brandon was awake and on a whim boarded the M104 heading down Broadway. He got off near Grand Central, but instead of going into the terminal he crossed Forty-Second and walked west the way he had just come. Now he was at the Circle Line, slightly sweaty and feeling anxious.

Jeff had never been to the end of West Forty-Second Street, where boats start and finish their three-hour tours of Manhattan. He toyed with the idea of boarding one, thinking that sailing around the island in one complete loop might somehow permit him to quit it for good. But Jeff looked at the schedule posted above the ticket window and saw he'd have to wait a couple of hours in a part of the city that didn't offer many places to kill time. Unsure where to go next, he stood idly against the concrete barrier between him and the Hudson River. The long gray water made where he stood cooler than the rest of the city, which was already hot and sticky now. Jeff was still crashing at Brandon's. When Jeff had arrived, Brandon said it was fine for him to stay for a while if he didn't mind a sleeping bag on the floor—Brandon didn't have a sofa, the place wasn't really big enough for one. Jeff told him it was just for a night or two, then he'd call Sam and tell him he was in town and coming over to stay.

"You can't do that," Brandon said.

"Why?" Jeff asked. "Someone already there?" He imagined first a new boyfriend and then, a second later, a caregiver.

"No. Sam's dead."

This news should have interrupted whatever Jeff was doing, but it did not. He didn't ask Brandon for any details at first, such as the immediate cause of death or just when his friend had cashed out. Instead he was overcome by the guilty thought: I was Sam's friend but, embarrassed and frightened by his illness, I let more and more time lapse between each of our phone calls and letters. And then selfishly, he wondered why hadn't anyone told him. Did he matter that little to everyone?

Later that night, more than slightly buzzed, Jeff did in fact ask Brandon just that, and the answer was: No one thought of it probably, or just as likely people hadn't heard from you in Nome or Siberia or wherever it was you went and concluded you'd run down the curtain, too.

"Fuck you," Jeff said as he took a swig from the fifth of Jack Daniels he and Brandon were sharing. He wondered what Henry was up to in Seattle.

"Yeah, fuck you," laughed Brandon in return. He got up with the bottle and put it away, something Jeff wouldn't have done in a million years.

On his sixth day in New York, Jeff took a nap on Brandon's bed. His brief visit to New York was turning into a long one. He led Brandon to believe he was busy with important errands during the day, but in truth he was idly trapped in his thoughts, marooned in New York until he knew what to do next with Henry's life and his own.

When he woke, the late afternoon sun had made the bedroom airless and hot. Jeff opened one of the two windows in the room and returned to the bed to lie down atop the balled-up bedspread and sheets. He tossed and turned and then found himself on his back looking up at the ceiling. There was an old-fashioned light fixture with some of its bulbs missing. Either the fixture was casting a shadow, or a stain in the ceiling ran in a nearly straight line to one of the walls. The sort of thing rainwater might have made. As he looked at the moody gray line it seemed to move, to squirm this way and that, growing wider at some points and thinning at others. Jeff squinted to see more detail. It was still moving, if ever so slightly.

Brandon came home with a bag of groceries. He grunted hello and made straight for the tiny kitchen. When he came out, Jeff was on one of the beanbag chairs with his hands locked behind his head.

"Hard day?" Jeff asked.

Brandon exhaled. "The usual. You?"

"Here and there."

Brandon threw himself into the black beanbag chair across from Jeff.

"Wanna get high?"

"Sure," Jeff replied. Brandon leaned forward the best he could in the formless chair and grabbed a joint he'd rolled the night before. He lit it and handed it to Jeff without taking a drag for himself.

"You have a leaky roof?" Jeff asked as he exhaled.

"Leaky what?"

"Roof. Leaky roof."

Brandon chuckled. "Leaky dick maybe," he said. "But no leaky roof. What are you talking about?"

"Look in your bedroom," Jeff said, trying not to exhale. "There's a stain on the ceiling."

Brandon turned his head in the direction Jeff was pointing, but without much urgency.

"I don't get it."

"A stain. On your ceiling."

Brandon stretched out his arm, motioning it was Jeff's turn to hold the roach.

"What are you talking about? And what were you doing in my bedroom? You pick up a trick today or something?" Brandon grinned as he teased Jeff, but his tone had betrayed just a touch of irritation at his houseguest. "Goddamn it. I better count the silver."

Jeff let it drop. Eventually they decided they were hungry. They went to Broadway to find some Chinese food. The evening was perfectly clear, the air cool, and you could even see stars. There were crowds of people on the street. "Full moon maybe," Brandon offered in way of an explanation. But when Jeff looked up, the moon was an odd egg-shape.

The next morning Brandon woke Jeff when he came out of the bedroom to make coffee. "There's leftover Chinese food in the refrigerator here," he said loudly from the kitchen. "Have it for breakfast if you want."

"Today?" Brandon said as he came into the living room with a mug in his hand.

"What about today?" Jeff said as he rolled over onto his back.

"Work?" Jeff wished Brandon spoke in complete sentences. "The library?" Jeff had told Brandon he was in the city to make revisions to his dissertation before attempting to publish it. But Jeff was doing no such thing.

"Probably." Jeff yawned as he crawled out of the sleeping bag and slithered onto the beanbag chair. He knew he had no intention of working on anything useful today, but why be honest now. Jeff was killing time in New York, waiting for some sort of epiphany that might never come. Brandon drank his coffee and left for the office without saying anything more. Jeff wandered into Brandon's bedroom and looked at the ceiling. There was no stain there now. It must have been a shadow or something, Jeff decided.

He walked everywhere, without a plan or the slightest idea where he was at times. At Seventy-fifth and Columbus he saw his

240

old late-night hangout, Ruskay's. He went to the door and pulled on the handle. It didn't budge. Jeff was sure the restaurant was open all the time. He took several steps backward on the sidewalk and looked up. It wasn't Ruskay's, or rather it wasn't Ruskay's anymore. The sign above the row of windows said "Rúelles."

Jeff was squinting at the sign when a woman walked up to him. She was dressed for jogging and was wearing leggings despite the heat.

"Opens at five."

"Huh?"

"Opens at five. It doesn't say it does, but it does. I work there."

"Oh, okay, thanks. It's not Ruskay's anymore."

The woman's face suddenly looked distressed, as if Jeff had said the wrong thing. "No, it's not."

"What happened?" Jeff asked, though it hardly made any difference to him.

"The owner sold."

"The owner, Richard?" Jeff said. He had known him to say hello.

"Richard sold the place after Ron died."

"You knew them," Jeff said with the finality of a command rather than a statement. Who is this woman? Did he know her, too? She looks like someone he might have known, but then so did so many other people he was passing on the street.

"I didn't. But I used to come here all the time. When it was Ruskay's." The woman's expression changed from troubled to smiling, and she turned to go.

"Thanks," Jeff mumbled. The woman waved one of her hands, her back already to him.

That night, curled up in Brandon's sleeping bag, Jeff thought about Richard and Ron. As he started to fall asleep, Ron's face morphed into Raul's, then one like Henry's. By the time the dreams came, all the men in Jeff's past had faces that resembled every other man's. Finally, Jeff's whole life looked like everyone else's, including that of a woman who wore leggings on a hot summer day.

For a week he roamed the city. Everything was old, dirty, on the precipice of decay and death. Why hadn't everyone left yet, as he had a year ago? Why was he back now? New York had no future; even its past was up for review. We had a dozen or so great years, Jeff tallied, and now they're over. His life had been free of mortal danger from the end of the Vietnam War abroad until the onset of an epidemic at home. A high lottery number had kept him out of the draft, but this time he wasn't going to be so lucky. He didn't deserve to feel cheated, it had been a good run after all, but he did. The men and women he passed on the street often had the same defeated look on their faces. New York went dark in his mind as he stumbled through its wretched, fresh history in neighborhood after neighborhood.

Jeff had lost count of the days, learning instead the irregular terrain of city by heart: level sidewalks requiring little physical effort, and the hills he struggled up like Golgotha. The faces of the strangers went by so quickly he couldn't make them out, and sometimes he panicked that what he was looking for was there, in the crowd he was racing by, dragged by gravity to the foot of an incline where the ground grew flat again. There, the rush of faces slowed down and he had a better look. Several times he thought he recognized familiar faces, but he didn't stop to remind anyone who he was.

One day he made an exception to his routine and briefly rejoined the world. He was in Washington Square Park and someone came up to him. A short, blond, muscular man, about his own age, walked over and reminded him what a good time they had had once.

Let's hook up again, he suggested to Jeff. I live in the East Village now, not far from here. Jeff could not recall where they had met before, or even if they had. Come back with me now, I've got good stuff. The man was one of Jeff's types, so he might very well have messed with him. I want you to do me. Jeff considered the invitation. He decided to forget his preoccupations for an hour and give his body over to manual labor.

The apartment on East Fourth was small and filled with hot air that didn't stir. Bright sunlight illuminated every corner. On a narrow unmade bed with sheets as white as a supernova, he mounted the man's smooth back and slid his slippery cock deep into the open abyss he was told he had screwed so well in the past. He thought he remembered the contours of this man, but he wasn't sure. The man clutched an open bottle of poppers as Jeff pounded him. He let his semen flow into him, leaving warm sticky tribute behind. The butt was endless, loose, cavernous—someone had visited there already today. The man soon rolled over and thanked him for stopping by, making it clear it was time to go. They had never used each other's name because neither could remember. Jeff pulled his pants on without taking a shower and went back to the sidewalks and his search. For what? he wanted to ask.

Jeff felt depressed and lonely after he left the man's apartment. He missed Henry and hadn't been able to reach him on the phone, or Nan for that matter, the couple of times he had called. What was he doing in New York? Life wasn't here anymore. Was it ever? Jeff found an empty bench in Union Square and began to catalog the big and little lies of his life, some he'd long told and others only recently. *I don't need anyone but myself.* They are the fables he invented to keep truth away. *That will never happen to me, I'm too perfect for that.* What truth? The lies were there because lies can hide but honesty is monumental. *I'll find love later, there's plenty of time.* Wait, what truth again? The falsehoods multiplied all around Jeff to keep the communicable at bay, just when he should have learned a sly contagion among men can make love possible as well as terror inevitable. *I will do this for you and not leave you alone with your dread.*

Now this ruined city was conspiring with Henry to make Jeff see himself. Henry and New York were demanding he banish pride

243

and cowardice to make room for *something else* in the world, something that will shatter his alone and let *another* see him as he is, in pieces and in pain; another who is like Jeff but not identical, similar enough to infiltrate the cells of his body and disarm fear, still different enough to make the singular of his life plural. *Henry, there's room for the two of us. The drugs and the drinking and the deception are not all we were promised, is it? You say to me: We weren't promised anything.* When we are gone, the two of us will recall what forks we took in the road, and the reasons why. Even our mistakes will look like the miracles they were. *Henry, lie next to me.* The chemicals we invited in and the viruses we did not race through our blood now, they are there because we are human. *Be with me, Henry.* The odds were always stacked against us, but so what. *I want to be with you.*

Jeff walked west on Fourteenth with his hands in his pockets. He let one of them play through the fabric of his pants with his soft cock, sore at the root after fucking. At Sixth Avenue he watched blue and white police cruisers race uptown, no doubt with urgent business to attend to. People in New York went missing all the time.

The phone rang a long time again, but no one had answered at the Yellow House so he was back to trying Tenth Avenue. He looked at the floor of the telephone booth. There were several pages of tabloid newsprint with dirty shoe marks obscuring the headlines. He let the old piece of paper stored in his wallet with Henry's phone numbers, past and present, fall from his hand and join the rest of the trash at his feet. He pressed one hand against the door to block the street noise. Just when he was about to hang up, he heard someone pick up.

"Uh, hullo?"

"Clark?" Jeff asked.

"No. Mike. Who's this?"

"This is Jeff. Yellow House Jeff. I tried calling your mother's place, but no one picked up. Is Henry there?"

"Where are you?"

"New York. Is Henry there? At your place?"

The voice at the other end fumbled.

"He's not here, Jeff. Where have you been?"

Jeff pressed the receiver closer to his face. "Is he at work? Have you got his number there?"

"Jeff, you need to talk to my mom, or Vinnie if you can find him. You need to get back here."

"Mike! Where the fuck is everybody? Is Nan with you?"

"Henry's dead, Jeff. A while now. No one knew how to contact you."

Jeff felt his throat constricting and his mouth going dry. His senses of sight, hearing and touch were suddenly out of sync. *Say that again?* The dial on the phone wasn't in focus. His palm gripping the receiver was sweaty. Was he hallucinating this? It didn't seem real. Jeff switched hands and replayed Mike's words in his head, one by one, hoping to make sense of them. *If only I hadn't left him.*

"They don't know exactly how he died yet, Jeff, other than he was shot."

His legs felt weak, as if they were about to fold beneath him. The floor of the phone booth was going to give way and he'd fall to the center of the earth. *If only I hadn't come here.* Jeff pressed the receiver tightly against his ear. *What has that little fucker gone and done.* Mike was still talking. The phone booth was hot and Jeff needed air. No one in Mike's house had gone to the funeral. *Listen hard to what he is saying.* Nan was staying for the time being at Mike's place but she was out right now.

Jeff had a lot of questions, but his childhood stutter had returned. He leaned back on the wall of the booth to steady himself. He began to hyperventilate. An emptiness inside him was expanding and making him light, ethereal, airborne. His head was going to hit the top of the phone booth.

"Vinnie and Greg have disappeared, and that guy Ryan too. The cops are looking for them."

245

Jeff looked through the dirty glass of the phone booth. *Concentrate.* Everyone rushing by him on the sidewalk was in a movie, and he was sitting in the dark watching.

"Something about a missing gun."

The colors were vivid, like in old Technicolor.

"The police are asking about you, too."

All the sounds on the street were loud and they hurt his ears. He tried standing up straight in the small booth, but fell back on the Plexiglas, shaking the flimsy wall.

"Jeff, there was a used needle in the room."

Jeff hung up the phone while Mike was still talking. He returned the receiver to its cradle and exited the booth in slow motion, as if his joints were old and stiff. Once out he wasn't sure which way to turn. All he wanted now was to sit down but there was nowhere he could. He started to slide down the outside of the booth, thinking he could rest on the sidewalk, but some cop was sure to come by and tell him to move on. You had to be in perpetual motion in New York and it exhausted him.

Jeff looked up at the sky and saw a jet plane headed in the direction of the airports. The fuselage was illuminated a warm orange color like neon but cast by a sun gone beyond the western horizon. It was packed with people buckling their seatbelts and raising their tray tables. He had a peculiar sensation when the traffic signal changed and he crossed the street with the crowd. He looked up at the sky again. It was hard for Jeff to signal his brain to move from one necessary task to the next. The plane was breaking apart. *I am made of air.* Jeff imagined the passengers screaming in terror, climbing over each other, each desperate to be the one to survive. A child's head being crushed by an adult struggling to reach the emergency exit; a flight attendant who should have been helping instead replaying the best lay of his life. *Jeff felt something let go of him.* Another flight attendant got an emergency door open but the passenger behind her pushed her out of the plane. Others plummeted thousands of feet, too. *Why am I falling as well?* Jeff

246

squinted hard and could see bodies, like specks of dirt, flaying their arms as they dropped. *My head feels like the pieces don't fit together anymore.* He kept walking straight ahead across the intersection. *Maybe Henry has died mid-air, and all that will fall is a lifeless body.* Jeff reached the south side of Forty-Second Street. *Did someone kill you in the Yellow House? Did you do it yourself?* He hesitated on the curb. The moving crowd parted around him. *Did you ask someone to do it?*

Jeff resumed walking and let himself follow the people in front of him. *Another couple of years, Henry, and it might have been me asking for help, nodding slightly as you approached me on the hospital bed holding a pillow.* Jeff passed a black guy selling fake designer watches on his folding table. They smiled at each other; even now, Jeff cruised. He was realizing just how close grief is to terror is to the desire for another, anyone, to save us from both. "Tests aren't back," Mike had said. Jeff didn't understand what tests he was talking about. *I am losing my mind and I can do nothing about it.*

Jeff took a taxi back to Brandon's apartment and waited for his friend to come home from work. When he did, Jeff did not share his news. His stutter was gone now, but he was still stunned silent as his emotions battled each other for supremacy. Theoretical things to say to Brandon dangled in the air in front of him, but none of them were utterable. Jeff was not so much upset as relieved at the quiet. It postponed everything. He knew he needed to make a plan, but it wouldn't be tonight.

They sat in the living room. Brandon produced a joint out of nowhere and handed it to Jeff as he exhaled the first toke.

"You got the steak knives, right? There's one more."

"Huh?" Jeff replied, taking a second to parse Brandon's sudden question out of nowhere. "Do I look like I need another steak knife?" Jeff sputtered in response while putting the joint between his pursed lips.

"You do. You don't have a complete set. Can't be gay without a complete set. Didn't you count them?"

"No."

"Eleven. That's all I mailed you. Things like that always come in an even number. As in a dozen." Brandon extended his arm to take the joint back.

"Where did it come from?"

"What?" Brandon asked. "The dope?"

"No. The knife." Jeff recalled Mike telling him there'd been a gun in the room.

"Oh, we found it when we were cleaning out the guy's apartment. Back of a drawer, I guess."

Jeff looked up at Brandon's ceiling and began to see Henry's face there in the shadows cast from the lights below.

"So, do you want it?" Brandon went into the kitchen and returned with a knife. "Here," he said. "Yours now."

"I'll just give it away," Jeff blurted.

Brandon shrugged. "Okay, fine. Give it away," he instructed. "I just don't want it here anymore."

Jeff knew he had just been told his time camping out at Brandon's was over. Gay hospitality only goes so far. He quickly invented a story about still needing to see a few old friends in the city. Brandon agreed to put him up for a while longer.

Soon Jeff looked like one of the lost homeless of New York, not so much because of the whiskers flecked with gray here and there, or the unwashed hair, as for the dull look in his eyes. In some parts of the city he became known. The crazy person who was the mayor of a nearby corner would nod at him, the chubby Latino who hosed down the sidewalk in front of his bodega near the apartment early each morning started to say hello, and in the Irish bar on Amsterdam, where he'd stop for a drink or two in the early afternoon, the other daytime drunks now accepted him as one of their own. Once he sat on a stoop on Carmine Street with an old Polish woman who unloaded the story of her son on him, until he stopped her when the son's story and his own seemed too alike.

He walked many miles in the following days. *When will I find him?* Jeff asked a God he didn't believe in. *This can't go on much longer.* He had overstayed his welcome at Brandon's. Then, soon after that thought, perhaps in another of his dreams, he did find whom he had been looking for. It happened maybe the tenth or eleventh time he crossed the intersection of Columbus and Seventy-second since returning to New York. Jeff was walking north on the east side of the avenue when he saw Henry coming the opposite direction. At first Jeff didn't recognize him. Or rather, for a moment he looked like so many other people.

Henry spotted Jeff at nearly the same moment. He stopped on the sidewalk and grinned. *Have you been searching, too?* Jeff heard a voice in his head that sounded like Henry's saying: "I fell from the sky and you were not there to catch me, but others *like you* raised me up." Jeff kept walking toward Henry, almost breaking into a trot despite how his callused feet hurt him. He could see that Henry had the start of a real beard. He reached up to his own face with one hand and felt his unshaved cheek. *There is a dark cloud in the center of his body.* He was nearly by Henry's side now, and Henry, smiling a smile that said everything never said, raised his arms to embrace his friend and steady himself for what was about to happen. Then Henry said, half to himself but loud enough for passersby to hear, *Come.*

And so the will of Jeff broke free from his body, *but did not ascend to the stars*, for it belonged to the earth and to Henry. Flying faster than his body could leap, the dark cloud sprung from his torso, ghostlike, flew the small distance between the two men and entered Henry through his own amazed chest, *I am ready for you*, dissolved into flesh, flowed through veins and turned the two of them into one and each one of them into two. Jeff and Henry would never be apart again in this life or any other. *Everything we did is forgiven us, Jeff.* In an instant, like cool morning mist struck by sudden sun, they both evaporated from the sidewalks of New York and no one noticed them gone, now or ever, because so many other people in the world still resembled these two young men.

Nan did not go back to the Yellow House until November. She parked on the street since the Hansen Bros. moving van took up the driveway. Trash, including her old globe of the world, was wet from the rain and piled high on the curb ready for the city to cart away. The front door was propped open and Nan walked in to a house now emptied of furniture. Once upstairs in her former bedroom, Nan put an empty cardboard box on the floor and sorted through what the movers had left for her. She wanted almost none of it and what she chose barely covered the bottom of the box. She walked out of her room and went into the one at the left end of the hallway. It was totally bare as well, which made it look larger than it ever had. Finding nothing, she retrieved the box and moved on to Jeff's room.

All the drywall and plaster had been removed, exposing tufts of wispy grayish pink insulation as well as old, threadbare electrical wiring. Maybe the police had done that. The door to the closet was off its hinges and leaning next to the frame. Nan avoided looking up, worried that pieces of Henry might still be on the ceiling.

She peered into the closet. It was dark and she almost missed seeing the things left on the shelf. Nan stood on tiptoe to for a better look. The first thing she recognized was a lime-green tennis ball, then a white athletic cup. One by one she took the objects down from the shelf and placed them in the box. All of them were things that belonged to young men; not just Jeff but Henry, too. There was an old copy of the *Post-Intelligencer*, with the story of an attempted bank robbery on its front page obscured by dirty shoe prints. She found candy refills for a Pez dispenser and at least a dozen postcards with Chilean stamps on them. There were two refrigerator magnets, one of them from Key West and the other a comic strip Snoopy. A flannel shirt was rolled up into a ball. She almost decided to put the book of matches from the Bush Hotel in her pocket, until she thought better of it and threw them into the box, too. She unfolded a piece of paper that had a crude map drawn on it, starting from an address in Fremont and ending in the Woodland Park Zoo. A shoebox had a half-empty bottle of bourbon in it. Further back were an envelope from the King County Health Department and a paycheck from Starbucks made out to the order of Henry Sosa. Leaning upright against the back of the closet was a hockey stick, too big for the box. Using her hand to feel blindly for anything remaining, she found some old Christmas cards held together with a rubber band. Finally she was surprised to find that old purple scarf of hers that had disappeared months before. She took it, shook it out and spread it neatly over the things now filling half the box. She folded the flaps closed.

The box was not heavy, but she had trouble getting it down the stairs. She might have shouted for help but did not. On her way down the front steps of the house she saw two men briskly approach from the direction of the parked moving van. "No," she said, "this box isn't going to California. It's coming with me now."

Nan opened the rear door to the Volvo and put the box on the seat. She waved to the movers to signal she was through. The skies were dark but there was no rain anymore. She wiped her forehead with her sleeve and went around the car to get in the driver's seat. As she pulled out onto Fifteenth Avenue, Nan decided she would tell Mike to store this box with him here in Seattle, in the Tenth Avenue house where he had let her stay these past four months. She'd tell him there wasn't room for it in her tiny Laguna Beach condo. The real reason Nan kept to herself: Some things should stay near the Yellow House and not be taken away or allowed to disappear. Jeff might come back one day, and want them.

ACKNOWLEDGEMENTS

One thing leads to another, if we are lucky. Jeffrey Sharlach led me to David Groff, who introduced me to Trent Duffy. Steven Caplan referred me to Robin Stratton, who gave this book not just a new ending but her patronage. Along the way Marlene Adelstein, Rachel DiNitto, Jeffrey Johnson, David Lapin and Ted Mack read the manuscript for me. Steve Ridgely not only read a draft, he went into his basement and made the first bound copy of it. Will Fleming gave me a very funny idea and Doug Lind found mistakes I would never have. Will Schwalbe offered me dismal advice about publishing nowadays (which was true), but Filip Noterdaeme cheered me with his quip about what eventually sticks to the wall (just as true). I also owe thanks to Sophie Linden, Joanne Erickson, and Corbin Lewars.

The wrestling scene in Chapter Ten is indebted to D. H. Lawrence's *Women in Love*, as is Chapter Thirteen to José Saramago's *Baltasar and Blimunda*.

I dedicate this book to the women and men of the real Yellow House.

ABOUT THE AUTHOR

Writer and critic John Whittier Treat has taught at Yale, Berkeley and Stanford, and is the author of *Writing Ground Zero: Japanese Literature and Atomic Bomb* (Chicago) and *Great Mirrors Shatter: Japan, Orientalism and Homosexuality* (Oxford). Relocating from New York City to Seattle in 1983, he was witness to the earliest days of the AIDS epidemic in the Pacific Northwest. Soon, he became involved with the local recovery community as AIDS affected gay men already struggling with addiction. Treat's fiction has appeared in literary journals, and his opinion pieces have been published in the *New York Times* and the *Huffington Post. The Rise and Fall of the Yellow House* is his first novel. Treat is now at work on a second novel, *First Consonants*, about a stutterer who saves the world.

Made in the USA
Middletown, DE
11 May 2016